Luke Warm, Thought Drunk

by

Chris DeVore

BookshopMH.com

Also by Chris DeVore

A Palatable Past
Catching the Flathead Monster
The Literary Detective

First Printing

ISBN: 0615922562
ISBN-13: 978-0615922560

for Hannah

for Mom and Dad

for Torrance, Lillian, and Evelyn

for writers and poets of all qualifications

ACKNOWLEDGMENTS

What follows has been written and rewritten over a number of years. So many people have helped it's difficult to remember them all in one list or measure their impact. It certainly won't happen in these couple of paragraphs. And it wasn't just editors and proofers, it was people who by their life, or words, have made me want to do better, be more thoughtful, and maybe even give a forgotten manuscript one more chance. Maybe you don't want your name in this book, which makes me want to name you all the more. I know this work of fiction somewhat defies a specific genre, but it turns out it was a worthwhile pursuit, even if just in the writing. What more can a writer ask for than to feel as though a writing project made a difference in his or her own life? My hope is that a few readers will feel the same; otherwise, I just feel selfish, which I probably should. So good.

To name a few of you: Hannah, Beth, Travis, Lenny, Pastor Dale, Kim Monnier, Jim Bird, Frank Monasterio, Tom Bennick, Truman Parker, Deena Trouten, Jeremy Johnson, Michael Johnson, Joe Johnson, Travis Strickland, Brad Johnson, Virgil Roehl, Michael Peterson, Brian Palmer, the Mountain Home Arts Council/The Literary Committee/*The Whistle Pig* literary journal, Calvary Chapel Mountain Home, and The Twisted Stixx Softball Club. I'll name a whole collection of other writers as well in the pages ahead.

INK SLINGER, ESQ.

He's never been just-right religious. He's always been either too religious or not religious enough. So. He said his prayers and he imagined walking to Boise. He said his prayers and he looked around, not wanting to be seen. He said his prayers and he took a rental car to a chain hotel. He said his prayers and he hid them behind the desk in a chain hotel. He said his prayers and he forgot his prayers and went to a banking trade show and pretended to be—and was, in fact, just moments into the conversation—interested in the newest innovations that would pay for six full-page ads or his next chapter, the new volume, his son's braces, his daydreams. He said his prayers and forgot them as a matter of habit. He moved on. He wanted to be something different than what he was. He wanted to be thoughtful. He believed being thoughtful was the highest calling. He had a new idea that he figured wasn't really a new idea, but at least unique. He lived in a small town and felt insignificant. He thought globally and lived locally. He got a cheap haircut, made sure to cast a vote in favor of the city council candidate who had visited his home late the night before, said his prayers, and drew up a list of changes to make in his life. They were simple changes. He ran through water because his days often required it. He wrote it all down because that was what he always did. He wrote it all down because words deserved to play after all their hard work without any union—or related workers' rights and benefits that an animated, educated, experienced advocate might provide. Words never called him master and he never called them servants. They were coworkers in an ever-evolving cubicle.

All this is backdrop. All these words amount to a peek behind the curtain. The curtain is small. The curtain is unremarkable. You might laugh at the view. It's all insignificant, but to those intimately involved, a tiny group: father, mother, wife, sons and daughters, elbows, knees, and toes. If you add it up, curtain after curtain, the sum is much greater than the world, greater than you might imagine.

Behind the curtain, in a moment among thousands of moments, the words assemble like this for the writer who just a few paragraphs before had been saying those prayers:

All writers—and by all writers I'm referring to those considered good and not so good at this craft people love to call wordsmithing (but it's not a dancing word), when it's really more akin to breathing deep, sneezing, or dumpster diving; after all, who is to say who is a writer and who isn't? A jury of our peers (or our own conscience), I suppose—so, to begin again: All writers get around to their own story sooner or later. It's just inevitable. You know, like long-term debt and the last page. They begin some place where lightening literally struck, say a tree just off Triggering Street, only to come around the bend and discover a familiar road full of delicately placed words. Even I'll get there someday, to my story. I believe it. But not right now. Not at the moment anyway. Right now, there is a debate going on in heaven and hell. For those of you who don't believe in hell, you've obviously never been to my attic in July. If you climb the long stairs of my neck, you will find a place where disillusionment grows for no reason and for every reason, despite how trite that seems. Visitors might wonder if what I am saying is some kind of hyperbole. It's not. The fact is I can't sit here any longer without considering the validity of it all. The big questions are questions for a reason and they are big because of their size and weight. I can't just sloth here and pretend I know what this is all about. I must light it all on fire and see what is burned up and what is purified.

I invite you to tell me otherwise only because I know you can't. It's not a challenge, really; it's just an opening line. It's just the truth. I'm no authority—not on this matter, or many other, I'm often reminded by editors and wives and children. I'm 30. I believe Jesus was beginning the legendary part of his life at my age, reconstructing the calendar. He was rearranging history, restarting time like an old Buick. Yet—here I am in a room, a hotel room, in Idaho of all places, taking a break from my life rather than fulfilling anything. I've run out of books to read, a travesty. I turn to the Gospel of Luke—that is how legendary this journey is. I turn to Luke because he's available. Isn't that how we choose our friends: based almost entirely on availability and willingness? I write on my computer because that is what I am paid to do.

I'm not getting paid for this.

I'm lying here. (On this sofa chair, I mean; I am being truthful.) I have a wife and three kids, one of them *on the way*. I miss them today, even how they drive me mad, even how I embarrass myself with useless rage. My love for them, it's nothing but maddening.

I have business in the morning. My shirts are lined up like better versions of me, certainly slimmer. The TV will be on soon. The world will remain a mystery. My authority will be unaltered. I won't be changing the world or restarting time, but maybe I will be trying harder. Maybe I will be funny, even really funny. Maybe I will make you laugh so hard the red wine will come out your nose. (Why are you drinking so early?)

I guess you can call me Ink. I mean that's my nickname. Some people call me Ink. I've had to work hard at getting them to call me Ink. I've had to ask my mother over and over again to call me Ink. Funny thing is now I hate the name. Seems cheesy. And when I say hate, I mean hate. I don't use that word lightly, let me assure you. Sometimes what we want so badly looks quite different when viewed from our lap. I thought a name like Ink might be a firm handshake or an MFA in creative writing. Turns out, I'm sometimes wrong about these things. I just don't have the energy to turn back time. I've already wasted so much, it's not worth doubling down.

Have you ever noticed how confusing this world is?

Do you read about current events in newspapers, on the Internet, in blogs by people named conspiracytheorist19822643?

Are you political?

I'm confused.

I'm not sure what my goals are anymore.

I go to church. I volunteer. I think sometimes. I even think for myself sometimes. I argue with my wife. She is smarter than me, but I am funnier. Well, that's an ongoing debate.

I start to wonder if art has a door. I knock. I step inside.

It is an exercise in devotion.

It is a call to congress.

With the door left open I am able to wrestle ideas. I am thinking of poverty. I wonder about Bible distribution. I wonder why Bibles rather than food. I wonder why every hotel, rather than, say, every street corner or cardboard box, needs a Bible. I know no cardboard boxes, but I pretend to. Why not bake the gospel into our bread? I'm not trying to attack my own beliefs (being lost affords you some leeway), but I wonder sometimes about the poor and not just the poor in spirit. The poor poor. I mean those without money or resources or a wealthy, beautiful spokesperson—the poor who we argue over like game pieces and then ignore. Do they need religion or food? Do they need Jesus or Christianity or public policy or judgment? What of these do I need? What do I have to offer and why? Why am I always being called an enabler? How do you get trapped in your own life even as you love it? I wonder about contentment. I wonder about expectations. It's strange how quickly we can lose ourselves—trap ourselves—in our own boredom. It's not really all that spectacular from a certain viewpoint, but with a microscope you can see the rift, the crack beginning to race and split and race some more, double. It's the little things that cause the big things. It's the smile uncontained that causes the affair. You're cheating on your own life. What can I do to change anything? I am just wondering how I can be dissatisfied and downright unhappy when my life is a comfortable, moderately expensive suit that most anyone would like to put on and then go to a party, maybe even flirt with the lovely brunette who's nearly 24, and pretend, pretend, pretend for just a minute or two. Can I examine the suit without staining it? Can I take off the suit altogether without destroying it?

I divorce myself with words.

Luke, you're a friend. Tell me what/when/where/why/how.

[A note to the reader: What follows is a journal or maybe a devotional of sorts. My thoughts verse by verse while reading Luke. I tell you this because some of you are expecting a narrative and I don't want you to be disappointed because of such expectations. I want you to be disappointed because of the writing and because you disagree with me. If you're a friend of mine—or MY MOTHER—and you were hoping to stay up all night reading a start-to-finish story, maybe you should just put this aside for a while until you can clear your head. Another thought is to read it like a devotional, my authority to write one aside, one day at a time. I'm not nor do I claim to be a Philip Yancey, Henri Nouwen, Donald Miller, A.J. Jacobs, or Brad Pitt, to name just a few people I am not. BUT. Ink journals just the same, and Ink comes to the Bible with his own style of bias, just so you know. Just don't hold my nickname against me. That's all I ask. And, you might want a Bible of your choice nearby, or a smartphone with a Bible app, or something, because I don't retype the verses. In case you care, the Gideon's Bible I picked up was KJV, but I also consulted NKJV, NIV, NCV, The Message, and NKJV study notes. I also listened to some great music from a number of my favorite artists, so you should too. Also read a bunch of Richard Hugo, Billy Collins, and Sherman Alexie poems. The right words in the right spot. Everyone has their opinions. Am I the only one who values good, great, and bad poetry? These are, in my mind, a few of the greats. I'm not. I also am one of three friends: a liberal, a conservative, and a libertarian. All three of us know everything. What that has to do with what follows: your guess is as good as mine...]

one

Luke 1:1

People are writing about it. Why not me? Do I have something to say? Am I a credible witness all these years later? Am I knocking and entering?

My wife and I, we fight. We experience disunity. We can be players in an event and come away impacted in a completely different manner. She believes the best in people. I distrust everyone. Why are they all out to get me? Why am I so unlikeable? Don't I deserve the benefit of the doubt? Why do I knee-jerk apologize?

Jesus is worth writing about, I think Luke is saying. He was there. A gang of people want to write about all that went on. People have been changed.

In the original language the word translated "undertaken" has many, esoteric meanings that the English language is inefficient in capturing. Crap. I made that all up. I have no idea about original languages or what I am talking about in general. I'm no authority, but on my own life. I'm not lying here reading and typing and interpreting. I'm lying here reading and typing and reacting.

It's the greatest story ever told. I'm out of books. I have a friend named Luke. I'm in a hotel. I don't need to watch TV.

Luke 1:2

Wasn't Luke an eyewitness? Maybe not, I guess. I thought I knew, but maybe I don't. What about these servants of the word? Is that referring to the disciples of Jesus? I remember that John says Jesus IS the word.

I would like to be a servant of the word. That sounds great. Even better would be the boss of the word. I mean, I could order the word around, get the garbage taken out every once in a while. I could tell the word a few things; maybe create a new life for myself with words like baseball and bestseller. I kind of enjoy the personification of the word—the word as a living thing; the word as a spirit. I can get into that. I feel that. Words are like magic. You put the right ones together and poof: You create love, worth, laughter, tears. Poof: people's lives have just changed. And for God... Poof: The world is created. Poof: people. Poof: everything.

Luke 1:3

Now it sounds like a great mystery. Luke has investigated the matter and is working on an orderly account for "most excellent Theophilus." Being a journalist—and on my good days even a storyteller—I want to write an orderly report. I want to have something significant to research, investigate, and orderly propagate. It doesn't have to be anything to do with me; it just has to be important eternally. Imagine the newspaperpro who got this lead: Jesus of Nazareth is fulfilling all kinds of prophesy in ways that don't really make much sense. Check it out. Twenty-five-hundred words should do it. In my son's math you might try 25 thousand, million, zillion.

Maybe this is all just a fantasy. However, I can already feel the joy and eagerness of Luke. He has a story to tell. I want to hear it. I want to be a part of his relational gospel. I want to meet the witnesses and characters and see them burst into song. I always want to be this optimistic. I never want to be this optimistic ever again.

Luke 1:4

Luke speaks of certainty. I'm reading for certainty. I'm open to it. Change my mind or confirm my thinking, I tell Luke. I'm your Theophilus.

Luke 1:5

I'm feeling somewhat tired all of the sudden. Tomorrow will be a long day. I brush my teeth, remember the young dental assistant who kept reminding me how treasonous my teeth are, swearing in open court that I grind in my sleep and don't floss enough. I look at myself in the mirror. The man looking back at me has some gray hairs and about 25 extra pounds in the middle I would like to punch away. I wonder why I am here. What is so important about analyst downgrades and loan modifications that I need to cover this trade show? I like credit and effective, honest regulation as much as, even more, than the next guy, but how am I impacting the world? One financial executive at a time, I guess. If I do my job well, then they do their job well, and then, well, some rich CEO gets richer. I spit into the sink. I take my glasses off, which are so filthy. My kids can't leave these glasses alone. They are always reaching for them and I protect them as if they are my cubs. I yell about them knowing better. I threaten them. I send them to their rooms. This life.

I'm on the sofa couch again. I'm drinking water and wondering if I will pay for it in the middle of the night. These thoughts, they somehow matter.

I wonder what it is like to be a priest like Zechariah in the time of King Herod. Is his the only job with real repercussions? I mean that is a high calling in his day, any day. He was in direct commune with God and not in the way we understand it today. He talked with God didn't he? Maybe I am making it all up. I sometimes wonder, however, if it is a tougher calling to give yourself over to the priesthood or become "blameless" and follow a calling in your own life. I mean, you're just weird if you act like a priest in an ordinary job. Everyone expects a priest to act like a priest. I don't want to be a priest or act like one. Then again, I don't know what I want to be or act like. Who does?

Luke 1:6

Both Zechariah and Elizabeth were obedient to God. Seems simple enough, although I can't imagine it, this obedience. I wonder what it meant in practice. Did it mean that they were uninteresting people, judgmental, or peace-loving weirdo do-gooders that never did laugh? Or were they those people we all love who listen to you and ask questions? Maybe at a party they would be so much fun and make you feel like the specialist person they ever met. Could this be them? Maybe they were unbending, yet wonderful. Not judgmental yet long in their convictions, racing after the very heart of God. It's a foreign concept.

I wonder how obedience impacted their marriage. I mean obedient people must make great partners. Or again, they could just be boring.

I imagine them, however, of one mind, one love. I imagine them spreading out a tablecloth and looking across it with joy and want of one another. I imagine others are there, the less fortunate than them. These people feel welcome; and well, like people for the first time in years. They are eating of the joy as well. Elizabeth is asking one man about his day, how he is surviving under the sun. Zechariah looks at his wife. He is biting a strawberry, yet he tastes only the best of her. He remembers their wedding. He remembers how she often asks him about his day. He remembers when he is unkind or judgmental or too wrapped up in traditions, how she says *get with it Zack.*

She spies his look. She smiles at him. She asks: What?

Luke 1:7

They were getting older now and no children.

They may have been sad or sick because of it, but by now my guess is they went ahead and planned for a life without kids. I believe in their time it was a bit of a disgrace to not be able to produce children, but it was what it was. This was their life. They were getting used to this old shirt. They were getting used to the stigma of a barren life.

My kids make me yell. My kids wake me up or throw a toy at my head at just the wrong moment. My kids soil their pants. My kids chew up blueberries and spit them on the floor. My kids make me roar like a lion and question my ability to be a man. At least I think I am a man.

Of course, I also wouldn't trade them for a game seven as the Dodger's catcher.

It's being away from them for just a moment that allows us all to survive. It's that *Eye Wove Yoooou* that keeps saving them and keeps them trucking. It's that moment when they are kind to each other or offer to share that cookie that makes you want to conquer the world.

Old shirt or not, this is our life.

Luke 1:8–9

Casting a lot sounds a lot like rolling the dice. Why if priests were able to communicate with God, tap into the Almighty, would they make decisions by rolling some dice or whatever? It's like me making a marital decision by flipping a coin rather than talking to my wife. Maybe the next time I have a really big decision, like let's say, whether we should have a fourth child, I'll depend on a draw of the cards, although actually I have no idea what I'm talking about. I'm shaking a Magic 8ball to figure out whether I have a clue. It came up: "You're an Idiot."

These things do work.

Luke 1:10

So Zechariah was burning some incense, a duty of the priest who had been chosen by the magic of the lot—okay, I'll let it go. People came together to pray. Why?

I don't know about this time in history, but I can think of all kinds of reasons to gather to pray and none of them are all that great. Sure, we might be together to praise and worship God, but although this is maybe most important, it is rarely the case. Usually we gather to pray because of tragedy and the fear of coming tragedy. We pray when we are suffering. As Americans, suffering is the most powerful enemy of all.

I can't breathe when I think of the times in my life when I have gathered with my family, our hands tightly clutched, to communicate our need to our God. I can see my mother. Her chest is rising and falling at the will of a machine. My world has been shattered. My brother is falling to his knees with the force of tears, and I envy him. Here I am stunned—I the deer, the shell of my mother the headlights. I can't exist in a world that can't hold onto her. She has been my hero since birth. I look over at my father, Hercules. He's on one knee, kissing her hands. My wife is with the babies. She is probably creating, inventing cheesecake. She bakes cheesecake when she's nervous. I want her here. I want my boys here. I don't want them here. I don't want to be here. My other brother asks if we should pray. He starts praying. That should have been me. When she was gone, I quit praying altogether until the next whiff of tragedy. There are always tears before prayer, both a secret.

Why am I writing this?

I'm sure it doesn't help.

Zechariah burning incense, my wife cooking, tears, and a gathering of worshipers, do they really have anything in common?

I guess it depends on what you believe and how you connect things.

Luke 1:11–12

And then there was an angel. And then there was fear.

I know I don't understand a few things about angels, when people are always so afraid of them in Bible stories, yet they seem docile enough to me. I mean startled by their sudden appearance I understand, but gripped by fear is another matter. Have we softened angels for easy consumption? Should I see a warrior or a gentle spirit when I picture angels? What is everyone so afraid of?

I saw an angel. I couldn't sleep. My heart was a drum set.

And another thing while we are on the topic of angels: I read about angels and I take them for granted. *Cool*, I think, an angel, nothing unusual really. *What?* (Italics added for *emphasis*). I mean I can't imagine seeing an angel. Alright, I'll admit it, nothing profound or poetic here; I just don't understand the fear.

Maybe we need to rethink our concept of angels, that's all I'm saying. Michael and Gabriel, those guys must have been cool. Nicolas Cage, now he was a GREAT angel. My wife **especially** liked him.

Luke 1:13

The angel says there is no reason to be afraid, but he had to know there could be a reason or that Zechariah was already scared to even mention it. Zechariah's prayer was answered. A son: John.

I remember praying and waiting for a baby. Before my wife and I tried, I just thought you decided to have a baby and poof: dirty diapers. It's easy really, but not exactly that easy. It took us over a year to get it right—for many it takes longer. It becomes a job, making a baby. This fact is incontrovertible proof that a person can ruin anything with schedules and rules and laws and regimen. However, even as hard emotionally as all that was, I think we are talking about an even longer timeline here. I think Zechariah and Elizabeth, though somewhat shamed by their inability and the stigma they carried, had given up on ever having a child. They were broken. A child wasn't in the cards. They decided to plan their lives for an alternate future, I imagine.

Zechariah's prayer? Was there only one? I bet there were as many prayers as hamburgers sold at McDonalds.

Wouldn't it just be easier to give up? If something seems like hard work or especially if the outcome is fuzzy, I like to go about planning for something else, or go fishing. I mean a concrete plan is always better than a muddy dream. Well, now that I say it... crap.

A son. John will be his name.

Imagine the joy.

Zechariah is full of fear. Can he believe this angel?

Fear.

Joy.

A son.

John.

Luke 1:14

Many will rejoice because of him. I can feel the pressure already. It's hard to breathe under such circumstances. I remember when I was young and nothing was impossible. What's changed? Me.

The reason I don't believe in miracles is my own fault. I don't believe in miracles because I was never able to predict or ignite them. I would swing at the first-pitch fastball and foul it straight back. I would take a step out of the box, breath deep, readjust my hands, and take the sign from my coach. I can remember a time when I thought every pitch had a shot at leaving the yard. Now I play scared. What if I... what will they think if...

Another fastball. They will rejoice. He will be a joy to you.

My kids are a joy to me one moment and I am yelling the next. There has to be a better way. What will my kids believe? How high can I hold them up? What can I give them to succeed? What is success? A home run? A bunt single? Humility in victory and in loss?

I step back in, looking for the slider on the outside corner. I try to let joy in even as I feel the yelling coming up in search of a target.

They will rejoice.

Luke 1:15

Your son will be great by God's standards; he won't drink alcohol; and he'll be full of the Holy Spirit.

Wow. I don't know what else to say. Wow doesn't even do it. The Holy Spirit, talk about a bundle of fear and ongoing arguments pertaining to that third of God.

I think there is a good rule: Never be jealous of your own child. This is definitely a high calling, one to be jealous of, proud of, but your children are standing on your shoulders and that is axiomatic. That is a high calling too, Tower-of-Babel high. Was Zechariah jealous after all his time, learning, and commitment to God? Or was he proud as punch? Maybe, he was thinking, *well no kidding, he is my son. He won't be a drunkard or even close. Not on my watch.*

He'll be great.

He won't drink.

He'll be full of the Holy Spirit.

The first is just amazing. It's a privileged existence. It's a blessed and important life. It's like signing a major-league contract from the womb.

He'll make a commitment. He won't be distracted. He'll live a healthy life.

I have no idea about the last. Is John going to be speaking in tongues all the time? Will he be shaking with the spirit, prancing around and out of control? Being filled with the Holy Spirit seems scary. Will he be prophesying? Will he be drunk with the supernatural rather than scotch? I've been in several churches that are said to be full of the Holy Spirit... once. However, if being filled with the Holy Spirit is part of the relationship, then we better give it a try. What could it hurt? I've made a colossal fool of myself.

I heard someone speaking in tongues. It sounded like gibberish. It seemed so fake: SHOUDACOULDAWOULDAFOUNDAHONDA... I'm thinking, *what?* Is this guy a car salesman? I felt ridiculous for him. My face was reddening on his behalf. I felt mean and judgmental. I was wondering if my Honda could take me far away from here.

Then the theme came up again: You don't know what you are talking about. Try communicating with God in English and see what happens.

It's early, but I'm tired. This is too much.

What does it mean to be imparted with the Holy Spirit, really? I feel so inadequate to decide. Do I really want to know?

How do you tell the difference between good crazy and just crazy crazy?

Luke 1:16

There's more: He'll bring the people back to God.
> Your son is crazy great.
> He'll do what you can't.

Luke 1:17

And still more: In the tradition of Elijah, he'll prepare people for God.

Wow. I'll say it again.

I'm not this kid's father, but all this talking of a calling, commitment, covenant, spirit, and power has me thinking about how inadequate my life is. I don't impact anyone. I don't prepare the way to anywhere. Where is my calling? Where is my coat?

I'm not going to be a priest and a third Elijah, but isn't there something concrete for me to do? Can't there be some reason for my existence?

How will I prove that this toil was worth it? Do I always have to come in first in a race to be significant?

I'll admit it: Most of what I do is in service of two contradictory goals. First to help people; second, to help myself. I really do want to help people. It motivates me. However, I also want people to like, respect, and admire me. This also very much motivates me. Left unchecked, everything I do will be to please someone. Every step I take will be toward the goal of people loving me.

I go to a get-together and afterward every look and word I examine for evidence of love and respect. Most of the time I wish I would or wouldn't have said that. I wonder if that person now thinks I'm a Cyclops? Am I a Cyclops? I turn to my wife, Cheesecake, on the drive home and ask her what she thinks about when Nancy or Eric asked about my new book and I went on for hours. Did they look bored? Was I talking loudly? Do you think they noticed this stain? Was my joke inappropriate? Do you think they knew I cared about what they had to say? Would it be okay if that goes in the book?

Every time I am in someone's doorway about to leave I am apologizing about something, wondering if I have overstayed my welcome. I even once apologized about apologizing so much. Okay, maybe I've done it twice. Sorry.

All this, I believe, can be attributed to a fuzzy calling and an underdeveloped faith. I am searching for my worth in all the wrong places. It sounds easy to fix, and it would be if my name was John and I was in Elizabeth's womb. Of course, then I would have to follow through on one of the highest callings ever called, which probably has its own troubles.

I liked this long line of words before I reread them.

Luke 1:18

We're old. How can this be? Seems fair to me. An angel announces all this about your family, and then you wonder how it is possible. This coming from a priest, though, shouldn't he be more up on the game plan? I like Zechariah. He's a priest, but he's also just a guy who's about to have a kid after giving up on the idea. According to an angel anyway. Okay, now that I write it down it does seem a little crazy. It also seems peaceful. It makes life's little annoyances seem ridiculous. It also has a message of peace with it: What goes on here really does matter. It's a tennis match. It's a love affair.

Obviously, I'm having a hard time with a comparison. I need to relate it to something today. An angel telling an old man he will have a son that will prepare everyone for God is not an easy pill to swallow without some contextual water. Okay, well, I have one. It's like having a lackluster college career, but getting a phone call on draft day six years and 30 pounds later to say the Angels would like to offer you a contract. In fact, you will be the catcher to prepare their young phenom, Jesus, who throws 105 mph, for the big leagues where he may just be the ticket to the World Series. That might be a shocker. Please, happen to me, please.

I pull off my glasses and run my fingers along my eyes. I wonder if any of this makes sense. I wonder if any of my questions can be answered. I wonder if this is worthwhile. I wonder if I am worthwhile. I look at the clock, take a deep breath, and keep reading. Maybe I'll just finish this chapter and then go to sleep. I never sleep on command. It's just something that attacks you or is wrestled from you.

Luke 1:19

I'm an angel. I'm Gabriel. Not believing me is like not believing God. I stand with God. I'm his fullback. If God were a pirate, I would be the parrot. This is good news. This is trustworthy news. I have been sent from God.

We often have to cite our sources or justify our authority on a matter. I can't think of a better source for any term paper, news article, congressional hearing, or prediction, than God told me. It's a message from the Lord.

Of course, you better not say such things unless it's true. Could you imagine facing God one day and him asking you about everything you have been telling people in his name? You wouldn't do it if you believed God is real. I think of all the people through the years spreading hate and justifying violence and persecution and prejustice in the name of God. I'm a little scared right now just thinking about it. I'm thinking of all the things I've said and done, how I've disrespected God, and I'm a little afraid. I think about me meeting an angel and him telling me my son's destiny. I would be afraid to believe because it is just so crazy and I would be afraid not to believe because if God sent an angel and I didn't listen what would be the repercussions? Crazy, I'm realizing, is a word I overuse. I own it.

Luke 1:20

You didn't believe so shut up and watch as everything I said happens just as I said it would. I said shut up.

Luke 1:21

Outside, everyone is wondering what happened to Zechariah. Isn't that how it always is? We feel the weight of the world in these expectations. Is he working or just goofing off? Zechariah is in there hearing prophesy from an angel and the people are wondering what is taking so long. I remember something about when Moses was up on a mountain talking to God. He took so long everyone betrayed him.

Actually, maybe everyone is concerned for Zechariah. Didn't they tie a rope around priests so if they died in there while doing their duties, the other priests could pull them out? I can't be making that up.

Anyway, it feels like a pressure cooker in there, talking to an angel about a son you never expected with people outside banging on the door.

I feel just like that sometimes. So what next?

Luke 1:22

I'm tired, but I'm a fitful sleeper. I read until I drop off to sleep or I don't sleep at all. The TV is an enemy of sleep. It could be a lack of oxygen, one doctor told me. It could be that I grind my teeth, a dentist said. It could be that I am under a lot of stress, a friend with a degree in psychology indicated. *Turn out that light and go to sleep,* my wife is famous for. I read and try to forget about all of these diagnoses just for a moment.

Zechariah couldn't speak. The people knew he had had a vision because of the signs he was making. That's a funny picture: a game of charades. The people didn't seem particularly shocked by the fact that he couldn't speak or that he had a vision.

I think not being able to speak would be horrible, but it apparently can't keep us from communicating.

I have a friend. He was injured in Iraq by one of those IED bombs. I visit him at his home, where his mom frets over him. He can't speak, yet he can communicate his needs some of the time, his love some of the time, his frustration most of the time. The theatrics of his hands and face communicate. His superior attention span when playing with his nieces communicates. His smile communicates. His tears communicate. His volume communicates.

Luke 1:23

After that, he went home.

After a normal long day I can't wait to get home. I can only imagine how Zechariah feels. Home is a sanctuary—most of the time. I can't wait to get home; and once home, I swear I will never leave again. At home, I am among those that know me and love me anyway. At home, I read a book or watch TV. At home, I don't feel uncomfortable about weird conversations or my sagging waste line. At home, there is a couch with exactly my imprint. At home, pants are optional, even discouraged.

All I need—love, food, shelter, protection, affirmation—I keep it in my treasure chest: home.

I imagine Zechariah walking briskly, almost tasting home. He will hug his wife and all the little stuff won't matter anymore. He'll communicate and Elizabeth will fret over him.

Luke 1:24

Maybe this is all worthless. I'm tired. I have work to do. But then she's pregnant. Elizabeth is going to have a baby! I find the strength I need to read on.

Luke 1:25

It's God! He did this! He has given me a life again and taken away my disgrace! Elizabeth is quick about giving God credit.

I am not sure how I feel about it. I mean, does she forget her long life wishing to have children? Does this make up for all the suffering and ridicule she must have withstood? Yes. It does.

I remember when my first son was born. I watched my wife giving birth and it was the worst thing I could imagine. She was in terrible pain all day, screaming out of control. I hated it more than I had hated anything in my life. And the women are laughing at me now. They are thinking he was just standing there. He didn't have to endure any of the pain. They are right. And I hated it still. Yet, when my son, Ollie, was born it didn't seem so bad. He made all that pain go away in an instant with a tiny wail. It was suddenly miraculous. He was grey and ugly, but all ours.

So I can imagine how Elizabeth felt. I can imagine her feeling the baby move inside her and thinking this wait wasn't so bad. Maybe, even thinking, God has perfect timing. I mean God creates; God is passion; God is a mystery; God is present when you least expect it.

This God, how amazing, how mysterious. She had taken some God drug.

I keep reading and remembering and think maybe things will be okay after all.

Luke 1:26

It's the sixth month and Gabriel has another message for another unlikely character.

I don't know about you, but I like this angel Gabriel a lot better than a stork.

I get the feeling that Nazareth, a town in Galilee, is kind of a strange place for an angel to go. It's kind of like Nineveh versus Tarshish; Tacoma, rather than say Seattle; Albany, rather than Portland; Mountain Home, rather than Boise; or Idaho, rather than any other place. What good could come out of Idaho?

Yet, I can't help but point out that I'm from Idaho. I've lived in Tacoma, Albany, and Mountain Home. I've run to Tarshish rather than moving to Nineveh. Of course, I don't expect The Big Potato to be anything like me.

Luke 1:27

Gabriel was visiting Mary. The first thing I note from this verse is that it's apparently very important that Mary is a virgin, since Luke says it twice. Virgin almost feels like a dirty word. I don't know why but it makes me feel uncomfortable. I don't want to think about virginity. I don't want to think about my forthcoming daughter and the word virginity.

I remember when I was in high school most of the guys knew who the virgins were. Typically, virgin girls were either a challenge or scorned. Nonvirgins were old news. Virgin guys were the butt of jokes. How did everyone know? I don't know, but we all did. There was a real significance then too. It kind of defined you just like it defined Mary. In small moments, it was respected; the rest of the time it made you really weird. It was either because you were a religious fanatic or because no one was willing.

I look at these young high-schoolers now and I scream! Figuratively. I had a reoccurring scary dream I was the catcher of our high-school team. I was up to bat and people were chanting, but instead of "Ink, Ink, Ink" or "Deuces, deuces, deuces," it was "Vir Gin, Vir Gin, Vir Gin." It haunted me, yet there was a line I didn't want to cross out of fear and commitment and many other reasons. I was afraid, thank God, or whoever was responsible.

And I had it easy, I'm a guy.

My daughter!

Mary was a virgin. It was significant. It was an even bigger deal back then.

I still squirm when I hear the word virgin. The word virgin, despite all the examples to the contrary, makes me think of prissy girls and ostracized boys.

Luke 1:28

Hi. You're very special. God is with you. Who doesn't want to hear that?

Luke 1:29

It kind of freaked Mary out. I guess you hear that greeting and then you are waiting for the punch line. At first I can't understand Mary's reaction. An angel has just said you are "highly favored" and the "Lord is with you," and you become "greatly troubled"? That just doesn't make sense. Then I see it. She knows there will be more. She knows that with this greeting will come a challenge, high expectations, a high calling. She's young and engaged and maybe she doesn't want all the responsibility of this. She just wants the life she's wanted.

I look at it in another manner: Some strange guy comes by saying strange things. And we can't forget that pretty much everyone that sees an angel is afraid and needs to be reassured.

Sometimes I want an angel and a true calling. I feel as though I am wandering—and wondering—around, barely touching the fabric of what should be my life. I feel aimless. Yet, I'm not sure I want a clear calling either. What if it is the wrong one? What if I'm not up to it?

I imagine myself as the best person I could be. There's a bat in one hand and the great American novel in the other. I realize no one would love me more. I realize I still wouldn't know who God is or what this life is all about. I realize that I still wouldn't listen or be listened to. I sneak out of my imagining and keep reading because these thoughts are playing ping pong with my heart, or whatever it is that inspires me to write and run and kiss my wife with passion.

Luke 1:30

I want to read more, but I am also disgusted with myself. I should be working on something, that's why I'm here. I should be preparing for the tradeshow tomorrow. I want to feel like I know what I am talking about. The life of a journalist is nodding your head and making note to research the topic later or look up that $10 word if you can spell it. When talking with financial professionals (a label of their own invention I'm sure, so I hope to one day be referred to as a language professional, word investor) I sometimes wish I could speak with such authority. I wish someone would be at awe about what I know like I am at awe at the moment. Sometimes I hear industry jargon and wonder if I will ever fit in. I should be researching, writing, and reading the competition. Save these things, I should at least be getting some sleep.

How long is this chapter anyway? Eighty verses!

I don't often call my wife on the road. We don't have much to talk about over the phone. We're too busy. We save up all of that conversation for when I get home. I step in the door and we see who can talk the fastest. We review everything even before the kiss. Why is the phone such a stumbling block?

Predictably, Gabriel said don't be afraid, God is on your side.

For some reason this verse makes me feel great. Maybe God is on my side. I get that feeling I get right before I write or right after I read something brilliant or Russell Martin hits a triple. I catch a glimpse of myself in the mirror. It ruins the moment.

Luke 1:31

You'll have a son. Name him Jesus.

Mary must immediately be thinking this is great, down the road a ways, when Joseph and I have been married for a year or two and saved up for a few sheep or whatever, a house of our own, then we will have a boy and we'll call him Jesus. How great to know this now, even while we are still engaged! Won't Joseph be excited when I tell him…? I've always wanted to be a mother. I always wanted to have a son. It won't be long. I wonder if he will look like Joseph. I wonder if he'll be a great carpenter. I can't wait. I wish it were happening now!

Luke 1:32–33

He'll be called the "Son of the Most High," and given David's throne. To be great is one thing, but this was altogether different. I can't even imagine what she felt, this young girl Mary. Did she know he meant Messiah? Did she grasp what Gabriel was telling her?

If she knew then that this child would save the world, how would she have digested the news?

If she knew this child would be born only to die, would she have wanted him at all? Aren't we all born only to begin dying?

Then she learns he will be over the house of Jacob and his kingdom will be forever. What a son! The life of a king has never been an easy one. Was she thinking he would wear a golden crown? Was she thinking of the tyrant kings of her time? Who would want their son to be a king given the track record of kings, even David and Solomon?

Even with these thoughts, it must have seemed unreal. I remember soon after I was married trying to imagine what it was like to have children. I remember not wanting to put undue pressure on them to be great at sports or interested in reading; and once born, it was hard to imagine them getting older. Yet Mary, young and not even married, was being told her son would in some confusing sense be the most important person in the world. As a parent, you have high hopes; as a parent, you have giant fears; as a parent, you do your best and try to do better each day.

Mary. What did you know? What did you feel? What did you believe? What did you fear?

Luke 1:34

But... I'm a virgin.

The phone rings. And I, of course, the fool that I am, answer it. It's a colleague from corporate—Seth—wondering if we can have breakfast in the morning. When I tell him I was planning to get something in the pressroom just before hitting the show floor, he lets me know that our boss thought it would be a good opportunity for "beneficial interaction." I guess I have to say yes, since I know the boss will be calling to check how the meeting went. Seth and I have had every dinner together on this trip, yet it's not enough. Sometimes I wonder if what we do matters or if who is in control matters more. The worst thing I could ever do is have an original idea and then spend some time working on it. My boss would rather that he gave me the idea and that I work on it twice as long as it would take. If I finish something early it's like I am stealing from him. *I paid for this project to take 10 hours and I want you to work on it for 10 hours.* What is even better is if my boss can think of a way to waste my time during regular hours, so I am afforded the opportunity to work in the evening. Since I am on salary, he believes this is like free work time. Or that's how I see it. I remind you, I'm often wrong. Okay... this is getting ridiculous, I realize it. I'll quit typing it, although I can't promise I won't continue complaining in my head.

Okay. Now I'm done. Unfortunately, I'm still an adolescent. I'm tempted to delete, but I can't. I'm too lazy.

Mary has a good point. I wonder how she knew that the angel was referring to now rather than in the future. If I didn't already know a bit about the story myself, I would think that was kind of a dumb question. Of course, the angel meant after you're married for a couple of years, not right this second. Yet, it's one of the most integral parts of the plan, a way for us knuckle-headed people to know it's really miraculous: a man born of a virgin. I sometimes wonder why Jesus wasn't just created from dust, but I think God wanted us to know he was willing to go through everything just like us, including birth, family life, a protective mother, adolescence, hunger, thirst, lust, everything. I can't think of what to compare that to. It's like me becoming an ant or a slug or maybe like Zeus becoming a fly to save all the flies. And that probably doesn't even give an accurate picture of the kind of sacrifice God made to become like us—to put on this old, grimy suit and show us how it can be wonderful.

Luke 1:35

The Holy Spirit will do it. Your son will be the Son of God.

There really isn't much to say about this. It is what it is. There are no analogies or similes with the required power, passion, whatever.

Mary must have been calm. It is the news that is so beyond our understanding and control that calms us. There is nothing she can do, so what is there to worry about? It is the things that we think we can control that cause so much trouble. This is a trouble-free, worry-free situation. However, now that I say it... I know I'm wrong.

Her life has just changed completely. Everything she thought and planned before can be thrown out with the pizza crust. Her circumstances have just been turned on their head. She is no longer Mary; now, she is Mary, soon-to-be-the-mother-of-Christ, one born to die.

I remember when my wife, Marty, and I found out we were going to have a child, everything and nothing had changed. Marty started cleaning up the house and I sat in front of the computer wishing I had something to write. Instead I researched child names, looking for a beautiful, not-so-popular name that wasn't hard to spell or easily used as a weapon in the teasing years.

Mary, would she be so different? Had her life not changed in this moment?

She must have been overwhelmed. Did she believe? How would she tell Joseph such news?

Luke 1:36

I'm a mess. There is so much to be done, so many stories to be told. Why am I doing this? Will this really answer any of my questions? I can't wait for my wife to read it. Marty can cut through the crap and figure out why I am writing such things. I feel as though the gospel of Luke has become a mirror. I look into it and I see who I really am.

Elizabeth is having a baby too, even though she is old and barren. If that seems impossible and yet is possible, could a virgin birth be possible?

Luke 1:37

Nothing is impossible with God. How long has it been since I believed nothing is impossible. I think that notion went out with Santa Claus. I hope my children still believe nothing is impossible. Is that how God feels? Does God wish us to believe nothing is impossible?

I've seen this verse on t-shirts—I've written it on my baseball caps. I've let it roll around in my head like a marble. I want to believe it. The weight of the world crushes this verse out of me and I wonder if I will ever believe it again. I'm as weak as everyone else. Suffering squeezes belief out of me. I can't watch my mother's slow, slow death and then believe nothing is impossible. Life, death, suffering, belief, impossibility. At times of birth and death, we come to believe different things, or do we? Suffering, I must point out, is also a major producer of belief.

Luke 1:38

I'm God's. I hope what you say is true. Gabriel leaves.

I wish I made quick/faithful decisions and proclamations like that. I would have been weighing the pros and cons against my fears like an equation, until at least a couple of chapters if not until the end of Luke. Amazing. Such solid, crazy faith. Can I even relate? I need to redefine or quit using that crazy word. Crap.

Luke 1:39–40

After that, Mary left in a hurry to visit Elizabeth in the hills.

Mary had to get out of there. She was unwed and pregnant. She was feverish with angel visions. She needed to get away. She needed to see someone who might understand, at least a little bit. After all, hadn't the angel said Elizabeth was also miraculously with child?

I would like to run away to the hills, to a good friend who might understand.

Luke 1:41

Elizabeth's baby leapt when Mary spoke. Elizabeth was filled with the Holy Spirit.

My wife is always trying to get me to feel the baby's movement, but I never really can. Not this early in the pregnancy. She is always irritated that I can't feel an arm or a leg or a bum. But to leap!

I know I've already said this, so I will only mention it and try not to belabor the point. I have no idea what it means to be filled with the Holy Spirit and I am a little afraid to know. As far as I am concerned if you aren't a little afraid of this part of God—The Holy Ghost—and what he apparently inspires in people, well then you really haven't put much thought into it.

I start to wonder why I am doing this again. I am too busy for this. Yet, I want to do something. I want to do something worthwhile. I don't know if this is worthwhile yet, but attempting to do something that could be worthwhile is definitely a step in the right direction, right?

Luke 1:42

Elizabeth shouts: You and your child are great.

I am expecting a daughter right now. The excitement is unbelievable. When people see my pregnant wife they want to yell, they want to touch her belly. Some people get so excited I find reasons to get busy, look away, or even run. I have a quiet excitement. I will hold my new daughter soon.

But this was different. These were words from the Holy Spirit. This was more than excitement, this was prophesy. Oh man, does that word make my skin crawl. Every movie seems to have something about prophesy in it. I don't like it. And yet, here it is in the Bible. Isn't the Bible supposed to be more down to earth, less crazy? Do normal (I'm trying not to use the word sane because I don't know what it means; I don't really know what normal is either) people believe in prophesy or just people that dress up for movie openings or learn fictional alien languages for their wedding vows? Well, apparently not. Not according to Luke. Apparently, prophesy also comes from warrior angels and old pregnant relatives that are filled with the spirit of God.

Luke 1:43

But, Elizabeth asks, what is so special about me; what have I done that the mom of the Lord would come to visit me?

It really does show a great deal of humility, this question. She sees more than a cousin. She senses the significance of the moment and her own insignificance in comparison. It is almost as if her life is complete in knowing she will have a son; and yet, there is more. There is more to the story and more to her role in the story. There is more, much more. As a side note, I hate when people brag. I want to say: I know you're wonderful; can we talk about me for once?

Luke 1:44

My baby leapt for you.

Luke 1:45

You're great. You heard from an angel and you believed.

So hard to describe how important or inspirational this moment is, these two women marveling about what God is doing. I remember in college we were discussing a certain text, it could have been Milton or possibly Blake, and the girl next to me, the one I had been eyeing all semester with all kinds of happily ever after, turned to me and whispered, "this is why I could never take those Bible-thumping Baptists, they always act like only men matter, and they use Jesus as a justification, which is all wrong." I smiled and hoped I didn't look guilty. I never asked her out to coffee or a movie, but I remembered her, that beauty that made my heart a punk fan. But every time I thought about her, I remembered her words. I came to realize none of us were really reading the Bible if we thought that this was its purpose, misogyny, and particularly the accounts of Jesus, who honors women, held them dear, listened to their testimony, tracked his lineage through them, first appeared to women after his resurrection, and so forth. If we thumped the Bible a little more often we might see that. Am I preaching? I'm scaring myself. But I will venture to say one more thing: The story the Bible tells is full of women—wonderful, faithful, strong, and lovely woman. It's the history of terrible fathers I worry about.

Luke 1:46

The Bible just amazes me when I look at it closely—no joke. I think of it as boring and outdated. I come at it with low expectations. I read it expecting ridiculous rules and straight-forward lessons. Instead I find stories and humanity. I read it figuring nothing is new under the sun; instead I'm over the moon. Okay… I'm losing me. I don't want to get caught up in this. I don't want to be coerced by my emotions. I want to be impartial about the whole thing. I'm the blank page. I'm Ink. Yet… I bring my own ideas and learned assumptions. How can I separate myself from what I read? How can I react without thinking first if my pastor or God or reason or wife or dad will think I'm saying something ridiculous or maybe even blasphemous? Is it possible to not be coerced in our thinking?

So Mary sings to God.

Luke 1:47–55

Mary rejoices at how God has taken care of her, an unwed mother. She knows she will be remembered through the generations because of God, because of Jesus, the holy one—her son. God is merciful if we fear (respect? See him as he really is?) him. God has done great things; he is opposed to the proud, even kings, but he holds dear the humble (Do gods do such things? Are gods attracted to weakness or power?). He favors the hungry over the rich(!). God is merciful. He keeps his promises forever.

This is Mary's song. Did she get it right? Does God look after the humble and hungry while passing over the proud and rich? In what world is this possible? This isn't the world I know. This is the opposite. Do I even want a world like this?

Yes.

Luke 1:56

Mary stayed three more months, then left.

Luke 1:57–58

Elizabeth has a son. Everyone heard and shared in her joy. Friends, family, and neighbors knew that it was only God that could give her a child. They came; they shared; they had a party.

Even though I've never experienced it quite like this myself, when I think of a father rejoicing over a new son, I think of blue cigars proclaiming it's a boy. Aren't all your friends there celebrating with you? Aren't you taking a pull off of one of life's luxuries, and grown men are hugging for the first time since the last child was born or the Rams won a playoff game? Isn't this what men do? Isn't it a party because the men still have energy and time to puff away?

Yet, after our son was born, I sat alone. My wife was sleeping after a great meal. I was looking at Ollie as he slept. I was alone. I was worried about being a good father. I was hungry because the dining area was closed. Alone, worried, and hungry, I was unable to sleep. I wanted friends. I wanted reassurance from someone. I wanted a cheeseburger and a giant-sized order of fries. I felt lost and needy and not up for the task.

A funny thing happened, though. I fell asleep. The next day I took my family home. The doorbell rang and friends dropped off food and asked to see little Ollie. I am far from figuring anything out, but Ollie is out of diapers. I don't think I could have even imagined it on the day of his birth.

Luke 1:59–60

The boy was to be named after his father, Zechariah, but Elizabeth named him John.

My wife and I love to argue about names. We argue about pet names and kid names for kids not yet born. I want to name kids and dogs and cats and fish after writers, poets, characters, and sports stars. My wife doesn't have alternative names per se; she just doesn't like the ones I invent. I am forever full of names; she is forever full of vetoes. I wanted Ignatius Popeye Slinger; we named him Oliver Vincent Slinger. I wanted Emily Dickinson Slinger; we named her, after much discussion, Ruth Christine Slinger. I came up with all the names. I argued with myself and my wife. I had a basket full of apples and she picked out all the rotten ones. When you find the right name, however, it feels like destiny. Not a naming as much as a discovering of the name they already had. We're finding the glass slipper that fits, not making a brand-new slipper from sand, soda ash, limestone, or borax.

His name will be John.

Luke 1:61 – 63

Names are just that important to us. They are a calling.

People were amazed because no relatives were named John. They wanted Zechariah to clear up the matter; certainly he had staved off madness in this matter. He was still mute for not believing in all of this, so he wrote that the boy should be named John.

I'm sore on my one arm. It tingles. My chest hurts. Momentarily I worry about a heart attack. I worry about dying tonight. It's like tiny ants running up and down my arms. The madness passes as quickly as it came. I worry about seeing my children grow up well, although I can't imagine them any older than they are today. I hold on to madness for just one more moment wondering what my wife thinks of me. Does she believe me to be a rash or calculating person? Am I really the love of her life or have I proven to be an uninteresting husband? I worry and then I try to put it away like socks in a drawer (clean?). There's no need. Who would want to know if they were uninteresting anyway?

Luke 1:64

Then Zechariah could speak again, so he praised God.

What does it mean to praise God? Do we yell out into the abyss? Do we speak in tongues? Do we fall to our knees in prayer? Do we hide away in a closet or wait until meal time and recite something our parents used to recite over a meal that we may or may not be thankful for depending on whether it is chicken wings or some new vegetarian invention that's supposed to help you lose weight and become better looking? Zechariah gave God the credit even though it was God that made him mute in the first place. It makes me think that it's sometimes more in our silence that we honor or praise God. If I understand anything, that is.

When I really think about silence, however, I get a little tense. Have you ever sat in silence? Have you ever been in a conversation and suddenly silence? Have you ever asked a question and then waded through the silence? Have you ever stood up to speak in front of a crowd at your mother's funeral and be faced by an open casket and an overabundance of silence? I actually think I hate silence.

I will try silence for five minutes.

Nothing is happening. I feel hungry.

It is kind of peaceful. I like this.

I have so much to do, why am I just sitting here?

Not bad, this silence thing. Okay. I will try it now without typing too.

I'm closing my eyes. It helps the silence.

I notice I'm breathing. Each breath is relaxing. I am able to listen to the still small voice.

Okay. This is getting weird now. I should feel as though I am wasting time, but I'm not really. This is great. Peace.

I need to do this more often.

Okay. I can't waste any more time.

Luke 1:65

Awe filled them. Everyone was talking about it.

Does this really happen? I remember in high school walking down the hall, a deafening silence like a loud buzz with the faint drum of my heart in my ears. I felt as though everyone was talking about me. I was sweating. I stunk. My fly was down. My ears were big. There's a laugh off to the right and it makes me want to run. I've forgotten a math quiz or a book report. My baseball glove is at home on my dresser. People know.

In dreams, I hit a walk-off grand slam and everyone cheers when I walk through the school doors. Girls are surrounding me.

These things only happen in movies and our minds, yet here news really was traveling that fast. John was a celebrity from birth with all its charms and expectations.

Luke 1:66

What is this child capable of?

When was the last time I believed in limitless potential? I am usually the one saying there is no way that is possible. I think of myself as optimistic. I believe in miracles, just not for me. Disappointment takes it right out of you. Wasn't I supposed to be a major-league catcher, or save that, the world's most popular writer? I'm not even an admired English teacher, my back backup plan. Anything is possible but happiness and contentment. Those aren't possible in my experience. Everything is possible when you are young. At 30, I'm not old, but I'm entirely more realistic. Sometimes I think that is a good thing, but do I really want to be the one remembered as saying that's not possible?

Should I, then, get caught up once again in these miraculous births, both John, and the other one that changed the calendar and according to some changed the world, everything?

And suddenly I have come to the end. These are all my words.

Luke 1: 67–79

Filled with this Holy Spirit, Zechariah sang and prophesied:

Praise God, the God of Israel, for he has saved us. He has shown his strength through the line of David, just as he said he would. Our enemies will never have us now. He has done all of this to be merciful to our fathers, to Abraham, and to keep his promises, particularly that we can serve him without fear all of our days. We can be holy. We can be righteous before him.

There is a pause.

I swear it was an angel visiting me!

Son. You will be his prophet, preparing the way for the one who is to come. Tell the people they are saved and forgiven. Why? Because God is merciful. Let them know that the sun is about to shine on us all even if we are hiding in darkness or almost dead. He will direct us to the path of peace.

It is a wonderful song, clearly inspired. It is a heavy burden like carrying an elephant.

I reiterate: This prophesy is a scary business.

Luke 1:80

John grew up strong in the spirit. He lived in the desert until his time had come.

Don't we all want a clear calling? Don't we want to hear from God about why and for what he created us, if such a thing is possible? Of course we do; but really, do we?

I've never taken these things all that seriously. The thing is it's a book about God; so, of course, he plays a major, magical role. In a book, anything is possible. It's all easy to believe. I try to take the story, the sentences, and even the words and shake them from the pages almost like shaking dirt from a favorite jersey or afghan. I want the words, the truth of all this, to permeate the world and be tested by its fires and smoke. I want to know if these stories, words, if the truth can survive in the world or if it will be choked out. The words have been born into this world by the beating of the afghan (or jersey) and I wonder if I can breathe it all in. I wonder if I can take that crazy step and be guided, feet and all, into the path of peace that Zechariah promised so long ago upon the birth of his son. I remember when Ollie was born, I could have sacked Troy—of course, those, once again, are not my words.

two

Luke 2:1–3

Caesar Augustus takes census of his people. Everyone has to register at their own hometown.

Thus begins the Christmas Story. I was reading this part to Ollie and Levi the other morning from a children's book and they were asking one question after another. Who is that? Pointing to Caesar Augustus. Is that a crown? Is he a king? Does he have a sword? What is a census? Why is Mr. August counting people? Can I have a snack? Something not healthy? Candy? Santa brings us candy! Let's do Halloween, Easter, anything with Candy.

If you believe the story, God uses any and every circumstance to fulfill his promises. He uses the census to put his men in place. I can't help but envision God strategically realigning his army as he begins the greatest story ever told. These shall be moved there; these there, and now it can begin.

No matter how much Christianity, especially Christians, are called into question, whether by me or those that have been wronged by people or institutions, there is no denying how amazing this story is. I've heard or read it at least a thousand times, but still I feel the anticipation rising up in me. The moon is up and across the sky signifying the idiocy

41

of being awake with so much to do in the morning, but on the other hand there's the story of Jesus. You don't come this far just to place the bookmark.

Luke 2:4-5

Joseph took his pregnant fiancée from Nazareth to Bethlehem because he belonged to the house of David—the adulterous, murderous hero-king who was a man after God's own heart.

Seems like quite an inconvenience to me. I don't go anywhere to be counted or otherwise when my wife is pregnant. Instead, I pack bags and make plans. I vacuum and put together bassinettes. I paint. I worry about everything. I try to get ahead in work so I can take a few days off. I do whatever my wife tells me to. I enjoy going out to fetch burgers and fries and ice cream and "something chocolaty" at all hours. I touch and feel the baby move... finally. She gains weight. I gain weight too. We're all very heavy. She is beautiful. I check the gas in the car. I worry about our brakes. I buy another car seat. I get talked into another class. I do what I am told. I eat and I worry. I do all of these things and more. I don't travel. I'm not counted. I don't do anything inconvenient for my wife's and new baby's sake. I get out of obligations and painstakingly negotiate time off. I prepare a clean, comfortable, and loving place for the baby. That's the plan.

Luke 2:6

The baby was coming, home or not.

I grabbed all those things that I had packed and planned and realized it was worthless. For the only time I can remember, nothing else mattered. I drove with my head in liquid. I could hardly breathe. I could hardly do much of anything. My wife, she seemed calm to me. She was calm between every contraction and even the contractions, she said, "weren't so bad." I ran around. I worried about details and if I was man enough for all this, the birth and being a father. Nothing else mattered. It was time. I didn't even call my boss. I caught sight of myself in the mirror and I was angry at my fat reflection for not looking more like a man. I felt like a man. Time, always an enemy, didn't matter anymore. I drove. I filled out forms. I held my wife's hand. I prayed silently. I did everything I had learned in the classes. I willed myself to be a better person, if not for this child and my beautiful wife than for what, whom?

I didn't even think about writing stories.

I held her hand. Although I felt like I was on the sidelines in the biggest game of my life, I approached it like I was the quarterback. I ran plays. I executed. I faked left, pitched right, and my wife ran through a linebacker on the way to the end zone.

I realized that I could never do what my wife was doing.

I prayed for her. I prayed for the son we would name Ollie. More than ever, during childbirth is an incredibly tough time to not believe in God, I found out. You really have to work at it if you want to do it right, this disbelieving. You have to treat atheism like a full-time job if you want to do it well—and let's be honest here, it's not worth taking an unbelieving stance unless you're willing to do it right and stake your whole life on it.

I mean not believing seems a lot like boxing. It's a dangerous sport. You let your guard down and here comes belief with a right uppercut and then faith knocks you out with an overhand left.

Luke 2:7

This is familiar: Mary has a son. She wrapped him up and put him in a manger. Then comes an even more classic line: because there was no room for them in the inn.

It makes me feel warmth. It all makes me feel peaceful and comfortable. I think of Christmas, a fire, my family, lots of good food, presents. Yet, something's missing isn't it? Is this the point—warmth and comfort?

I guess I need new eyes.

Maybe from Joseph's point of view, I'll see something new.

I'm Joseph. My wife is having a baby in a barn because we can't find anywhere else to stay.

I'm feeling colder now.

After she has the baby—our son!—we put him in a boxy feeding trough for lack of a better place. The animals come to eat and drink and find a baby. They go away angry. I feel worthless and cold.

This is the beginning. This is our story.

God chose this? This is God's story? He was conceived out of wedlock by mysterious circumstances and then born in a barn?

My mother used to ask me all the time if I was born in a barn, demeaning me just enough to slam the front door on my way out.

Luke 2:8

There were shepherds just down the block guarding their flocks in the darkness of night. Mysterious business was a foot.

I could keep reading to get to the angels, but I'll stop here because something has struck me. We quickly move away from the birth and are now speaking of shepherds. What a story. It's not about kings and royal births and purple robes. It's about regular people, if not lowly people. It's about shepherds and dirty sheep with the hint at the possibility of wolves and other trouble under the starry night sky. It makes me feel as though I could have been there. That could have been me watching the sheep, lying under the night sky—rather than in this sofa-chair meant for someone half my size and with a heftier title—listening for predators or counting sheep until my eyelids were as heavy as two oxen.

Luke 2:9

See previous thoughts on angels and their ability to inspire fear.

My best friend, a recently married college roommate that lives across the American landscape from me just beyond the Louisiana Purchase, just called from a crackling cell phone that sounded like a cheap firework. He's frustrated about a recent manuscript I sent him to review. He's on some noisy vehicle of public transportation yelling about poetry. I can hear *why poetry, why always poetry? Why can't you just tell a story?... off topic... makes no sense... crackle... crackle... crackle...*

I laugh to myself. I have no idea. I want to squeeze those answers from myself. I imagine getting me in an interrogation room and really exploring some of these issues. Whenever I'm feeling distracted or abstracted or obtuse, a poem enters the story like a burglar through a side window. I wish I could have thought of that before our connection was lost. He'll call some other time to renew his disapproval about how I handle my retirement account. Just because he has an MBA, he thinks he can...

The dress you wore was blue.

I noticed my feet. Empty. But—
I know you know the piece and part
And can piece that part and of course
I'm stalling now. Your secrets. The music.
Something blue.

You remember. You know the dress you wore
was blue and full of lessons.

Luke 2:10

Don't fear. I have great news for everyone.

I imagine they sit up from where they have been hiding in the grass. One shepherd looks at another across hundreds of sheep. *News for everyone?* All I ever hear is sheep gossip about wolves and terrible lies.

45

I'll tell the truth at some point. I didn't come to Luke randomly. I didn't run out of books. The truth is... well, I wish I knew. I got some bad news. It wasn't shocking or astonishing, just the kind of news that has you grasping. Plus, I reach for discontent every day like a cigarette. I breathe deeply and cough. It saddens me to hide the truth behind pretext and fancy footwork. I parry. I don't understand why it's all this unruly. I can't explain my favorite moment—my wife in that blue dress—any more than I can explain emptiness.

Luke 2:11-12

Let's see, this is where it might be helpful to know more about words such as theology and prophesy. My interpretation is this: A savior, the one people have been waiting for—the Christ—has been born right where he was supposed to. However, here's where it gets a little strange: The baby is wrapped up in an animal trough, no throne in sight.

What strikes me is the angel just assumes that the shepherds will go see this baby. When you get there, you'll know this is the baby because he'll be wrapped in some old clothes and lying in a manger. Apparently it was a foregone conclusion that they would go see him. There's no doubt. This event is so amazing even the shepherds are leaving their sheep. Yet, why is it the shepherds in the first place? Why are they the chosen? And, why is the Christ in such an ordinary, dirty place? Do shepherds ever leave their sheep?

It's just the first time this Christ will overwhelm and underwhelm.

People's lives change forever, but not the people you expect. The savior comes according to plan, but he's a carpenter's son rather than a warrior's. This savior refutes all preconceived notions. This savior is like no other. This baby in the barn, mixing with animals, shepherds, virgins, and angels, is either God or something else entirely. This is either the beginning of the greatest story in all of history or another myth for another dusty, outdated book that could be a good decoration in a fine, upstanding house.

Luke 2:13-14

A choir of angels! Glory to God! Peace!

Let me first say that the "!" is like an enemy to me, but when one is required, it is required.

My first reaction is to squirm. It's this kind of stuff that makes me uncomfortable. Just when things seem simple angels appear and give glory to God and peace to men like a bunch of cheerleaders at the Superbowl. It makes me think of those after-school specials. You wanted them to be believable, but then the storyline goes crazy, such as a young boy playing detective or the ninja. Anyway, I squirm. I squirm because I want to believe, but then this. How could I explain to my friends that I believe in a choir of angels? What would Steve think? How hard would Allen laugh?

There are lots of things that you can explain away and rationalize before people, but a band of angels is not one of them. Either it happened or it didn't. I can almost believe left alone, but when I think of co-workers, friends, and my father, the belief seeps away like so much embarrassing sweat. Still, angels, peace, God... it's no small matter and I refuse to let it be. I choose angels over emptiness every time.

Luke 2:15

The angels went back to heaven. These shepherds decided amongst themselves to go see what all the fuss was about. Angels, God's representatives, had come down to tell them what was going on after all, and it wasn't often they were up on divine scuttlebutt.

I don't know what is stranger, the angels and their message or who they decided to tell. It just seems a lot like a political committee going out Old Snake Road to tell a few recluse farmers that President Obama is coming to town for a speech. It just doesn't make sense. Even that doesn't compare. I can't think of anything that is this ridiculous or less strategic. Yet, I have to say one thing: It was enough to convince the shepherds, who would probably never leave their sheep for any reason, to go investigate. That seems significant.

It's a story for the common person. It's an amazing cheeseburger, not a pretentious $35 steak with sides not included. Great, now I'm hungry.

It's all upside down and backwards.

Luke 2:16-18

The shepherds hurried. They found Mary, Joseph, and the baby. They told everyone they could. Everyone was amazed.

News worked a bit different back then. I envy those shepherds. Their whole world changed, bam. They got swept up in it, this great story—the best thing to ever happen in this world. They found God first, and then they went and told people. I wish I had a story like that—one I got swept up in and told everyone about. I would keep writing draft after draft until it was just right. I would have loved the look of amazement. I don't write about amazing things, and even if I did, I wouldn't see those who read about it. I remember the first article I ever wrote was a quarterly report of a small analyst firm that was thrice gobbled up, been in Chap. 11, and since liquidated. I poured my heart into the adjectives, the numbers, and particularly the headline. I took a step back when I was finished and took stock of it. Nothing. I electronically handed it in and that was that. It was edited down to bones and dust and soon an issue was out. They forgot to add my bi-line. The article went out into the world like a child at 18, and I never heard from it again. It was prodigal in nature. I envy those shepherds. They had a gem and they knew what to do with it. If I had a gem like that today, and went to tell people, they would ignore me. I can imagine nice families seeing me coming down the block. They run inside. They turn their lights off. They hide. They call their friends to tell them about how masterfully they dodged me. Others leave me a love note that says don't you dare knock. So in my imagining, I go back to my desk. I make rich men richer by strangling all life out of the words before I send them off on a barely seaworthy boat bound for the seven seas of commerce.

Luke 2:19

For Mary, these moments were like treasures. She collected them and pondered them in her heart.

This is one of the most beautiful moments in all of literature. It was God. It was also her son, whom she loved more than her own life, no matter the circumstances or his incarnation and destiny.

I remember every detail about when Ollie and Levi were born. It is treasure. I never knew I had such a capacity for love. I feel self-conscious writing it down. I keep looking over my shoulder, but it's true. When your child is born, you know for sure there is a God, you see love more clearly, life looks different from every angle, and you without a doubt know you would do anything in the world to protect them. Everything's new. It's treasure.

Luke 2:20

It was just like the angel had said, no exaggeration. The shepherds returned, praising God.

There was no need for hyperbole; in fact, these incidents would set a new standard for hyperbole. The truth was better than fiction, and you didn't need to be a shepherd to know it. The birth. The story. The unbelievable truth. Could it be that Luke got it all right, this account? Was he careful in gathering facts? Did an editor make revisions that changed the meaning? Can we trust the Bible after all these years? I wish I could know for sure.

Luke 2:21

They named him Jesus, which is the name the angel had given him before he was even conceived.

It was all going according to plan, no matter how ridiculous the plan sounded. They trusted the plan. They didn't doubt. Mary had a son. Joseph had a family. Jesus had parents. An angel told the truth.

Naming is very important to me. I ponder name meanings and how I might honor people by using their name or the name of their parent. Names can be like an Old-Testament blessing not only to the one named, but to those she or he was named after. One might steal this blessing with soup, for instance.

Doing a quick search of Jesus it means *God will help* or *God rescues*, which may be the meaning after this Jesus took it as his title. There is power in a name. I say Jesus even now and I see how it impacts people. I say Jesus and people smile, laugh, or cry. I say Jesus and people squirm. I say Jesus and the world stops. At the name of Jesus, the world takes notice. There is power in a name.

Luke 2:22-24

Honestly, I don't understand much of the Jewish law as it relates to purification, consecration, and sacrifice. Sometimes this language can even be exclusionary for people who are interested in God, but don't know the lingo. Language sometimes feels like the currency by which we can bless, curse, exclude, or love.

The way I see it, Mary and Joseph were committed to being obedient. Even with everything that had happened, angels and prophesy and shepherds and stars and mangers, they didn't forget to show their devotion and commitment to their God. It seems as though through sacrifice, according to the law, they dedicated Jesus to God. But what do I know really?

When Ollie was born, we took him before the church and they prayed for him. They committed to being his spiritual family. I hadn't always been a good part of the body, so I was thankful. I hoped we could all always be this close. I was nervous. I thought they were going to baptize him, but it turns out only some churches do that as babies. Maybe I am the only one that didn't know that. I go to church and I even try to pay attention, but not growing up in one, sometimes I am blind to the most elementary facts. I read the Bible. I question the worth of church. I look at myself in the mirror. I ask questions. I read.

I dedicated my son. Jesus was dedicated by his parents.

I wonder if they will say of me, he was a churchgoer, a religious man, a Christian, a reader of the Bible, a flip flopper, merciful, judgmental, misguided, anti-intellectual, committed, enjoyable, loud, quiet, good looking, open minded, loving, guarded, generous, dedicated, respectful, saved, strong, unbearable, beautiful, funny, astute, practical, unique, heavy, obtuse, strange...

Luke 2:25

Another mystery afoot: This righteous man Simeon is new to the story. He is waiting for the comfort of Israel? He was full of the Holy Spirit?

What could possibly come next? It seems like the old and the new are colliding. Is this what has been hoped for all along?

This story has everything, even the old, wise man who had seen it coming and was waiting. Isn't this the case in all great hero stories?

I'd like to talk with Simeon. I'd like to buy him lunch and hear what his life was like. It has the feel of a great prologue about to pass into chapter one.

Luke 2:26

He'd see the Christ before death, he was told.

It was written on his heart that he would see who would save it before he left the world. If he is anything like me his first thought would be, why me? Why this old man with the withered bones and disappointment splashed across his face? Was this his last comfort before he went home? I'm sure there is more to say on this, but what? What can I say? You'd have to believe, bet your whole life on the Christ. Did he ever think, how will I know him? Why did Simeon recognize Jesus when so many others didn't?

The moment was on fire and I
wanted to throw wild waters on it,
maybe a river from my youth gone
rapid. I see it now, the oxygen
between these words—a borrowed line—
burning up while
only everything remains. My bones
old as night. Faith, maybe a friend now,
running down and between and through,
my heart pumping it out and attempting
what might tumble. I recognize it all. I hold
it above me, maybe. Kings, they call them.
Kings they are not. The moment burned and
a light emerged. Isn't it strange? Isn't it old? Hasn't
the fire just begun, always been? I'll see it. Now, I know
it must be true. A child changes me, all. A final
word, oxygen burned. A final word, finally come. Don't go
into the future, future you. Stay here, now, fire

Luke 2:27-32

Only the facts are needed. Simeon, apparently keenly in-tune with the Spirit like an AM radio station, knew when to be at the temple. When he saw the baby Jesus he grabbed him and started talking to God. (I'm laughing imagining it all. I stand up, no longer tired. I close my eyes.)

Simeon, with Jesus in his arms says: You were right God. You kept your promise. I have received the peace you promised before I am dismissed for the day and forever. I see the salvation, here it is. It will be for Israel. It will be for those Gentiles. It will be for all.

I can see Simeon holding up the baby, wild. I can see father and mother with fear and awe. I can't help myself. I'm nearly dancing. I'm caught up in the moment. I'm 30 and I want to do something with my life. I'm 30, and a great deal is still before me. I'm 30 and optimistic and almost ready for bed, but not yet.

Luke 2:33

That they marvel is not surprising. What is surprising is that they didn't snatch their child back and run for the length of the Bible. Instead, Mary and Joseph listened. They marveled.

Luke 2:34-35

There was a blessing. Simeon told Mary that Jesus will be the cause of the falling and rising of many in Israel and will also be some sort of sign that will be argued over. These events will show what is in people's hearts. There will also be a sword. It will not spare you at all.

Good thing Simeon blessed them first. He told Mary a tale that reminds me of Beowulf or King Arthur or Star Wars or some such thing. Your baby will cause a lot of trouble, saving many and changing all. Some will believe, some not. Hearts will be filleted. Victories will be won. It will tear you to pieces. And Mary, I'm sure she stored it all up. She showed faith letting Simeon hold her baby. She showed faith not grabbing Jesus back and declaring, *not my son, over my dead body*. Wouldn't she want to protect him, them all, from such a fate? Certainly. Wouldn't we all? But she had been visited by an angel and proven herself faithful. Still, it amazes me. I might have taken Jesus far away in hopes that I could bare his trials for him. But. He had a better father by far.

Was this why my son was born, to cause trouble and to die?

Faith is a funny thing. You can't see it, really, but you know it all the same.

Faith is a hilarious thing really, just like love. You know you have it when you start acting all wacky. Obviously, Joseph and Mary were in love and faithful. Simeon too.

Luke 2:36-38

Anna was also there. She was an old profit, who lost her husband while young. Tragedy. So she married again, the temple this time where she worshiped and worshiped more. She also waited for Jesus. Once seeing him, she told everyone about how Jerusalem would be saved.

I remembered Simeon, but not Anna for some reason. She was 84 and still carried the pain of her husband's death so many years past now. This I can't even imagine, could any imagine unless made to see? Her life was dedicated to the temple. Her life was dedicated to fasting and prayer. I sometimes think of prayer as a selfish act and fasting as a ridiculous one, yet this was Anna's life. And because of this dedication she could see things others couldn't, or that is how the story goes whether believed or not. What does it mean to pray? What does it mean to fast? Is it just talk and lack of food? Not to Anna. She thanked God. She saw his mercy amongst pain. She was waiting too for Jesus. She recognized him as a gift from God. Her message is powerful because her life was stuffed full of patience and hope. I stop. I can't move on. Do I have time for this? Should I be focused on more pressing matters such as work? Sleep? Food? Interest rates? Or my children's favorite: birthdays?

How can this be? Her message was one of power and mercy. Do I listen? Do I hear it even now? How hard is it to believe in Simeon and Anna, and the destiny they read in Jesus? Is this all just a great, economic story for a reader such as me so many years now gone measured by death and dedication and waiting? Is this what we should look back upon and also forward to? Can I just read and then move on or should I allow my life to be impacted? Oh how important this—I—have become. I liked it better when I could laugh it off and not see how it pushed me. I like adventure better than dedication and subsequent decisions that must be made if I am going to look and discover. Why am I a part of the story now? Isn't that against the rules of journalism? What is journalism if it doesn't impact our lives? Shouldn't it be about something new, not something as old as pain, redemption, and stories for countries gone by? Is this task greater than sleep? Why so many questions? I grow tired, very tired, and yet... what is redemption really? Must I have tragedy and patience to see? What is sight? So many questions, so little sleep. I must move on. I must quit. I must read on. I must stay here. Maybe pray. Maybe be ridiculous for once in my life, or is it quitting that is ridiculous? I hope to rewrite this, me. I hope to write again. I hope to change. I hope to stay the same. I hope. I hope. I hope. I'm confused. I'm just pretending I am the person I want to be. Does that even mean anything? Questions.

Luke 2:39-40

After that, Mary and Joseph finished their temple duties and went home. Jesus grew up. He was filled with both wisdom and grace. The grace of God, Luke called it.

That's it. All this happens and they just go home. Jesus grows up. I guess I expected more. I guess I expected questions. I expected a long trip home with confusion as a companion. Am I the only that is confused? And the story moves on with or without me. I tag along because what else am I going to do at this point?

The TV switches on next door.

It's loud.

There are three of them on the other side of the wall.

They are having much more fun than me.

Luke 2:41

A personal note: I need to exercise and eat better.

Mary and Joseph went to Jerusalem every year for Passover. What a holiday. Isn't that the one where the people celebrated that their children were spared from the angel of death? I seem to remember that they smeared blood on their doors as a sign. What a sign that must have been. There has already been blood shed here, no need for more.

I make light of it because I don't understand the times. I don't understand the word sacrifice and there is a big part of me that likes my ignorance. Make a joke and run away.

Chicken wings and nachos be the death of me. Didn't Israel eat bitter herbs during Passover as a remembrance of the Exodus? I'm not making that up am I? I need an Old-Testament diet: no sausage and lots of bitter herbs. Would it be okay if I dipped the herbs in wing sauce?

Luke 2:42-43

If you are wondering I am not a lawyer. Technically, you don't have to be a lawyer to add Esq. to your title—that is just the common usage. My boss added my moniker and Esq. so it might give me an air of authority, which, of course, I badly needed. It's my balk move. No one ever calls me on it. The runners don't advance, rather they stay off balance. It's strategic. It's dishonest. It's within the rules of the game.

They went to the feast when Jesus was 12. On the way home, they couldn't find him.

My worst moment as a parent was the 45 minutes I couldn't find Ollie in the mall. He was three. He ran and with each stride put my heart in a blender. I thought all the worst thoughts. I knew I was the worst parent in the world. I called his name. I recruited friends and mall security. I was embarrassed, but was willing to be embarrassed to find him. I called my wife, friends; we panicked together. Cheesecake.

To say my heart was drumming in my ears is to completely understate. I have never felt so lost, hopeless, useless, afraid. I would now give him a thousand toys. He emerged from behind a rack of clothes. I hugged. I cried. I took deep breaths. I wanted to tell him everything was okay and to teach him to never do it again. I was at a loss. I wasn't a very good parent. I hugged him and said I loved him. I told him to never do it again. I marched him to the car and we talked all the way home and we tried to figure it all out. He said he was mad. I said I was mad. We tried to forgive each other. I told him he meant everything to me. We negotiated a truce. I waited for the night to fall. I watched him as he slept. I promised myself and God to do it all better tomorrow—to not lose my temper or focus. I made a lot of promises I could never keep. The world was out of control.

My wife baked a German Chocolate Cheesecake.

We ate.

We talked.

We yelled a little, cried a little.

She is a much better person than me, no doubt.

She would never lose a kid.

A dog maybe, but never a kid.

Luke 2:44-45

They traveled for a day. They looked for him among and with friends and relatives. They went back to Jerusalem.

They must have been frantic. I am sure there are explanations dependent on cultural differences or rituals, but how could he be missing a full day before they realized? Seriously.

Luke 2:46-50

The next part would almost be comical if I couldn't remember what it felt like to search for a son. Jesus is no regular boy. It gets a little mythic.

Mary and Joseph don't find him for three days. They must have been half dead with worry by then, worst-case scenarios attacking them day and night. Jesus was in the temple courts holding discourse with the teachers. Everyone was amazed that he could hold his own in the spiritual ring. He was a heavyweight at 12. Even Mary and Joseph were astonished and they knew the story. Still, he was their son. He was young. Mary's fears, it seemed, had turned to a bit of anger. This I can understand. She wants to know why Jesus would put them through all of this knowing full well how it would terrify them. I can hear words I have yelled about being the parent, the authority, the boss. "I can't protect you unless I know where you are. Get in your room and stay there until you are ready to listen." But Jesus. He wanted to know why they were searching. He thought they should know he would be in his "Father's house." I don't care what you believe about Jesus, that was a dagger. "You're not the boss of me."

Jesus was about the business of God. Twelve and already you've lost control of him. Ollie is five. He's sometimes out of control. He's sometimes obedient. He's sometimes insightful. He's sometimes terribly disobedient and illogical. Mary and Joseph had to raise God. They were Jesus's parents, but really they had no authority, but what he gave them.

Mary and Joseph didn't understand what Jesus was saying to them.

Parents are all the same.

Or as the Fresh Prince says "Parents just don't understand."

This is like a wedding, something borrowed, something blue, something from an early-90s sitcom.

Luke 2:51

Jesus went with them to Nazareth. He was obedient. Again, Mary stored it all in her heart. Her heart was like an attic.

They acted in obedience, even Jesus, which must have been trying with all he had to do. Mary knew the story was significant. She saved it in her heart. I think that all parents do this. They try to remember every moment with their children. I try to remember their birth, how much I loved them then and now. As we prepare for another child, I remember. I store it up. This is my story. This is our story. I love my wife and children. I remember for all of us. I grow tired, but I want my life to change. I realize my need in good and tough times. I always remember and try to do better. When I think that this or that past is the only that holds the perfect moments, I remember the future. There is so much ahead. There is so much to do. There is so much to be. All I have to realize is that I don't really understand, but I can do good. I can love. I can forgive myself. I can live rightly. I can't control much, but what I can control, I must do well. I must remember. I must move forward. I must change. I must remember. The storage of these moments is the storage of time. The storage of this time is the storage of my treasures. The storage of these treasures is the storage of the future. I store. I cull. I go home. I try to be obedient. I move forward. It's all I can do. I can stand on the shoulders of those who were before me and ask my children to stand on mine.

We all have a story.

Luke 2:52

Talk about less is more: Jesus grew up both physically and mentally. What else happened? I could never get away with this. Give me some details. If you don't know, find out. Come on, Luke. What pub do you work for anyway?

Jesus found favor from both God and man. Is that even possible? It's either one or the other, isn't it? We really did skip a lot.

It's late. I'm tired. I need poetry in my life, if just to irritate a reader. One stanza. I can do that. You can survive that.

If I could read my life—one more
page gone gray and annoying—I would
have a poem worthy of afternoon showers.
I only have three more lines and words
to fill them with. I give up. I can't write
anymore. The libraries are flying south.

three

Luke 3:1-2

There are lots of important people who do lots of important things, denoting history and place like a bookmark, or better yet a yellow highlighter. God's word came to John, the son of Zechariah who hangs out in the desert like a long-haired hippy who snacks on the land. Whenever I read history it is based on the most important people and events, or maybe just the most powerful people and events. We put things in context by what a president did or which war was being waged. Yet who changed the calendar and the timeline most? How did a man who chose powerlessness become so important when money and power are the currency of history? I'm no historian, but it doesn't make sense to me, unless of course the unthinkable... it was so true it was undeniable. That's too easy. However, something was so important that the accounts were kept sacred and have been maintained and protected throughout time. Apparently; I remember being told in literature classes that the translation and accuracy of the Bible through time is unparalleled. No other book even comes close, further evidence depending on your point of view. Anyway, I'm off chasing rabbits, but no one would argue this: These times were remembered. I have to ask myself a simple question: Why?

Luke 3:3

Crazy John of the desert began preaching baptism and repentance for the forgiveness of sin—always a popular topic.

What a dirty word, sin. Nobody uses that cuss word anymore, sin. I am not sure what it even means. What is sin? It's a political debate these days. People use the idea of sin to exclude. That is sin, so you can't be a part of my church or team or clique. Isn't sin supposed to be the great equalizer? Aren't we all supposed to be put on the same team by sin? Aren't we all sinners? We're either sinners or gods. If sin is dirty then emersion seems appropriate, but, then again, what is baptism and how important is it? I feel like I am on shaky ground here. With every word, I know I am making someone angry. To say such and such is a sin is to lose a friend. To say such and such is not a sin means losing a friend. I don't want to lose any friends! It makes me wonder what Jesus will say. He will say something conclusive, right? He will clear up the debate and unmuck the waters, won't he? What will he tell me is a sin? For what reasons would I allow John to put me under the waters? Isn't this same practice a form of torture? Hold me under water and I will tell you all of my secrets. Is it wrong to feel the need for continual baptism, yet be afraid of the act? I feel an emptiness that I want to fill. No matter how good the day is, it is never good enough. I know there should be more. I feel lost. I feel a need for water. I fear the water. What is sin? What is truth? Does sin separate me or include me? Again, questions. Again, dirt. Again, water as cleansing and torture. I stand at the shore and I wonder if I will remain standing or if I jump in, will I drown or swim? Is this a clever image or ridiculous? Will I ever know? I keep writing, the words and ideas before me forming a river that both invites me and challenges me with calm pools and rushing waves.

Luke 3:4-6

Isaiah's words are like a poem! Is the reader getting angry? You hate poetry don't you? The prophet is recorded as saying something like:

There's this guy in the desert calling out to everyone that they should prepare some kind of path for the Lord that is straight and flat—no hills or mountains, for they will be no more. Rough and crooked roads will be made straight and smooth. Everyone will see God's salvation.

Are we the roads or will the trip be simplified for God and for us? I'm somewhat confused, but it's beautiful. Everyone, everything will be saved and made easy, simple, straight? I can't help but want to rewrite it again. Am I the same man as when I began?

I'm hearing a voice among the dust.
The voice is speaking for God. It says
prepare for the Lord and be ready for
change. Valleys, hills, mountains, hearts
beware. Everything is about to be changed.
High will come down, low up. Prepare.
All people will be saved. Prepare or be prepared.

I'm no mountain. I'm not even sure I am ears.

How do we prepare?

Luke 3:7

I'm not having fun anymore. Crowds are coming to John to be baptized, and he is chastising them. He calls them a brood of vipers. He asks them who has warned them to avoid the wrath that is to come.

Prophets are often the best reason to ignore the message. People who have a message are often mad. Prophets are often hypocrites. Prophets don't stop with hope, they move quickly to condemnation. People heard his words, recognized his words, and came to John. He called them evil.

I feel condemned. Why John? We've heard what you have to say and we are coming to you, isn't that enough? What more do you want?

Isn't it baby vipers that eat their own mother?

This really should be a conversation among friends, say over dinner or coffee or even a couple of beers, rather than between a writer and his computerized words. But you do what you can do, but you don't just drink the Kool Aid.

Luke 3:8-9

John continues. Your repentance can't be a single act but a lifestyle. You may claim that because your people have been promised salvation that you can act however you want, but God says otherwise. Even the stones can replace you at any moment. Where's the hope?

John's not done. Here it comes: You're a tree. You either produce "fruit" or get chopped down and burned. I can see the people leaving the church as I type this. Why? Are our lives that bad? I fear the axe.

Does fear produce faith or does love produce faith?

Why rule with an axe?

Do I believe in the axe?

What would my life be like if I knew an axe was being swung?

Is that life? Is that my suit?

I'm a tree.

Luke 3:10

Every time I begin to believe, I run into the axe. The axe keeps me running rather than setting down roots.

The crowd asks John: What can we do then? I ask John the same. I start to wonder again who this axe-swinging God is? Are other people reading this? Are Christians reading this? Will the path be prepared through the clear-cut of sinners? God as Weyerhaeuser?

Luke 3:11

I feel like I have stepped on a landmine. I'm frozen. If I just would have left it all alone, I wouldn't be here, balancing on John's words, wondering what kind of savior this is that clears the trees to save the forest. Maybe my questions are sealing my fate. The axe. Even as I write it, I don't really believe it. Is there really an axe?

John answers: Share your clothes and food with those in need.

Give and the axe will be put away.

Wow. Giving is important; it's salvation's requirement... or at least the outcropping of salvation... "the fruit." God is asking for repentance and charity. He wants this tree to share the sun and soil. He tells of an axe for those without fruit.

Luke 3:12-15

This is a strange story full of strange characters. Tax collectors come for the water. They ask what they should do and he says don't be greedy. To recap: give and don't be greedy. Then soldiers. John says: don't extort or falsely accuse, be content with the money you earn. To recap: give and don't be greedy. I'm hearing the ten commandments. The crowds aren't running away, they are coming forward. I don't see fear. I see openness. What is attracting them, is it fear or hope?

Luke says the people are expectant. What John is saying reminds them of the promised Christ, could that be it?

Luke 3:16-18

John says: I have water. But this other guy has the Holy Spirit and fire. I can't decide what troubles me more the Holy Spirit or the fire. John says this guy who is coming later is much greater than him.

If I didn't like the image of an axe, I surely don't like the winnowing fork. This next guy will be gathering wheat and burning up the chaff with a fire that will never stop burning. This hungry fire. Good news? Is there another option besides wheat and chaff? Which am I? John had many other words. Good news? The harvest is here.

I'm no farmer, but I understand that before the harvest the fields are full and afterward, everything has been cleared and is no more. I know this life won't last forever, don't I?

Luke 3:19-20

John gets specific, maybe too specific. He speaks of Herod's sin. Herod was one of the four rulers with power over John. It makes me believe his message, if he is willing to take it to the highest levels. I seem to remember this sin, which reminds me of David somewhat, about Herod taking his brother's wife Herodias. John also said he was doing many other evils. John announced it. He said even Herod needed to repent and be baptized. Wow.

So the next part isn't much of a shock: Herod locked up John.

What time is it? I'm afraid to look. I really do need to hit the sack soon. Does anyone say that anymore? My gramps used to say I'll tear you up like a sow's bed. I should bring that one back.

I was in church just a few days before. I was fidgety and Ollie and Levi were even worse. Cheesecake was pretty bad too, but she's large with child. The sermon was about Jesus. It asked the question: God or maniac? I looked around. I had to bring my dad to this one. His theory is every sermon should have the same title: You know where you are going. Sunday School was easier. We looked at a passage in Genesis concerning the character of Joseph. We all agreed. We talked quickly. We prayed quickly. I was thinking of lunch. People offered prayer requests for other people. I tried to remember everyone's names. I couldn't think of anything I knew about them other than their dislike of other religions. I turn my ears off, or at least to low, with this talk. I won't participate. I will argue over truth, but I won't flippantly dismiss anything others hold dear. How heroic of you, I think to myself. I know I am a hypocrite. I should be the hardest on myself and my church. I should be the hardest on my country. I should hold us to the highest standard. I should believe with confidence and let my life reflect my belief. Of course, that kind of belief leads to rulers and imprisonment. What is scarier than prison? I can't think of much. All this to avoid the axe or the winnowing fork. Are those my options? An axe or craziness and imprisonment?

My father and I got a couple of western cheeseburgers at Carl's Jr. We discussed church a little and the onion rings a lot.

Then we went fishing. Crappy. Small mouth.

Cheesecake took the kids home. Sleep. Food. Sleep.

Luke 3:21-22

I'm not quite ready for this passage. I think I will go down to the vending machines and see what I can find. I hope for chips and chips and chips. I run away from Jesus's baptism, the Holy Spirit, and the booming voice of God. I run. I chip. I'll be back soon when the moment seems less strange, insoluble.

I'm back from the long, dark hall, fingers orange. I'm ready—I think—to try it again. There is a lot of pressure, tangible weight and the ridiculous word responsibility. I'll just tell you what I am reading and leave it up to you. Here's the story:

Even more people were being baptized, the water splashing with sin—the fish must be drunk. Jesus came. He was baptized too in those same waters. Was he the one John spoke of? I was sitting there, trying to write this but my back was hurting. I couldn't find the right spot. Jesus was praying. His prayer was personal like a conversation between two coffee patrons. Familiar, you might say. Abba. I didn't even notice heaven there until the door was opened. There was this wavy dove that came through the door, coasting down until it was mixing with Jesus. I'm not sure if you are seeing what I saw. I read and I see. This wavy dove was the Holy Spirit. I gasped. There was water. There was heaven.

There was a dove. And then there was a voice that I almost recognized. This voice said: "You are my Son, whom I love; with you I am well pleased." The voice had timber. It wasn't a matter of belief or even fear. It was a matter of awe. *Have you ever felt awe?* I asked. *At the dentist*, someone said. I said, *this is no time for jokes.* I couldn't remember anything but this moment. The voice had a son. He was in love with this son. He was pleased with this son. Since my own son had made me watch the old Star Wars trilogy about 20 times with him, reciting the lines during the last few showings, I came to think of Darth Vader and Luke. I came to think of how it didn't really relate at all. I came to think of what an idiot I was for even bringing that up.

I had a story here. I began writing it. My lede was: Jesus was just one of many in the water stirred by John the Baptist when heaven opened, a dove descended, and a voice boomed. It was for him. And so it began.

I looked down at the orange of my keyboard. I tried again.

Crowds, tax collectors, soldiers, and a man named Jesus tried the waters stirred by desert John this morning. It's difficult to describe what happened next. I, like many others, just watched as the sky seemed to open up to any possibility. God came down in the form of a dove—this reporter is as shocked as you. Let me tell you, the story is far from over. There was a voice coming from nowhere or maybe everywhere. I am afraid to write it, but it reminded me of the hand on the wall, something like the voice in the sky. I understood the voice, and you will too.

"You are my Son, whom I love; with you I am well pleased."

I don't remember what happened next. How's that for some great reporting?

I just couldn't do it. I couldn't describe it. So, I did what I always do. I moved on, promising myself I would go back and fix it some other time. Sometimes I do. Sometimes I don't. That's it. That's how it works. Mostly, I don't.

Luke 3:23-37

After that, Jesus began his ministry. He was 30. Imagine the hope for my life this becomes. Though still young, I am tempted to think that this is it for me: The best years are behind. I had baseball dreams. I had writing dreams. The reality is I was a bench player for a mediocre college team and I've wrote three novels that were quickly buried. I want again those impossible dreams. I don't believe in anything that is impossible anymore. Is this what is called maturing? I want none of it. Yet, arguably the greatest man to ever walk this earth started it all at 30. Is this possible? I should be successful by now. I should have a red-stitched ball in one hand and maybe a pen in the other. I should have a uniform and a signing schedule. Why not? Days are not dreams for me; instead, days are but schedules. I get past the empty part of my day on small miracles that aren't really miracles at all. I don't know what to look forward to. Some days, truthfully, I can't wait to get out of the house, only to wish I was back in it when I leave. Here I am at a tradeshow I have been looking forward to in small ways wrapped in escape, wasting sleeping hours, and none the better for it. After this chapter I will go to sleep. I look in the mirror. I see me. Some would call this a victory: A spiritual journey that culminates in the finding of one's self. I look at me and feel empty still, the search not over.

Then there is history. God is before time. Jesus can track his family all the way back to Adam and then God. I wonder about all of these people. Some I know. Some have stories. Some have great character. I want to tell stories about great men or contentment or something. I know little of my own history. What could I gain by knowing it? I see a king. I see many kings. I see a man knocked around by life that was victorious in the end, saving his entire family. I see a crazy man in a crazy boat full of animals. I see the first man that sinned. They all sinned, that dirty word again. Some believed; some were faithful; some murdered; and some wandered. How do we measure our lives? by faith? by our stories? by what we did or did not do by the time we were 30 or 33 or 100? What is the measure of a person, his family, how he viewed the world? Tell me, Luke. Tell me. Someone, please, tell me.

I wander around the floor. I have coffee in one hand and a notepad in the other. I ask vendors about trends and innovations. I see the hangovers drooping. A man hangdog, and hope that isn't me. When a representative of BoA or Morgan Stanley or Oppenheimer or The Wall Street Journal stops by I somehow end up on the outer edge, listening. I move on. I see huge credit cards. I see investments and dream scenarios. I see fire places and big-screen TVs, model homes bigger than my own. I see maps and charts and earnings expectations. I see eyes. I see mirrors, extra weight, sweat, red. I see lives I could never afford. I see the word NEW on every professionally designed sign. The housing market is down. The economy is in the wind. Everyone is sour on foot traffic versus yesteryear. I haven't found my story yet. I interview a new player with this year's big entertainment hit. It will make my life easier, my parties more exciting. I try to imagine this in my life. I imagine the friends I could make. I stifle a laugh. I look at what I am wearing. It's a nice shirt and pants I bought on sale. The shoes are old but shining for the occasion. I feel like a misfit. I wear my press badge and hope it is impressive. The sweating has already started and I wonder how I will survive this and find that right angle I have been searching for since seven years ago when I took this job on a hand shake and all brands of hopeful words. I think of Luke and my hotel room. How far away they seem now. I will be back soon, I tell them. I wonder what this vendor is really dreaming about as he gives a canned response to my canned question: This new product can do this new thing, increasing turns for every retailer in every channel of trade. Invest. Up two points. I nod. Another: I wonder what she has waiting for her back home. I wonder about her stories. Is this the job she always wanted? What would she rather be doing? Does she take me seriously? Do I take myself seriously?

I want to be reading. I want to be writing. I want to be turning two at a crucial point in a crucial game. I want to see my wife and kids running at the door as I set down my suitcases. I want to figure it all out and tell a story that makes a difference in this world that has done nothing but offer me these riddles. There are stories buried everywhere. I pour over the landscape looking for just one.

What trends are you seeing in this challenging economy? I ask. And

I wink to this other guy, like we have some inside knowledge that other chumps just dream of.

four

I'm back. My shirt is off. I take every moment and review. I get angry with myself over errant words. I wonder when I will trap some confidence. I am setting up cages everywhere.

I see the Bible. It is open to Luke. I turn on the TV instead. Luke is looking my way. I tell him to look somewhere else. There has to be someone else more appropriate. I think about a taxi and imagine myself riding to any bookstore.

Luke 4:1-2

I'm not ready for this. I know that, but I'll try. It's extremely difficult to turn the spiritual into plain words. What kind of formula is there for such a transformation, translation, exchange? It's like turning water into wine. How can I state plainly what is hard for me to even read?

The facts: Jesus was being led by the Holy Spirit away from the waters of his baptism to the desert. He had just heard the booming voice and now he was out in the middle of the desert with the devil. Is the devil real? What is worse is he doesn't eat anything for forty days. This I can't imagine. I can imagine his hunger and dizziness. Was it the snake again? I don't know if I really believe in the devil, but that doesn't make sense. I hear people's arguments. Many say they can't believe in a God that would allow suffering. Many say the devil is a myth. Can you have it one way and not the other? Look around, do you see nothing? I do see a war between good and evil. It's raging inside me. If I believe that some things are good and some things are bad, why? Why do I always do what I don't want to do, while not doing what I want to do? Now who's spiritual?

The devil inside, I have no doubts about.

Luke 4:3-4

Temptation, while it comes in many forms and angles, seems to boil down to a stew of greed, sex, and food. Just turn on your TV.

I try to imagine the devil, red with horns? Too obvious. The devil has to be more sly and cunning than that. Is the devil an elaborate ruse personified? I have several politicians in my mind now. I don't know if that is fair or not. I see the devil suited up with slick hair offering me a ten-year, 100,000-mile warranty on an over-priced Ford Mustang, orange as the fruit. He tells me he is willing to not make any money on the deal, but he can't take a loss. Will I sign in blood? Will I be a guitar hero? More subtle than that I bet.

The devil tested Jesus too. He wanted Jesus to prove that he was the Son of God. He knew Jesus was hungry, so he told him to turn the stone into bread. How could Jesus possibly resist? He could shut the devil up and eat with one stone. It was two birds if I've ever seen it.

Jesus said the scripture says man needs more than bread.

Jesus didn't need food; he needed God. Now that is faith. I have trouble doing anything when I am hungry. My wife calls it the Slinger grumpies when I haven't had my cheeseburger. He also wasn't one to do tricks for hire. Jesus seemed to reveal himself and his motivations in his own time. He wasn't concerned with the calendar; he was abolishing the calendar.

The devil—such a strange concept really. God's opposite. The whole dynamic seems to be equivalent with this statement: The opposite of love is not hate; the opposite of love is indifference. I might add to this: The opposite of love is also sometimes disillusionment, confusion, and even subterfuge. The opposite of love is a ticking bomb well hidden. The ticking like a lullaby.

Luke 4:5-8

The devil offers Jesus the world in return for his worship. Jesus responds that the scriptures say to worship the Lord your God and serve him only. It's almost lawyer-speak. Rather than say I will only worship God alone, he quotes the scripture, the law.

Why exactly is the world in the devil's hands? Is that an illusion or true? Did sin do that? In Job, God gives the devil a long leash in order to prove the faithfulness of Job. Is that what he has done with us as well?

How many people could turn down this kind of power? What if it wasn't the devil offering it directly? This cosmic, cryptic exchange is strange to me. It has the feeling of *A Christmas Carol* in its other-worldly, didactic nature. How often do we get a ring-side view?

I look over and see my smile in the mirror. My features are so strange. Does your reflection ever surprise you? I'm at it again.

A colleague drops by. I hear the knock. He says turn on the news. We sit on the edge of my bed and watch. The newscaster tells us that thousands are dead in China, thousands more are trapped, after an earthquake that has demolished most everything. Everyone is without shelter and food and family. I watch and want to move on with my life; for this, I feel the guilt. I look over at my colleague. Amazing, he says. He's at least 15 years older than me. He's been selling ads since the launch of our second pub. I wonder momentarily if he is looking for a sales angle. His dark hair is cut short and the gray gone since last I saw him several months prior in Chicago. I look back at the set and see a nurse helping a baby with a head wound. I'm not sure whether to internalize the news. I'm not sure whether to replace this baby with one of my own so I might at least guess at the pain. I look at buildings, homes, and lives demolished. I see estimated numbers beyond my comprehension. As many are dead or trapped as the city I live in. I can't quite comprehend. He asks if I am watching this without looking over. Yes, I say. I'm going to call my wife, he says, and leaves the room. I lock the door behind him and wonder if I should call my wife. I watch the news. I take a shower. I try to mourn. I replay my life. I reach for a half-

empty bag of chips. I look around the room and see its comforts. I wonder why them and not me, only it's but an intellectual question; it's not real at all. I wonder if I was a better person would I feel more. I let the guilt and pain pass through me like a long drink from a steaming cup of coffee. That's all I can do. I sit. I watch. When I can't do it anymore, I read on. I try not to think about what I can do because the answer is either nothing or it would change my life entirely too much.

Luke 4:9-12

I read the verses three or four times. I couldn't focus; details escaped me. I read them again.

This is all I could see: Now the devil quotes the law. Apparently quoting the law doesn't make it right. He says angels will protect you Jesus. If you really believe, you can jump from the temple and the angels will save you. Take a leap of faith. You have faith don't you? How tempting it must be to prove someone wrong, why not?

Jesus says don't test God. I'm sure there are volumes written about this third temptation by smarter men and women than me. I don't know what to say about it. Maybe having faith in God is not testing for testing's sake, but to trust when faith is necessary. Daniel didn't throw himself in the lions' den; Joseph didn't sell himself into slavery; and Esther didn't offer herself to the king. But when it happened, they put their hope in God. However, there are others, such as Gideon, which did test God. How do we know when it is the right time and when it is the wrong? Blah. Waxing intellectual seems so inappropriate with the news playing quietly from what I have pushed to the background. What if the devil had said jump from here and you will save everyone? I guess Jesus did something just like that, didn't he?

Luke 4:13

It's one of those comic-book, Star-Wars, super-villain exits. This isn't over. He's already planning for his next strategic opportunity. He already has the cross in mind.

Luke 4:14-15

Jesus returned to Galilee. Everyone was hearing about him. He began teaching now too in the synagogues and people were praising him.

Jesus is able to resist the devil and quickly he becomes a public figure. He is even allowed to teach in the synagogues. I don't think I'm assuming too much in thinking that not just anyone is allowed that sort of privilege. How has he come by authority and influence so quickly, particularly in such a historic establishment?

I don't even think this relates besides I miss her. I met my wife in college. Martha—I call her Marty or M or Cheesecake—was one of those soccer players, 5' 4" and legs as defined as Latin. I was walking down the hill to campus. She was running across the green chasing a cross-field pass. I watched her glide across the ugly ground. It was beautiful. That was it. That's all it took. Sure I fell in love all the time with women and motion, but this had staying power. It was both.

She kicked and missed. The ball rolled, stopped, then caught a hill and came down to the chain-link fence. She came closer. I looked down and kept walking. Love. Moments. Motion. I thought, she must really think a lot of herself the way she was waving at that group of guys. I kept walking. Then like a detective, and not a creepy one (or maybe a little creepy), I found her all over campus until I could nearly predict where she would be. My roommate Virgil thought me a fool. Foolish, yes. Time moves. Motion falls in love with motion. It was both.

Luke 4:16

Jesus went back to Nazareth, where he was raised, and went to church on the Sabbath. He stood to read.

Is this how it usually works? Does everyone get a chance to read? How come I am never asked to read at church? I could do a good job. I could follow the punctuation, taking breaths in all the right places. I have a strong voice when I want to. You might call it booming. It might have timber. Would I have to wear a tie? Would I be nervous? I can imagine looking over the crowd and hearing Ollie or Levi's laughter. I see older people straining, so I read louder. I notice my uncle out there under the huge bulbs. Uncle Mark hasn't been to church in ages. It must be Christmas or Easter. I've lost my place. I don't know about this reading gig after all.

Luke 4:17-19

Jesus was given Isaiah to read. He read something like this:

I know he's there, God. His touch.
His spirit. His anointing.

He says tell the poor   about me.

He has a message for prisoners,
the blind, and the oppressed.
It's   freedom.
It's sight.
It's release.

This he has me telling.
I am an   usher.

This is the year God   likes.

Luke 4:20-22

There is a palpable pause—a pregnant pause—as Jesus rolls the scroll of Isaiah and returns it. He sits. Everyone is looking at him. Estimating him. Fastened like bright lights on him. A spot light. Jesus says: This scripture has been fulfilled today right here, right now, as you listened. The pause was a full pause. A beat. Faith was a term buried in those words. People who desired something new sat. Listened. Were locked in. Some wondered about the power and grace of his words. "Isn't this Joseph's son?"

Luke 4:23

I'm not sure what Jesus means by what he says next, may be some kind of prophesy about how a person is viewed in his hometown—not always a hero. He says to the group that they will soon be quoting an old proverb: "Physician, heal yourself!"—isn't that quoted when he is going to the cross?—"Do here in your hometown what we have heard that you did in Capernaum." Sounds like a test. This is something that I have learned and I am not sure if it is true with everyone: Faith is not a frog. Faith is not something to be dissected or tested to come to some kind of hypothesis. Jesus wasn't looking for a tryout. He's not made to order sunny side up. Faith is just that, it's faith. It's not a science and science is not faith.

Side note: You don't need to choose between them.

Both are magic, treasure.

Luke 4:24-30

This is one of those passages that is just amazing in how it erupts. People are in awe of Jesus, thinking he speaks with such authority yet... don't I know his father, didn't I see him grow with my own eyes, isn't he just ordinary like the rest of us?

Jesus says no prophet is great in the eyes of those in his community. He says even though there were specific needs in the hometowns of great men of faith such as Elijah and Elisha, they had to leave the area in order to feed and heal.

It all changes then. The community of believers becomes an angry mob. The church becomes a gang.

They were angry, furious at Jesus's words. They took him by force out of town in order to throw him off a cliff. Murderous. He spoke. They wanted to murder. Am I missing something? Had he attacked them and they were defending themselves? One thing is Jesus aligned himself with the great prophets, which is never a good idea unless it is true.

But if they did know him since birth, how could they turn on him so quickly? Pitch their good friend's son from a cliff and get back to the service?

I was laughing about the ridiculousness of this passage at the beginning, but now I am angry. No wonder the church gets a bad name. Maybe the church came by it honestly. This is insane. Seriously. I can't believe this and how quickly the whole thing escalates to corporate murder. He, by their own admission, grew up among them. Was a son of their tribe. No mercy. Murder will make it better. Murder will teach him, everyone.

The next part almost sounds sci-fi: Jesus walked right through the crowd and went on his way. A ghost.

Luke 4:31-32

Jesus gets back to business. He goes to Capernaum and teaches. People don't understand—are amazed—that his message has such authority.

There is just something about Jesus, and what he says, that is different from anything else. His words have a life of their own. His words heal, inspire, and transform. He is young, but his words are old. Luke reports.

There's this picture I have been painting.
It's a picture of the inside of my mind.
It is a strong shade of red.
It also reminds you of yellow.
There are all of these pieces and chambers and monkeys.
The ears are all wrong.
There's this picture I have been painting and it's stored
here where only I can find it, but it's still a picture, and
I like to think it might be beautiful, true.

Luke 4:33-37

Demons. I never liked horror movies. I was never interested in ghost stories. I like to sleep. I have a really difficult time wrapping my mind around demons and spiritual warfare. Sometimes I think Christians made it all up because their parents said they couldn't play role-playing games like Dungeons & Dragons. But then, like most things, I actually read the Bible and have to rethink things. It gets confusing. It gets downright strange and unbelievable. You have to read the Bible to believe it. So here goes:

There's this man with a demon.

One step back. I am really trying to internalize this and not just gloss over the thought of a possessed man. Is he a Tasmanian devil? Does he have super strength and a raspy, creepy voice? Does he levitate? I have no idea, but one thing is for sure: this demon recognizes Jesus.

The man with the demon is yelling: *Ha! Here he is. What are you doing here Jesus? Yes; I know who you are. Why are you here on earth, Holy One of God? Have you come to destroy? Is this the end?*

Jesus, unintimidated and even unsurprised, tells the demon to quiet down and come out of the man, which he promptly does.

This is the Bible? Exorcism? Seriously? Has anyone else ever read this and felt a little weird about it all?

The people there at this time were amazed too. They wondered about Jesus and his teaching. They wondered about his authority and power. His words free. His words command. His words are pregnant with immeasurable power.

It was an amazing story. People told it to any who would listen.

Luke 4:38-39

I've forgotten even about myself. I'm tired again. I don't want to get up in the morning for another show day. I miss the routine of my family. I miss. I miss. I miss. Have you ever thought that nothing turns out or up like you thought it would? I remember when I thought all I wanted to do was be a role player on a college baseball team. Right away I was antsy, grumbling about not being a starter. How's that for life?

Jesus then went to the house of a man named Simon, whose mother-in-law was sick with a fever. In an act that makes one wonder why God doesn't just heal everyone in an instant, Jesus "rebuked" the fever and she was well. The mother-in-law immediately stood up and started waiting on them.

It makes me wonder why the hard way is sometimes the best way. Healing must be the most wonderful gift to give and to receive. Right up there with love.

I've just hung up the phone. I stare at it in disbelief. A staff writer has just called. He's working late because of me, he says. I wonder why he felt the need to call. He had to tell me that my last article on bank-backed recovery was uninformative. He suggested more research. He suggested I call a few more analysts. He wasn't impressed with my adjectives either or my use of the word emphasized, which he called sophomoric and over intellectualized. Does he remember I am above him on the organizational chart? I've hung up the phone, but I can still feel it in my hand. I can't write anymore. I can't do anything but turn on the TV and forget about all of this. I can't believe he called to tell me how inadequate I am. One call from me to the senior editor would have him in lukewarm, if not hot, water. It's that important to him. My biggest fear: That maybe he's right. I stop typing because a Seinfeld is on. At least Seinfeld isn't inadequate.

Luke 4:40

People brought to Jesus their sick friends and relatives and neighbors. Jesus healed them.

What can I say to that? Can you imagine? Maybe your wife is sick, has been for years, and you're so heartbroken because of it, it's hard to even breathe. It's all just wiped you out. Yet, one day you hear of a man who heals. How could life possibly stay the same? Now your child. Now yourself. Goodbye, you tell cancer with the smile of a champion, or just any old buffoon.

Jesus also continued to exorcize demons. They came out yelling he is the son of God, the Christ. So he kept them quiet. I still can't get my mind around this being in the Bible rather than, say, a horror movie. It's worth saying again.

Luke 4:42-44

Jesus went to be by himself. The crowds followed him because they didn't want him to leave. They wanted him for themselves. Jesus told the crowds that he must leave so he can tell others of the kingdom of God. That is why he was sent. So he kept preaching in the synagogues of Judea.

Sometimes it is difficult to keep to why you were sent or commissioned, even why you were born on this earth at this time. At first it's exciting, and then you hear of some other way and think it sounds good too, maybe worth a try.

I have had many careers and dreams: baseball, writer, teacher, journalist, book slinger, well loved. At the first sign of adversity, or even the rumor of quicker success, I lose track of the train I was on.

Chris DeVore

Unlike Jesus, I am always questioning my purpose.

I am attempting to keep it all together
with a tube of ugly glue. That's as plain as
I can say it. Do the words I write become
an airy picture for you to imagine?

If my life was just a collection of words
what might it say? Would it tell you how
much I watch for myself in the birds or
clouds flying overhead? My daughter sees
the moon or an airplane and yells to me.

A better father might have been paying attention
to more than words and his own wants.

Can words remind you of music hidden between
the branches you are lopping? The apples are falling
with a thump never to grow bigger than an egg.

From up on the roof, I see my daughter climbing the
ladder and I yell to her with all the fear of the past
several weeks when we have put the house up for sale and
are feeling more optimistic than the housing market
should allow. We can't help it.

There should be more but there is only this: I help
her down and the fear subsides. I think of more
words and try to put them together. I look into the
sky and see nothing but the sun peeking between
the remaining leaves and apples.

Okay. There's that, but it has no commitment. Here's something else entirely:

Misusing the Word War

Go to war the words say, but we
signed some treaty long ago that was archaic
the day we penned it. We've always had our noses in
the liquid law. Leave room for air.

I must be able to write what I must write.
I must be able to use every word at a moment's notice.
I must fall in love. I must.

I look out my window in the middle of the
day and find the moon up and as smug as
a toddler.

The moon.

Must I battle these words to the inevitable, bitter end
just because I saw her again in the middle
of the day walking past like she did so very often
before, of course, I drove away forever
only
  to
    stumble
back with a piece of paper and a quiver of
words I swore I would never puke again?

I thought puke.
It was an idea.
It felt like an idea.

How can you be smug? Your language and
your day-time moon is reckless and terribly feckless.

If there was a
need for an answer there would be no need
for your question because
you would already know
or not know.

You already know.

The words are playing games outside in
the snow. You want to call them in to warm
by the fire, but you must let the words do
what they need to do. That's the only way
the monosyllabic will become polysyllabic
one day.

All that and I thought I was done, only to
find myself here in the middle of a party. It's
someone's birthday I am sure of that. The beer
is good, better than most, better than the peeping-tom moon,
that old reckless chump.
I'd tell you about it, but I'm required by some new law
I don't quite understand (who does?)
that words are only to be used by those that
earn them. Language is a type of currency, which
is just another class issue. It's a regime, a diction dictatorship.
Grammar guerrilla warfare. Seventh-grade teachers armed
with moony smiles.

I did love her.

But the moon is still out there. It must be tired from
working around the clock like my father's stories.

The moon is on the swing shift. I don't know
where this is going. I drive home with my wife. I
love her again for the first of many times. It's her
legs. It's her mind. It's a number of things mixed
with words warring inside me.

First-draft poems aren't really poems at all. We write them to get rid of
them and hope to never see them again. How do we get from this to
something real?

five

Luke 5:1-3

Aren't we all just lifting up rocks and pulling weeds, looking for what we can only call meaning? It's hidden. We give up too soon. It can't be meaningless.

Jesus was standing by what must be a familiar scene. It's the Lake of Gennesaret. People were crowding in on him and listening to his words from God. According to Luke, Jesus looked out on the water and saw two boats, possibility. The fishermen, who were washing their nets and going about their business, had left them on the water's edge. Jesus got into Simon's boat and asked him to pull out from shore. There in the boat Jesus sat down. There from the boat, he taught the crowds.

People listened.

Being listened to is maybe one of the greatest feelings there is in this world. When you talk, people stop what they are doing and deem your thoughts—you—important. It's amazing. On the other hand, I have spoken many a time over chatter. I have been talked over and wounded. This is possibly my wife's greatest gift to me. When I talk, she listens. She makes me feel important. If I say I desire something, she makes it happen. If I offer an opinion, she listens until I have completed a thought. She responds accordingly, which is not always positive, but is always careful and caring. She takes me seriously despite my ramblings. What else could you ask for?

However, most people don't do so. You can measure a person's wisdom by how he is listened to. Jesus speaks with the highest authority. People listen. Where others see problems, he seems to see possibility. He sees solutions. When Jesus sees crowds and boats and fish and nets, he sees opportunities. There is a picture of a lake and a man in a boat. The man speaks. It is beautiful.

Luke 5:4-7

I think my favorite kind of story is a fish story. Salmon. Bass. Pike. Shark. Perch. Crappy. I love to hear them. I love to tell them. My father-in-law can tell a fish story so well you can smell the huge bass on the barbeque and taste the added salt. He can make the one-that-got-away into the all-night affair, a romance between lovers, a joust. Knowing how to fish is only half of it. Who believes fish stories anymore?

I do.

After teaching, Jesus told Simon to try another fishing hole and lower the nets for a catch. Given that Simon was the fisherman and he had been cleaning his nets earlier, he probably didn't want the advice or to have to clean the nets again. He wouldn't tell Jesus how to raise a roof. Yet. He listens. He tells Jesus he will do as he says only because of his authority on life, not on fishing. Simon had been fishing all night without success. He was tired. He was defeated. He had already spent extra time taking Jesus out in the boat. Yet. It wasn't a time for common sense or worrying about needs. It was a time to do. It was a time to leap. It was a time to fish.

Like all good fish stories, they caught so many fish it was breaking their nets. They called for help, and the fish were so plentiful both boats were sinking. This wasn't just a great fishing trip. This was great riches for them. Fish overflowing. But this isn't a story about fish.

Luke 5:8-10a

Simon Peter and his partners, James and John, the sons of Zebedee, were floored. Peter felt unworthy, telling Jesus to go away because he—

Peter—was a sinful man.

Jesus's soon-to-be disciples were utterly amazed at what he had done. Peter thought Jesus had made a mistake: *You've got the wrong man. I'm full of sin. You don't want me. I am not worthy of you, your miracles.*

Sometimes I feel entitled to everything, sometimes nothing. Sometimes I ponder freedom; sometimes I use it up like coffee grounds and then pitch. Repeat. In the face of God, I might run. I might tell God he chose the wrong man. I might just be unprepared for the fullness of the undeserved blessing that would tear nets and capsize boats.

Luke 5:10b-11

Jesus told Peter to not be afraid. He said from now on Peter would be a fisher of men. Then Peter, James, and John pulled in their boats, left everything, and followed Jesus.

I can't think of anything that could make me drop everything and go. I'm still trying as I type this and I can't think of a single thing. Not for new love; not for a major-league contract; and not for money. I wouldn't drop everything and leave my family for any of these. I might consider a proposal and discuss it with my family. I might spend a sleepless night considering a new opportunity. I wouldn't even think twice about new love, it just doesn't seem possible. What was it that made these men leave everything, particularly after what must have been the greatest catch of their careers?

Fishers of men—I always loved that. I liked to close my eyes tight and imagine men being caught in a net of words. I imagined saying things so inspiring that men forgot themselves and followed. I imagined music so beautiful that it physically pulled you in. I imagined a truth so accurate that no one could deny it. Fishing for the hearts of men, that's your new life.

Luke 5:12-13

The truth is... I have no idea what I am doing. I'm spinning around like an aimless top. That's no good. I can't see that. I'm writing, but for whom? I'm working, but why? I like the sound of the typing. I like process and documentation. I like to think that sometimes I add words together that have never been together before. It's a wonder how I can sit here and write and also think of the most eternal of matters and each of my family and how I miss them and how much I'd love some chicken wings and a good movie. It's a wonder how our thoughts swim around our mind like a school of hungry trout and I barely notice. I barely dip my line.

There was a man covered with leprosy who sought out Jesus and begged him for healing. Jesus healed him without hesitation.

Anyone would hesitate at the sight of leprosy. How did this man even know Jesus could heal him? I seem to remember that people with leprosy were severely shunned and separated. It was a step of faith to first realize the need, identify the one who can fill the need, and even be bold enough to approach him even though you culturally shouldn't. Is there one of us without leprosy?

Luke 5:14-16

Jesus told the man not to tell anyone, but instead to offer the sacrifices that were required under the law for cleansing. However, the news—as it often does—spread anyway. People whisper. People talk. *I wasn't supposed to say, so don't tell anyone. It didn't come from me.* My wife calls this a Slinger secret. People came to Jesus for his message and for healing. Jesus was often retreating, in search of hidden places, prayer.

It's hard to get anyone to listen to anything but bad news. Jesus did it, though, because Jesus was the real deal. So many scams these days it's extremely difficult to know who to trust. Trust no one, not even your feelings, they tell me. I can't help it. I want truth. I want peace. I want healing. I will believe even a rumor of it.

Luke 5:17-19

The phone rings. Something in me swells up and I answer. My wife. Neither of us can turn it down to a lower gear. We talk over each other. No, you first. We begin to argue about how to deal with Levi's nap and bedtime. He's been skipping his nap just fine, but falling asleep just after (or during) dinner. We must, for some reason, figure it out right now. I have visions of being the greatest father, but then I look at the way I am. Missing each other always leads to an argument. I can't wait to get off the phone. I can't wait until these words splash off me and I can get back to imagining the romantic moments when I get home. I imagine my wife meeting me at the door with the crescent-moon-shaped smile that was the highlight of our first few dates. I imagine me as the father and husband that I might admire. I imagine myself beating up the self I am imagining. I'm a fool. I can't wait to get off the phone with my wife, so I can imagine this other version of my wife that I am able to mold into what I want her to be? I say goodbye. I say, love you. I still don't know how to fix the sleeping problem. I do now know, however, that I "always try to fix everything when I should just be listening." Isn't that the truth? Cars and houses can be fixed. Humans—well, it's just not the case. We can make suggestions, but not changes. I wish I could take this heart to the shop for a major overhaul. I wish I could think well as if I was eating better. I wish I could practice the art of kind words like I was riding a bike. I wish I could do what was right in difficult situations like I was lifting weights. I wish my insides were a picture of health.

There was a crowd of teachers around him, so several men who were carrying a paralytic could not get to Jesus, who was in the house. The men went up on the roof and lowered him down.

It's a crazy scene, the kind I like to avoid. But what friends this man had! They did what it took to get their friend what he needed. Is there any better description of a friend? I like to say that I would do anything for my friends, but... It's just one of those unbelievable acts that hits you in the stomach, the chest, and even around the eyes. This is exactly what the world needs. This is exactly what can be done. I hope I don't let any hurdle—physical, emotional, intellectual, or self-provisional—keep me from lowering my friends through the roof to get him or her what he or she needs.

Luke 5:20

Oh how clever I think I am writing this. I sit here laughing at my own jokes. I sit here trying to escape life. I sit here feeling like a rodent that has to climb through and out of the hole it is stuck in. The words are my claws. The words are my claws. The words are my claws.

I used to believe I could do anything. Do you remember when nothing was impossible? I find myself recycling that line as if it will take me back to a day that never really existed. Back then I couldn't wait to grow up. What is with this life, it just never fits. Is anyone ever content or are we all just pretending?

The TV is on, but the sound is down all the way. A woman is lighting a cigarette. She cups her hand around the small fire to protect it against the wind. It's a beautiful, delicate moment. I have no idea why she is waiting there outside the restaurant that promises the best steamed clams in town, but her slight movements suggest a song. She dances like nothing else exists. She pulls the cigarette from her lips and blows smoke out into the night. I envy her. The camera pulls back and I see the entire city. It could be any city; it could be any song. I can almost touch it. I can almost hear it.

I know I am way off topic now, but stay with me for just one moment. I have a small dream. It's small but important to me. I want to write something of significance. I want to walk into a bookstore or a coffee shop and see something I wrote make someone laugh or cry or tell their friend. I want to see something I wrote spark a conversation. I want to write something that makes someone do something they wouldn't have dreamed of doing. I want to write something that in some small way impacts a life. Is that too much to ask? Is that weird to write such a thing down?

Meanwhile, Jesus, a man of action, sees the faith of the paralytic and his friends. He tells the paralytic that his sins are forgiven. I know what happens next. I know the crowd will question his authority. They will wonder if this man should be claiming to forgive sins. Isn't that unique to God?

Luke 5:21-26

The Pharisees and teachers of the law call it blasphemy as they consider it in their hearts. But Jesus knew what they were thinking, so he asked them why? He wanted to know if it was easier to say your sins are forgiven or get up and walk. Maybe he was saying, can you do either? Or what do you know of this kind of power? Jesus wanted to know if the Son of Man had such authority on earth to forgive sins.

It was all about authority then. Jesus had the authority. He told the paralytic to get up, walk, and go home healed. Amazingly, the man immediately stood up and went home praising God.

Everyone was amazed and they all began praising God. They all realized they had seen a remarkable thing. What else is there to say? How can I add a single thing to this account?

Jesus healed the man. Jesus had the authority. I guess what is left is to believe or not believe. Only that.

Luke 5:27-28

The Bible always eludes me. I sometimes get the impression I am chasing a lost dog that seems to stay several steps ahead. This bulldog roams the neighborhood, doing his business, but can never be caught.

I don't write because I am a writer. I write because I want to be a writer. Someone smarter than me once said the only thing you have to do to be a writer is to write. If you write, then you are a writer; if you quit writing, then you are no longer a writer. I think the same might be true for a person of faith. It's humbling to try to be faithful enough to believe. It's not a set of rules, really. It's about believing and trying. I'm not a model Christian. I'm sometimes no kind of Christian at all if it is only measured by action. What is a Christian, but some sort of openness to God? I'm not a Biblical scholar. I don't understand or have authority or great faith, but I try. I try to read and learn and do my best. It's not enough, but it's something. You try to be that good person you want to be. You may never become that person, but you can keep trying. I guess what I am trying to say with all of this is that I read the Bible and write about it not because I have understanding or am a great authority on anything but my own experiences, but really because I want to be a good person and a good writer so I pretend I am. In pretending maybe I get one step closer—or maybe not—but if I quit pretending, then I quit. I don't want to quit.

If I write poems am I a poet? Do you have to write good poems to be a poet? If I stop writing poems can I ever be a poet?

Okay, where was I?

Maybe we are at a scary part now, callings. Jesus went to a tax collector named Levi, at his place of work, to ask him to follow. Levi followed.

Just like that: Jesus asked, Levi followed. This must be faith then: Someone asks for you to follow and you follow. Someone comes to my work and asks me to come with them and leave my job, how do I respond? I say something about having work to do and keep working. I look over my shoulder to see if my boss is watching. I look right and left to see how other people are responding. A tax collector? Does anyone dare ask anything of a tax collector or maybe an IRS agent or his boss, the politician?

This is yet another spot where I might just read on without really thinking it over. It all seems simple, but is it? Would we drop everything? What is so compelling to Levi that he would drop everything? Even that question seems too simple. Is it simple?

We must press on, despite the quicksand.

Luke 5:29-32

Levi holds a party and a large group of tax collectors come. Teachers and Pharisees complain about Jesus and his disciples partying with tax collectors and other sinners. Jesus responds: The sick need a doctor not the healthy. I've come for the sinners not the saints.

More questions: How can that be? Why would a prophet come for those who need faith and not the faithful?

I always thought God was for those who go to church not those who should go to church. Who feels welcome in a church other than those that attend regularly? If Jesus is the CEO of this religion, then why wouldn't he go to the churches for recruitment? What kind of religion is this anyway?

I'm frustrated with my lack of insight. I didn't want to write that down. It's part of the story though. How can I write without discovering anything? What is the use of writing without coming up with anything new? I really thought I would record answers not more questions. These actions are simple, but the reasons are not simple. How do I examine the what/where/when/why/how when the how is so simple? Are people more complicated than "will you follow? Yes." Isn't there more? Where's the indecision? What priorities are being weighed? How can I fill in the blanks? I don't make a decision—big or small—without great deliberation. If Levi's actions are a model for men of faith, I'm afraid I'm found wanting. I couldn't do this. I couldn't just follow. I've heard the term blind faith, but I know I can see. Is this blind faith in action? If so, how do we become blind? Do I want to become blind? How does a parent or a son give up their sight? Geez; how do I make the simple so complicated?

I take my glasses off. The last afternoon of the show is over; I type up and email an article. I head home in a blue rental car. I listen to an audio book. I forget all this ever happened.

I remember later though. Some kind of magic has a Bible open on my nightstand. It just so happens that the fifth chapter of Luke is staring up at me. I tried to go on with my life, but there it is. The Gideons don't mind if we take those hotel Bibles do they?

Luke 5:33-35

It's been a month at least. I'm typing again only to type. I try to quit but I just can't; this writing is like a carton of smokes.

Everyone in authority is always questioning Jesus. Other disciples are disciplined. They pray and fast. Your disciples eat, drink, and go willy-nilly. What's the deal?

No one says it better than Jesus: "Can you make the guests of the bridegroom fast while he is with them? But the time will come when the bridegroom will be taken from them; in those days they will fast."

Don't you see? This is a special time. This is a wedding or a party or a celebration. Don't you see that we should be extravagant? Don't you believe in extravagance? The time will come for fasting; don't wish too much for that time.

Luke 5:36-39

I haven't written for several days—maybe a month (again)—because of the next passage and how much I don't understand it. It's this whole business about wine and wineskins and old and new garments. You can't put the old with the new, I get that, I think.

So don't ruin the new to fix the old because it just won't work. However, there is more here than just ruining the new to fix the old, there's also this wine analogy. It says—I'm only trying here—that if you attempt to contain something new within the parameters used for the old, the whole thing will burst... but sometimes, in the case of old or aged wine versus new wine, the old is better anyway. So new is new and old is old, each having their benefits. I'm fairly certain Jesus is referring to the old and new covenants, which are mutually beneficial, but can't really be used in tandem or measured with the same stick in all cases. Or does one fulfill the other? Isn't there a new and old testament? Is the old thrown out because of the new? Am I anywhere close here? Maybe Jesus was just talking about clothes and wine, ha. Who am I to say really? I have a case of should have quit writing a sentence, paragraph or lifetime ago.

My wife and I were up half the night discussing a new job and a move. I applied for a position in another part of Idaho figuring I wouldn't be considered. It's a writing gig for such and such a bureau, and anyway, I'm not considering the job really, but it got us thinking about change. We argued. I yelled. I threw a book with my name on it. I want to say it was an accident, but I meant to throw the book. My picture on the back cover was pissing me off. I went downstairs for several minutes and then came back, hangdog a little. My wife tried to apologize! I was the one...

I always thought I would be getting on with my life by now. I used to think baseball. I used to think writer. I'm thinking bookshop now with a little writing on the side. Everyone wants a bookshop at some time in their life. Everyone has had a friend lean over to them in some dusty, old building full of used literary dinosaurs, and say, I could see you sitting back there running one of these. At that moment an old man looks up from his game of solitaire and sighs. That would make you happy, they tell you. We laugh it off. We always do. That would never happen to me.

I'm having a difficult time relating all of this to wine and clothes and the Jewish Law and how Jesus changed everything, but there must be something that relates them because the two thoughts were joined in my mind. The idea of a nacho lunch was also looming.

six

Jesus is walking through a field with some of his disciples and they are eating grain. The Pharisees want to know why they are breaking the rules of the Sabbath. Jesus answers, of course, with a question: Have you never read about David? About how he and his companions ate consecrated bread when they were hungry? Then Jesus ends with: The Son of Man is Lord of the Sabbath.

Sitting here in my chair after a half day's work, with a half pastrami already eaten and a shower yet to be taken, I read this passage and get a little confused. Why are the Pharisees following Jesus and his disciples through the fields? Is it that important to see if they might misstep? Also, aren't they doing some traveling on the Sabbath as well?

Jesus responds to their criticism with a question about their knowledge of the scriptures, which was basically their profession. Haven't you ever read about David, he asks. Yet, he knows that they have it memorized. So what's more important memorization or synthesis and integration? Wasn't Jesus saying, you know the law by heart but does your heart know the law?

Then he says it more plainly: I make the rules. It's my Sabbath. Mine.

I look back at my sandwich. I love Miracle Whip and jalapeno mustard. I've never been all that hungry in my whole life. I like to think I am neither a Pharisee nor a short-sighted disciple. I like to think I would never be involved in such a story. I sit here writing and eating and sipping coffee and I don't really know where I belong or how I relate to such talk. I don't think of rules; I think of calories and how unfair it is that my waistline expands. I should run more, walk more, something. Every day is like this. I stop the days from running right into each other. I keep wondering what I am doing here. I go to church on Sunday and people tell me to read my Bible and pray. So I'm reading my Bible and trying to pray the only way I know how: by writing stuff. Is it helping? I'm not yelling as much. I guess that's a start.

I watch football and eat pizza on what is left of the Sabbath these days. I'm not a tough guy, but sometimes I feel like there's a voice inside saying rest is for the weak.

Luke 6:6-11

It's one of those strange stories of the Bible, this one. At first look, I flippantly tell myself, of course heal on the Sabbath day. Heal all the time, around the clock. But then again, I don't know if my mind can comprehend healing. I know my church today would have problems with healing any day of the week, much less from a Sunday morning guest speaker. Could you imagine the scene that would make? Leave it to the televangelists, I say. But if you can heal, then heal.

Jesus knows what's going on. He was teaching at the synagogue. A man was there with a shriveled hand. No one really cared about the man or his hand or even the Sabbath, but they were thinking about how to accuse Jesus because people liked him. Jesus knew all of this. He knew their hearts. Unlike the coward I would be, Jesus doesn't skirt the issue, he brings it out into the open. He takes the opportunity to teach a lesson. He has the man with the shriveled hand stand up in front so everyone can see. He asks the question of whether it is against Jewish Law to do good or evil on the Sabbath. He pauses, taking time to look at everyone in the crowd. You can almost hear the words, "He without sin should throw the first stone" or "I am the way, the truth, and the life."

The people must be uneasy in their seats. He catches their eye, reads their thoughts. They squirm. Jesus then answers his own question. He heals the man. Easy as that. In what should have been a joyful moment when hairs stand erect and crowds cheer, all that is seen is grumbling. *This Jesus has too much power. He's leading our people astray.*

Live rightly. Heal if you can. Do good. Save lives. Give credit where credit is due.

The stone falls with a thud, thud, thud, splash.
This rock marks the end of a large march through
heavy terrain and triumphant air. It's amazing how
abruptly it comes to an end. The cliff but one more
reminder. A clue requiring an investigation, a great
adventure maybe. Your heart is drumming now to
a punk beat. This is it. They're all here, all silent in
admiration. One more step and you could fly, but
sadly only for a moment. So there it is. It is what
it has become. The beat slows to hard rock, then
Bryan Adams sings a tune you know well. You sing
along, backup to your own life. The morning is as bright as the sun will
let it be. And you're bright too. Warm and cold at the
same time, the sun and wind in a mighty battle. The
stone jumps back up to you without any discernible
sound. You throw it out to sea.

Luke 6:12-16

Jesus prayed and chose the best from among his pupils. Is there more to say? Jesus prayed the night through. Did he catnap? It was so important to spend time talking to God that he spent all night. That says a great deal. I've skimmed the surface of that before. And what might be just as important is that something significant must have come out of his time with God. This all-night experience led him to choose a close group with which to accomplish his mission. It was go-time and these were his warriors. It was a motley crew of brothers, fisherman, doubters, a tax collector, and one, if not several, anticipated betrayers. It was Lord of the Rings. Only through prayer and council from the Almighty could such a group be assembled. To say, this election was one of three: crazy, random, or inspired. Maybe the jury is still out. One thing is for sure: Sometimes it takes some crazy, random, or inspired ingredients to make a great soup; also, to make a stew, church, or chili. I add cilantro to most things. I love the smell. Add cilantro to your Buffalo wings. Seriously. Cooking has a bit of magic to it. When I get into the kitchen, I can feel the power. I begin with an individual part, add others, and soon I'm creating something completely new. I'm adding a little more Johnny's Seasoning Salt and it's done. I've concocted. I've steeped and brewed and mixed and broiled and deep fried and marinated. I've given feet, arms, legs, eyes, and brains to the body of my meal. My wife comes in and maybe asks what smells so good and I maybe tell her she wouldn't believe me if I told her the strange way I have mixed a little bit of bitter and sweet and sour and spicy and everything to make such a perfect feast. To this she might say *it doesn't smell that good*. And to that I might laugh or if someone has stolen my horse that day, I might frown and take it all wrong and nothing she'll say afterward will sooth the pain I have poured over my day.

But Jesus prayed. He prayed all night. And then when he was done with his prayer, he chose them. Twelve of them. The chosen ones. His friends. Soup.

Luke 6:17-19

People came from all over the region, the known world, after that to see Jesus. They wanted to hear his message but they also wanted to be healed of their ailments. And who could blame them? According to reports people were cured of everything from diseases to mysterious evil spirits. People crowded Jesus because everyone who touched him felt his power and was healed.

This section couldn't be more understated. What a report, and so matter-of-fact. Is this so mundane? Or is this amazing? I find I want to fill in the details. Write about the long distances and difficult terrain people traveled to see this man that may not be a man at all. He may just be wisdom and power personified. He may just be magic. He may be just everything that is right in the world. When you're sick, possessed, or just crushed by the weight of existing at all, why wouldn't you be curious?

You hear from the fisherman down the shore that a man is speaking about a whole new ideology and the people who see, touch him are being healed, wouldn't you maybe take a peek for yourself? I would think so... Today, however, everything under the sun has been discovered. Wisdom can be found anywhere and in anything. Faith is watered down like a bad whiskey. People know about Jesus. People have chosen sides. I have to say many people are attempting to make Jesus a political figure just like they wanted the Christ to be so many years ago. It seems nothing has changed. Ask someone down the street about Christians and you probably won't hear about peace, love, and grace, you'll hear about the conservative right, a moralist agenda, hate, discrimination, war, free markets, small government, lower taxes, tea parties, and a great deal more. Christians, particularly evangelicals, are more and more throwing their hats into the political arena in order to "save our deteriorating and vulnerable country." Some criticize me for not being more involved in this fight. Some tell me I should solidify my beliefs and take a stand. They say I am either with them or against them. I get dizzy. I see a Jesus that loves and offers free gifts of healing. I see a Jesus that came for the sick and not the healthy, which I take to mean morally, physically, spiritually, or politically. Admit you have a need and this man has the cure. Touch him and be healed. Can it be much simpler?

Politics... hate... unforgiveness... marginalization of peoples... those are ingredients that will quickly ruin a great soup. Make it so bitter there's nothing left to do but pitch it all.

Is this what we need to do? Shall we embrace, twist things to how we want them to be, or pitch it all? I have no answers to these questions. I'm not even sure where to begin. But I can say we should stop making the same mistakes as old as dinosaurs and Christopher Columbus. Live thoughtfully. Oh, now I have all the answers it seems... I'll choose charity over hate every time.

Luke 6:20-22

As if it wasn't enough, then comes the words that could change the world. A revolution. Jesus says the poor are blessed. He says it's the poor who are the rightful recipients of the kingdom of God.

In my mind there is only two ways to see it, either God is amazingly generous, giving to those in need the greatest gift, or it is those who need that depend on God and receive a full share of what he has to offer, which is, well, everything. Either way you boil it down, it's the poor that will sit at God's table and eat too, and after eating they'll sleep in his mansion. Even more, where they are sleeping won't be in the guest room, but in the master suite. Being this kind of poor sounds a lot like being rich. And wouldn't you know, there's more.

Those who are hungry, according to Jesus, will have their fill, and those who cry will laugh. He calls the poor, hungry, and sad, the blessed ones. Some have called this an upside-down kingdom. I don't care what you call it; it works for me. Who hasn't been poor, hungry, or sad? Who hasn't felt need and tried to hide it in shame, thinking they are not among the blessed? Jesus says don't worry, you're blessed and will continue to be blessed beyond your imagination. There's more...

Luke 6:22-23

...but it's more difficult to swallow. Jesus says you're blessed if you are hated and excluded and insulted and thought evil because of your association with him. How is that a blessing? Honestly. I'm serious here. How is being hated, excluded, insulted, and thought evil of ever a blessing? I always want to be on the right team, but I wouldn't call it a blessing. The greatest people ever to walk this earth have always been met with strong resistance. Great people see a need and work toward change. A desire for change creates great opposition. Opposition sires hatred, exclusion, insults, and the title of evil. It's part of the territory. There's no doubt at all that good is worth the battle, but I still find it difficult to say that the battle is a blessing, hidden or otherwise. But as I slow down the stream of words being typed, I read on and find Jesus has more to say on the matter. Jesus says rejoice because when the battle is over there is a reward, which is pretty good: heaven. Okay, I realize how much I sound like a religious fanatic right now, all this stuff about heaven and The Great Reward, but it's hard not to be caught up like a trout in these words. The promise is so great you want to open the package. I'm evangelizing myself, I'm embarrassed to admit. These words, so stuffed full of hope. These are old words, older than Columbus, yet so new; newer even than my almost-new daughter.

Sometimes we cause suffering, but that has nothing to do with it. We should know the difference. We should know when we're just being a jerk.

I take a deep breath and try to remind myself that this is just a moment among a thousand of its brothers and sisters. No words, no matter how well they are strung together like popcorn on Christmas morning, can make a bit of difference concerning truth. Things are either true or not, aren't they? So I breathe. I look across my kitchen, at the cereal I've left out. I think about looking in a mirror and how I know I haven't changed. I still need to shave and shave off a few pounds. I've still got anger problems and a heart and mind that roam as they please. I remind myself of how incomplete I can feel. In other words, I remind myself of reality. It doesn't do a bit of good to splash optimism across my face because it only lasts for a moment. And a moment never lasts. What does last is need. I need answers. I need optimism. I need happiness. But only if they are stone real and lasting.

I hit a triple, but get reality stuck in my cleats when rounding second. I jump up, grab my keys, and run to the car to pick up my oldest from school. Well, I'm going to do that after I stop this typing.

Later I go to church, then to Wal-Mart afterward. There isn't as much a difference as I would like.

Luke 6:24-25

How do you respond to such words? How do you pour them into your life? People that take such writing lightly aren't reading it.

Then Jesus takes a right turn and says watch out for potholes.

He says if you're rich, that's it. Don't expect more. If you're rich in this life, you're riches will run out. And then what will you have?

Also, he says, those who are well fed now will be hungry later, and those that laugh now will later mourn and weep.

It seems to me—and I assure you I am no authority on the subject—that it is more about attitude and spirit than anything else. It depends on what you consider riches or hunger for or laugh and cry about; is it the lasting and eternal or the short term?

It's a tough message... unless you're able to unlisten to it.

On the other hand, it's not all about attitude and spirit; sometimes it's about feet. Sometimes you need to give and help. If you are rich and well fed and laughing, have you given enough, helped enough, been concerned enough, loved enough?

I find myself sighing a lot lately. I find myself getting through days as if something better will come up. I find myself having rehearsed conversations. I feel as if I am the drip running down my coffee cup. When do the good days start?

Luke 6:26

I would say that one of my unconscious—but, at times, very conscious—goals, at all times in all places, is to have people like and speak well of me. I go into a work, party, or church setting and the show begins. I want people to like me. At the first sign, a scrunched nose maybe, someone disagrees with my clothing or sentiments or how I drink my coffee, I try to change. I try to be what they might like. I try to turn down the volume and reevaluate. I'm a bit nervous. I'm talking a mile a minute. I'm sweating. I wonder what she thinks of me. I wonder if he and I could be friends. The ride home is torturous for my wife. I ask her what she thinks about this statement or that look. I wonder if she thinks people like me. I wonder if she would consider me smooth or rough or likeable. I'm afraid of opinions. I want to be perceived as a nice guy. I never realize that it's not totally in my control. I navel gaze, but I never want to look in the mirror, too painful.

All this confession to say that I don't understand why Jesus would say woe to people that all men speak well of because that is how false prophets are treated.

Is my goal to be a false prophet?

I suppose upon contemplation that I understand that pleasing everyone means compromising, and being one person at one point and another at another point. I suppose upon further contemplation I understand that doing what is right is not always popular. I also know that my need for approval is about as healthy as a Big Mac. When you're hungry anything tastes good. When you're thirsty you'll drink muddy water. When your heart feels—or worse is—empty, you grasp for any positive word. It's not enough. It never will be enough.

It still stings to not be liked.

It's at this point I would like to say something wonderful. I'd like to make resolutions and keep them. I'd like to go out and do something big. But something big isn't required. Self-examination sprinkled with small tweaks of attitude is what the recipe calls for. It comes down to what you personally place value upon. After all, it's not money that has worth, but the value we place upon it. Same goes for you and for me.

So let me try this on for size: It's not what people think; it's what some people think of me.

Luke 6:27

But you haven't heard anything yet. The next statement blows the ship out of the water. Jesus says love your enemies and do good to those who hate you. Can you imagine anything more counter to how life works? It goes against everything. It changes everything. It throws justice out the window like an apple core. For a moment I try to imagine what it would be like to love an enemy and do good to people who hate me. It's not a pretty picture. It doesn't inspire me. Yet, if everyone would do it, it would change the world. I'll admit that. But the first people to try will be pulverized. I wish I had better things to say. I wish I was inspired to write beautiful words, but I am not.

Luke 6:28

It doesn't get much easier: Bless those that curse and pray for those that mistreat you?

Luke 6:29-31

And here are some more tangible instructions: If someone strikes you, let them strike again; if someone steals from you, offer them more of your stuff. Has anyone ever heard of Jean Valjean?

Give to all who ask.

One of the greatest lines ever spoken: Do to others what you would have them do to you.

How can you argue against that logic?

All I can say is I'll try.

I wish I could say that I have been writing more faithfully or religiously or consistently. The truth is, I haven't. Life gets in the way like a half-done home-improvement project. I wish I had more time. Actually, I wish I made more time. I have enough time if I wrote rather than read or watched TV. I want to do everything. I want to do nothing sometimes. What's the worth? Why am I doing this anyway? Am I a better person?

Luke 6:32-36

I'm a bit sensitive today because I went to a party last night and said all the wrong stuff at exactly the right time. I felt horrible later because I said things when I was nervous that I now wonder whether they will hurt feelings. I was being sarcastic. I was attempting to be funny. I was trying to be honest, but it ended up exploding in my face. The details don't even matter because they're embarrassing.

When I get over myself, I read Jesus saying that it's no great thing to love those who love you or do good in return for someone doing good to you, or even lend to people that will surely pay you back because everyone does that, even the people you don't like do that. Instead, Jesus says love and do good to your enemies. He says lend to people with no expectations. He says that if you can do that, then there will be great reward, and if you are kind to the wicked and unthankful, you'll even be a son of God. His summation is this: Be merciful like God.

I am trying to survive this life. I can barely take care of myself. I have a need for writing, but no purpose. Honestly—and this would definitely not go over well at a dinner party, I will assure you right now—I want to do good, but only to people I like and am not afraid of, which means only my friends. That's the truth. How could I ever put Jesus's words into practice? In theory, I agree. I agree wholeheartedly in fact. But my life is not a theory. My life is not high minded. My life is a series of moments where I make split-second decisions about what to do next and then next and then next. I never decide to waste a day on TV or at the bar. I just do it. I never seem to do what my priorities are. I do what is easiest. Believe me, I don't write this down easily. I put my kids down in front of the TV to work one day on finishing an article. Fairly soon, it's a habit I have to break because I am doing it every day. That is not my priority, but that is how it plays out. I walk across the street or screen a phone call because I don't have the time. I haven't spoken to my so-called friend for months. This is life. These are those moments. How do we take big ideas that we agree with, theories that we buy into, and break them up and add them to each moment of our day?

Luke 6:37

Do not judge or condemn, but rather forgive. This is one of those crazy verses. Don't judge people. Don't condemn people. Forgive people. Isn't this what Christians do? They judge if someone is doing right and wrong, and they condemn the wrong. Is Jesus really being relativistic here? Or is he saying as some have suggested to "hate the sin but not the sinner." That's still a value judgment. I kind of maybe think he is referring to people's salvation. It's not ours to judge the fate of others. Besides, I like forgiveness much more than judgment and condemnation. Sheesh. I feel so inadequate to respond to such a statement. However, I do think I understand the spirit of the statement. I can say that I don't think anyone is doing a very good job of it, but maybe for a select few. Did I just judge? If I did, I forgive myself. Ha! I never forgive myself. I can't even pretend I do. I am the most difficult person to forgive.

I just can't seem to find the time lately. Something comes up. What is so worthwhile about all this anyway? I want to make a grand gesture. Maybe, move to some woods and write until I'm done. I think of this while I am on the couch reaching into an empty bag of chips and wiping my hand on my shirt. I feel like getting up and doing something with my life. I really think this dramatically. I am dramatic. I love huge. However, it's the day-to-day that gets me. The tug and pull that we call living. Anyway, that wasn't even a complete sentence...

Luke 6:38

I'm still here at the Bible with two baseball-sized eyes. I am told that if I give it will be given to me. Listen to this: A good measure, pressed down, shaken together and running over, will be poured into your lap. Sounds like a recipe gone twisted. Maybe it's from the barkeep's bible. This line is amazing to me. It's so poetic. It's so beautiful. The more I read it the more I love it. I think... I believe it means that your charity will be the measure of you. I can't tell you how in love I am right now. I am in love with anything and everything. This is what I was looking for. This is why I climbed the mountain.

The last thought of the verse is it will be measured to you how you measure.

This seems like the natural law of it then.

Hear it again: A good measure, pressed down, shaken together and running over, will be poured into your lap.

Don't miss it: A good measure, pressed down, shaken together and running over, will be poured into your lap.

Thus is life. I can't say it better no matter how I try. TV on.

Luke 6:39

How do we know if someone is blind? How do we know if our own eyes are open?

Luke 6:40

What does it mean to be fully trained? Off the top of my head, this must have something to do with how we choose our teachers. If you can't be above your teacher, you better pick a teacher worth aspiring to. Is that it?

Who is a teacher to me?

I have been waking up every morning in some sort of a minor panic. It's like my life is on a path that I didn't pick. It's nothing like the movies. It's nothing like any book I have ever read. It's nothing like stealing second in a big game. My life is a like a series of small decisions made without a lot of thought. My life is like a series of small bites at a buffet without a thought for nutritional value or the marathon I'll be running later or maybe I'm already running. I'm blind and I know it and I don't seem to care even though I wish I did.

We moved. I don't want to say too much about it because that is not why I am writing. But we did move. I got a new job at a new publication, which is supposed to change my attitude and change me and change everything. I hope it does. But it won't. It just won't. I'll still yell and do lousy things and will not be the husband and father that I would like. I love my wife. I love my three kids. I love them. That is why I am typing. I feel empty. I want to do better and fill up. But I don't want to fill up on just anything or just everything. I want to fill up on just the right thing. And sometimes I think that Luke has it all. Other times I don't think about it. Other times I do whatever I want to do and fill up on whatever I want. The hardest part about really jumping in is the people I see that claim to have already made the leap. They are not always fun. A new town means the same problems. I wish I could tell you about the great love affair I am living. The truth is, however, that I have a lot of thinking and writing to do. It's exciting and boring. It's both.

Luke 6:41-42

I've heard this verse a lot. Usually it's used as a reprimand. It's also true. Why can't we offer the grace and mercy to others that we offer ourselves?

It's really interesting to me that Jesus goes on to say that if you remove the plank from your own eye you will better be able to help your brother. I want so terribly to help my children be great people. One of the many things in the way is my collection of planks.

I should tell you that my children are beautiful little geniuses.

Luke 6:43-45

I should shower or shave or work harder. I should write beautiful and terrific stories about beautiful and terrific people and moments. I should tell you about my first beautiful and terrific day in months. I should write about what I know.

Instead I offer this: What I think it all means. It's the only suit I have. I take this seriously. I write when other people shower and shave and get on with their lives. I only want to get on with my life if my life is worth getting on with.

Jesus tells of a tree and of a man's heart and words. He says trees are measured by their fruit, and man, his heart and words. By the fruit and heart and words, you can tell if each is good or evil. We already know this to be true, he tells us. We pick fruit from fruit-bearing trees, not thorn bushes and briers. What you store up in your heart is what comes out in your words. Be careful, I hear. Save carefully, I hear.

I sit back and think because that is what I do. I sit back and think and also write it down because that is how I often do it. How will I be recognized? How will I know what is fruit, what type of tree I am?

I write stories most days. I make phone calls on time and ask what I hope are good questions. I record what I believe is profitable. An editor tells me yes and no in red ink. I try again. I polish. I hope to bear fruit. I read the book of Luke and try to figure out if it will bear fruit in my life. I store it up.

Luke 6:46-49

Jesus also seems to be asking similar questions. He wants to know why people would call him Lord and not do what he says. He wants to know if his words will bear fruit in us. He asks and I ask.

He tells a story. He says a person that puts his words into practice is like someone who builds a strong foundation for a house. Those who don't listen are like people who build a house right on the ground. When the storms come, which they will, some houses stand and some crumble. I hear it and wonder if I am finally building a foundation.

Am I becoming a bore? I am truly wondering. The truth is that people who care too much become a bore. They aren't the life of any party. They talk too much. I wonder if being well liked will always be my ultimate goal or if there is another for me. How ridiculous I have become. I get swept up. I go crazy for each moment. I can't help but feel the weight of this life and the two men that are warring inside. I want to be a good man. I am willing to keep working at it. I am willing to put aside how I feel about myself in order to be what I ought to be. But... I just can't help pondering what I might become. I might become a monster to myself and to others. I might just let all this make me believe in things that will put me on the outside. I just might have to change so much of me that there will be so little left that I like. I am whatever I need to be at the moment in order not to cause a wave. I interview and observe and attempt stories. I love and parent and do what feels good. That is who I am. Who else could I be?

Where is the poetry in that?

seven

Luke 7:1-10

When Jesus was finished with his lesson, he entered Capernaum and was confronted by friends of a centurion. This centurion knew of Jesus. He knew of what he was capable. This centurion sent his friends to speak with Jesus because his servant was close to death. This centurion loved the servant and seemed to be out of options. The friends said the centurion wanted Jesus to come and perform a miracle, a healing he was apparently famous for by now. The friends said the centurion was worthy. He loved the nation and built their synagogue. Jesus agreed. The emotion is palpable. The centurion is desperate. He loves his dying servant. He reaches for Jesus. He is willing to believe. The friends love the centurion, plead for him, them. Jesus is willing.

The centurion sends yet more friends to Jesus. He fears he has asked too much, troubled too much. He knows the time restraints. He humbles himself, saying he is unworthy to have Jesus under his roof. He says he understands to some degree Jesus's authority. He knows from his own experience that people follow the orders of those in authority out of love and fear. He knows he only needs Jesus's word and it will happen.

Jesus marvels at his faith. Jesus says he is more faithful than even all in Israel. The friends return. The servant is well.

We document such happenings, but have trouble swallowing afterward. What does it all mean? How could it really have happened that way? When my son's heart seemingly stopped during childbirth it was only a matter of minutes. I pleaded with God for life. My heart stopped and I was willing to sacrifice all. I was willing to believe. I prayed and prayed and died. Nothing really mattered. I pleaded and called it prayer. I thought nothing of being humble. I didn't think of power and authority. I just pleaded and prayed and promised I would figure it all out later. Those minutes choked me and choke me still. The nurse panicked over the phone within earshot. She called out for the doctor. I couldn't believe how our lives were changing.

They found a heartbeat. They rushed to get him out.

I felt nothing.

I wasn't sure who to thank.

I cried with my wife.

We took deep breathes.

The doctor said we must proceed quickly.

I got back up. I did nothing but try to calm my wife. She did all the work. She produced a beautiful son. I laughed and cried. We were exhausted (surely my wife more I feel the need to say, though obvious). I didn't know who to thank. I thanked everyone. I wondered if I had seen a miracle. No one marveled over my faith. My wife did it all. The doctor did it all. I wondered who else.

Luke 7:11-17

This story about faith, and how it reaches out and touches me right where it hurts, inspires me so much I go right out and join a men's Bible study. If this story was about my life, I would describe each person in detail: what they look like; how they part their hair; what politics rile them up; what verses make them cry; who has deep, dark secrets that aren't as deep and dark as they think they are. I could tell you loads. Of course that would break the men's Bible study covenant. What happens at this Bible study, stays in this living room. We eat pizza, read the Bible, and drink a murder spree of coffee. The first day someone is crying when I show up. I look at my feet. People say hi, nice to meet you. The man who is crying continues his story from the middle.

I wonder if I am the only moderate here. We tear through the verses in Romans. I interject from Luke once, using my new-found familiarity like a badge. People talk about cussing and drinking and all kinds of things that other people do. I do these things. I try to hide behind my slice of pepperoni and mushroom. These guys really read their Bible. I wonder if they are ever as scandalized as I am by what they find. That wasn't supposed to be there. I must be reading this wrong. I remember what my friend told me: If you don't say anything, you don't have to be embarrassed about what you said. I keep quite. I hide. I marvel.

Not much later, according to Luke, Jesus travels to Nain, and a large crowd, including the disciples, tag along. He's not even to Nain when they confront a funeral procession. The son of a widow has died. The two large crowds meet. Jesus, Luke calls him the Lord, says don't cry because, as Luke tells us, Jesus's heart "went out to her." He goes right up and touches the coffin. He says to the boy get up! The boy sits up and speaks. Jesus gives the boy back to his mother.

Not surprisingly, everyone is in awe. They recognize this act and praise God. People start talking amongst themselves. A great prophet has appeared among us, they say. God is here to help us, they say.

The news travels throughout Judea and places elsewhere.

What can you say about that? The dead rise. As much as I want to, I can't even imagine it. I've encountered death myself. The tears can never be taken back. I've never seen anyone come back from death. It must have been pandemonium. When a baseball team comes back from seemingly insurmountable odds, I marvel. What about if they won the game after the game was already over? (It's against the rules!) That would be something in and of itself, but that—even though impossible—is no equal to this story. This story is bigger than the words that explain it. This is the type of story that mixes up your life. This is the type of story that makes you sell everything that was your old life. This story leaves nothing of the old. There is only before it happened and after it happened. I imagine everyone changed. I imagine the type of person I would become. I want this story to linger. I want to believe this story and change. If I believe this story, what then? A healing I can swallow, someone stealing from the grave just gets stuck in my throat. What else?

Luke 7:18-23

John the Baptist hears about these things from his own disciples. He sends two of them out to speak with Jesus. They say are you he or should we expect another? Jesus replies: Tell John about what you see and hear: that the blind get their sight, the lame their legs, those with leprosy are cured, the deaf now hear, the dead are alive, and good news is told to the poor. In other words, see what I am doing and judge for yourselves. We are what we do. Then cryptically, Jesus says, blessed are those who do not fall away on account of me.

I'll admit it, I'm dumbfounded. So much Jesus does. He cures. He loves the poor. Also, seriously, what does it mean that the man who doesn't fall away on account of him is blessed? How could you fall away because of him? Wouldn't you join because of him rather than fall away?

To the best of my ability I come to this conclusion: Don't think of Jesus as something new, only a continuance of who was already there, whom you already follow—God. Don't create a new religion, commit to the one you already have. Don't create a new God, see the God you already follow. To John specifically: Don't quit what you are doing, do it better.

John was watching for the messiah. Jesus says, did you find him?

Again, I'm at a loss, but maybe you're used to that by now, whoever you are. Maybe you have come to expect it. I am waiting all the time for that one thing to happen that will change me, that will be so big and amazing that I can't help but become a better person. How will I know when I bump into it?

Luke 7:24-28

Is there nothing new under the sun? All poetry bows down. We write it because we have to. It only makes sense—it never makes sense— written this way, painted this way, sculpted this way. Why is so much of the Bible poetry and story, yet these are considered lesser genres by most Christians? Are they misunderstood like John, like Jesus?

After John's people leave, Jesus speaks to the crowd about what they have witnessed. He asks what did you go out into the desert to see? Was it a reed swayed by the wind? Well, if that's not it, then what? A man in a nice suit, maybe. No those people are in palaces. So, what then? A prophet; yes, a prophet and more. About John it was written that a messenger will be sent ahead to prepare the way. There is no one greater than John that have been born of women, but the least in the kingdom of God is greater than him.

Jesus can always drop you on your head. None is greater, yet everyone in the kingdom of God is greater. How do you even begin to explain that? It has to go back to what you are using to measure a man. Is it his appearance? Is it his house or clothing? How can someone be the least and the greatest simultaneously? I don't know, I'm asking you.

I walk around the house, which is empty and quiet. I wait for my wife and children to come home. I want to tell them about what I have read. I want my wife to explain it to me. I want to romance her with my day. I want to play imaginative games with my kids. I want my day to overwhelm me until what I read and what I do mixes together so well that it becomes one substance and that one substance can be understood. Later, I wait for the night of the men's Bible study. I want to hear about other people wrestling with life for a blessing. By the time, it comes about—like most things—I have forgotten my fervor and can't recreate it. I watch the clock until it's over. I go home and watch TV. I drown out the dialogue going on in my hellish attic.

When the kids sleep, I sit around and ponder how to be a better parent. I look over at my wife as she washes the dishes. I want so badly to say something that will overwhelm her, something that might remind her of why she married this sloth that types and types and types and reads and watches TV and and and.

Luke 7:29-30

Some sort of schism is created. The people acknowledge that God's way is right after hearing Jesus. Luke notes even the tax collectors acknowledge, and I can't help but hear the distain in this side note. These people come to this conclusion because they were baptized by John. However, the Pharisees and experts of the law, all of whom, by the way, were not baptized by John, reject God's purpose.

It's amazing to me how often the experts reject. They know all too well. They won't be swept up by it all, the unseasoned new. Old good, new bad; so they won't lower themselves so far as to believe some infant thing. They know the law. If they don't see it, it's not there. It takes a great deal of humility to admit to seeing what everyone is seeing without the gift of expertise. Are sinners closer to God than those that admit no sin? Apparently so, Luke indicates. Even the tax collectors, he says. Even the IRS guy, he says. Even that sinner in front of you at the airport security shouting at someone for the crowd's benefit, he says.

Luke 7:31-35

I'll paraphrase the next part because I've caught a bad case of creativity this morning. I warn you now.

Jesus says something that makes me write it this way: To what should I compare this generation? You are like people yelling out to each other: Didn't you hear my song? Why didn't you dance or cry or laugh? John followed all the rules, neither eating or drinking, and you called him a devil. The Son of Man comes among you eating and drinking and he is a glutton and a drunk, a friend of sinners. Wisdom is proven right by all its children.

It takes all kinds. Figure that one out. I'm not as creative as I once thought. Two paragraphs ago I had a grand plan. The words are bullies. They gang up on me and make me self-conscious. They punch me from the inside.

Jesus speaks of a generation that finds any reason to reject. They reject all but their own song, all but their own way of life. I can see it. This message needs no update. This is today. You drink too much, you drink too little. You live this way and that way and it doesn't measure up to my expectations. You are too religious, not religious enough.

But wisdom is proven right by all her children.

I see two possible interpretations of this and by interpretations, I mean, my takeaways, it's not as grand as the word interpretation implies. I am sure there are many more. I see that wisdom produces and reproduces. Just like a poem is born from the marriage of a poet and an idea, so is wisdom the father and mother of right living. Also, a poet doesn't sire only one poem. His love affair with ideas produces many poems, and only in all his various words can the worth be measured. So it might be also true then, that wisdom is the mother of many children, each of whom reflect that wisdom in a different manner. One boy might reflect his mother's good teaching by going without, while a daughter might show us the moderation taught by her father. Isn't resisting overindulgence a discipline too? Right living may look different for different people, but it still points to the source. Am I even close here? Wisdom produces; the product is various, but from the same source. Wisdom produces children. The proof is carried by ALL of them. Not one, all.

I reach out for wisdom and stuff it in my pockets. I hope my pockets will hold.

Luke 7:36-38

I think this is important in its own little way, although I don't show it by the time I invest. But, it's important to me. I can see how it has impacted my life, how I think more rather than just do. I've also lost at least twenty pounds not having to carry around regret all day to work, to the grocery store, out to dinner and a movie. It's nice to have a backpack full of thoughts rather than homemade, strawberry guilt.

So here is what I am doing about it: I'm setting aside time. My original idea was a weekend retreat to really do it right. However, a retreat is too easy. Fitting the Bible into your day is another animal all together.

Anyway, 9 to 10 PM. That's what I will set aside. I feel a little panic in my gut because that's TV time. So we'll see. It might be worth it.

I say a prayer then: Please God make this worth it. Amen. (There was more, but this catches the spirit of the thing. The rest is between me and God.) That sounds like a secret, it's not; or maybe it is. Secrets. Secrets. Secrets. Words. Words. Words.

So, with that out of the way, I read one of the most moving passages in all of scripture. It's so intimate; I almost want to look away. Read another passage or another book. A Pharisee has Jesus over for dinner and a lady with a bad reputation comes over too. She sits at Jesus's feet, cleaning them with her tears, kisses, and a whole jar full of perfume.

I don't like feet.

Also, I don't like dirty feet.

In Mexico, I got habanero juice on my face and it was bubbling and spreading to my eyes. No amount of water or fit throwing could stop the burning. A woman rushed up to me. I didn't know her and I didn't speak her language. She pulled her hair from a bun in the back and wiped my face with it. There was a mother-son intimacy to this act. There was a lover's intimacy to this act. There was a concerned and purposeful intimacy to this act. Then she left. It was startling and didn't make sense. It also worked and I loved her for it.

This woman in Jesus's story, she loved much, of this there is no doubt. Hers is a bold, emotional, passionate, humble, and extravagant love. She broke in on a dinner. She cleaned feet. She cried openly. She kissed. She spent a great deal of stored-up riches to honor Jesus. What a private and precious scene. His feet no doubt caked with the duties of his day. It brings to mind that Jesus was willing to do a similar act for his disciples, to which Peter replied, *no way*.

Luke 7:39-47

The Pharisee begins to doubt Jesus. He believes that if Jesus was really a profit (prophet), he would know that it is a sinner that touches him. Jesus reads his heart.

So Jesus, according to his way, tells a story. He says two guys owe this other rich, corporate guy. One owes him a few thousand, while the other owes him, let's say, fifty thousand. (Sorry, I can't off the top of my head work out the exchange from denarius to dollars, but you get what I mean.) Neither of them had the money, but the rich guy cancelled their debts anyway. So Jesus asks the Pharisee, who of the two loved the rich guy more. He said the one with the larger debt. Jesus said, you're right.

Now Jesus turns to the women. He says, look at her. I'm in your house and you haven't offered me anything for my feet, while she has cleaned them with her hair and tears. Jesus also says, you didn't kiss me, but she has never stopped kissing me. You also gave me no oil for my head, but she has poured perfume on my feet. You see, her many sins have been forgiven because she has loved much, but those who have been forgiven little, love little.

Love and forgiveness are mixed together so well, you can't taste one without the other.

I see a real irony here. The more forgiveness, the more love, but in order to be forgiven much you must owe much, sin much. So, the more sin, the more love? Obviously, not, but what then? And then I see it. It's not the amount of sin, for we all sin enough; it's really the amount we admit to ourselves and to God. Sometimes you must examine, to find it. So admitted sin=forgiveness, which=love.

Luke 7:48-50

Jesus looks at the woman. He says, your sins are forgiven. The other guests (I guess this is more of a party than I was picturing initially) are in awe: He forgives sins? Who is this man?

Jesus tells the woman it is her faith that has saved her. He says go in peace.

It's no small thing to forgive sins. That's in the job description of governors and presidents and gods. Which was Jesus? He surely doesn't seem to hold a governmental office.

Go in peace, he says.

Peace.

Jesus had washed her clean. Not just her feet, but all of her. It boggles the mind really. Go; be new. Start over. Have the peace that can only be obtained by having a clean bill of health.

All cancers are gone.

She loved extravagantly, and extravagantly was she loved.

It makes you want to do something outrageous and wonderful.

eight

Luke 8:1-3

Jesus was traveling with his disciples from town to town with the good news of the kingdom of God. Also with them, Luke reports, were a number of women who had apparently been cured of evil spirits and diseases. These women were supporting them out of their own means.

It needs repeating: A girl turned to me during a university class and said, *See, I can't believe like these crazy Bible-thumpers that all this stuff about Jesus and his disciples is important. I mean, where are the women? I know there were important women around; I've heard reports. Yet those white men who wrote the Bible left out the women. Those stupid misogynists.* She was beautiful.

I didn't say anything. What could I say that would matter? After all, I was a white male and I was known to thump the Bible now and again.

But reading the Bible now, the women do play a key role. They wash his feet and are forever remembered. They follow and support his ministry. They are the first to see him after he died and rose. They are witnesses. I'm not sure what all this means and I'm not sure where my classmate was coming from really. She may have had good reason to be angry with the whole thing. We were studying snippets of the Bible as a cultural and literary text, but it was hitting her where she lived. At least she was thinking about it. At least she was interacting with it. At least she was willing to take it seriously. I tended at the time to just read and accept, never to think. Be thoughtful, I told myself, but I couldn't help but rush and watch TV as much as my schedule would allow.

I feel insufficient for the task at hand.

Luke 8:4-8

Jesus told a parable to the crowds. A farmer was sowing seeds and some fell on the path, but were trampled and eaten by birds. Other seeds fell on the rock and died without water, among the thorns and were choked out, in good soil and yielded one hundred times more than were sown. Jesus concluded, you who have ears, hear it.

I imagine the crowd full of farmers, who are nodding their head in agreement. They must have wondered why a farmer would be so careless to sow seeds in anything but this excellent soil that could produce so much. I'm no farmer, but a hundredfold sounds like a tremendous crop.

What could it mean to them? Were they the farmer or the seeds or the soil? Are these the lessons they came for?

Luke 8:9-15

The disciples asked for the meaning. It strikes me that they were thinking, and that they also had easy access to the teacher. Without both the inquisitiveness and the opportunity, they might have missed the message.

Jesus says the secrets of the kingdom of God have been given to you, but I teach others in parables so that though they see, they may not see, and though they hear, they may not understand.

Why?

It's difficult to understand why there is a distinction or why a parable was the chosen vehicle for Jesus's teaching. I'm not sure I can explain other than to use the very parable as an example:

Jesus says the seed is the word of God. Those along the path are people who hear and then the devil comes and steals the word from their hearts so they won't believe and be saved. Jesus speaks of the devil casually as if he is a given entity. I just can't take the belief in this being so lightly. I see evil, but it's never pure evil and the devil is a difficult concept to grasp. There is good in all, it seems to me. Is there really someone out there working against this message? Is the devil like a crow that wants nothing more than to eat the seed so people might not grow in their knowledge of God? This type of diligent opposition seems to prove the importance of such a pursuit, but can I really grasp this being? Can I wrap my mind around a person so bent on opposing this message he stakes his whole worth on it? We see glimpses of this man called the devil and he is like a Lex Luther. It reminds me of the first few chapters of Job when God and the devil argue about the faith of Job. Why is it so important to both, being who they are, that people have such faith?

Then there are the rocks, who are people that receive the word with joyfulness, but they have no roots, and when tested, they fall away. Joy isn't really joy, it seems, when it doesn't overcome opposition. Whenever you put your faith in something, your trust will be tested. I've loved three women romantically and although it's not worth the time, energy, or words to explain in detail why I loved and why I only married one, I can say that one love passed the test. One love had roots. One was a love that led to commitment despite the struggles of life. This final love that led to marriage and children was such a different animal, in fact, that I can easily say that it is clear to me now that I have only loved once. Adversity only made this love stronger. The more difficult it gets, the closer we become. I know this type of love must seem like a fairytale when I attempt to describe it so plainly, but the truth is, the difference is plain. It's so plain that no description will ever do it justice, but I will try. It's this: The bond is stronger than any particular circumstance. My wife is willing to hold tightly when it would be easier to let go. One quick example might be helpful. I'm an idiot and I do idiotic things. I say things I don't mean when I am angry. I yell. I don't even like myself. I talk and talk and talk, and yet she listens. She holds tight. She loves this idiot. She wants to share it all with me. She wants us to be better people and she is willing to work at it. It's not all fun, but she's willing and she never quits at it. What do I offer? Hopefully something. I hope I offer the same as these. I commit to these ideals as well. What is good in this world is so hard to explain when it comes down to the bones of it, but I can say it is made of commitment and hard work and a love that is able to see right from wrong and fight for the right even when it isn't easy and even when it isn't our first inclination. I don't know if I've grasped it all with these words, but I do know it when I see it. And I put my faith and hope in it. I let it break me and save me. I let it undo me and redo me. I attempt to give and I attempt to receive. I fight; I yell; and I commit to it no matter what comes along to try and snatch it away—even if the thief is sometimes me. Is the message of this parable so different? Will it produce hundredfold?

I've come to believe that life is not this simple and is this simple. It's both.

The thorns represent worries, riches, and pleasures that keep the seeds from maturity. What a list. How are worries the same thorns as riches and pleasure? All of these choke out the truth. I worry. I want riches. I seek pleasure under every rock and moment. These are the things that take the place of the good news. How can this be? Can it be true? Is there something better? I want to say that I place more emphasis on finding the truth than on riches and pleasure, but does my life say so? Do I really believe that worries are the sign of thorns in my life or that I am simply a conscientious person? Worry, like a video-game zombie, steals my sleep. What then do I put my hope in? Is there some formula for success in this life?

The good soil is a picture of the noble and healthy heart that not only hears the good news, but treasures it and preserves, allowing the message to produce a bountiful crop. We only need to ask but one question: Is this really what we want? And not just in our dreams but in the details and the moments of our day.

We peek behind the curtain and hear the words of Jesus to those closest to him. We find ourselves inside the tight group he chose for himself and he speaks plainly. He never wavers or doubts his own message. I look at his life and his words. I so strongly want to accept and let my life show it, but I also see how so much would need to change and so many people wouldn't understand. I see how I could be the soil but I don't know if I am. I don't know yet if the seeds are worth it. There are secrets in my soil. They aren't even interesting secrets, they're just mine and I hold them tightly. I want to write about the person I wish I was, instead of the person I am. The work and the growth to be done will only play out over time. Geez. It's a mystery to why I even allow myself to write these things down. I can't even connect this to the small moments of my day. What I do with my day doesn't seem to fit with such deeper meaning. I eat and sleep and go to work and complain and argue and shop for groceries and read a book I wish I would have written. These are the ingredients of my day, not a search for truth. I go to church and I pray when I really need things. I balance my checkbook and wish my money didn't go this way and that like a thousand tiny creeks. I worry about how I am raising my children. I take them to school and t-ball and the park. I watch a movie. I go to a Bible study. I get annoyed. I get angry. I make doctor's appointments and call mechanics. I order books online. I eat dinner in haste. I play peek-a-boo. I change a diaper. I lay awake and think about words and how I might put them together in such a way that it might mean something. I tell stories and talk too much. I make detailed reports to my wife and she listens.

Luke 8:16-18

Sometimes I really wish I was traveling, writing specific details about new places I was seeing. I wish to live the exciting and detailed life that is easily transformed into a great piece of writing. Instead, I sit here typing on a computer trying to conjure interesting travels from thin air. No Edward Abbey am I. I'm nobody of geographic significance. I'm the big man in my house. I'm the tyrant at his royal computer.

You don't hide a lamp—you display it. After all, Jesus says, nothing will be hidden or concealed. He concludes then that we should take care in how we listen, and that based on these observations, he or she that has will be given more, but those who don't have, even what they think they might have hidden away, or snuck in their pockets for later, will be taken away.

It's difficult to even untangle all of this. I get that a light is to shine, and that you can't ever hide your true nature, and after all God knows everything anyway. Where would you hide from him? Many have tried. It's never worked.

So maybe Jesus is saying live thoughtfully. Be careful what you sign-up for. There's even a hint that those who can accomplish some, grow some from the seed of God; to these people much will be added, but to those who only pretend, all will be stripped away. That's all I got.

I'm sitting here. I'm tired. My eyes are heavy. I don't want anything tonight. I don't want to be anybody or come up with any new theory. I just want to be. I just want to be content with what I have. I want the phone to ring and for it to be a friend from across the country or across town. I just called because I missed you. I just called because there's a great band playing in Boise tomorrow night and I bought us tickets. I want a phone call and then I want a bed so soft and safe I don't remember falling asleep and I wake up with the energy of my kids. I want to rouse them from sleep and suggest a waltz in the fresh snow. Okay. Never mind. I've gone too far.

I used to read from this perch, but
now I make all good parenting
decisions from the toilet.

It's the only time I have to myself
because the kids are afraid of
being tricked into baths or potty-training.

I use that fear to my advantage. I use that
fear like bricks. These bricks are
the foundation for my little kingdom.

It used to be baseball, fishing, or writing
that sent me running across a hairy
sky with platitudes I myself couldn't follow.

I understand love.
I understand the power of coffee.
I understand that it doesn't matter what I say the children will always
believe that the universe has at its center one little girl and two little
boys who love to play and color pictures and pretend they are
superheroes.

I understand this. I know this. I see my wife
swallowing a mountain of laundry and dirty
diaper covers. I yell from the bathroom that
I will be right there even though it could be
a lie because I have just had an idea and I am
over the moon. I always mean it to be the
truth. The toilet makes me lie. The toilet is a
winter retreat, but it makes me lie. I never
lie at any other time. Not to anyone other than
myself and the toilet that holds me quiet, but
thoughtful.

If you're sensitive to these types of things, poetry can invade your life at
any time, like a mosquito or a bad pun. It will sit behind the door, or in a
tree, for hours just to jump right in. It sucks your blood. I kick it off my
shoes before I go inside or shut the car door. Some people hate poetry...
but how can you hate poetry when it is willing to invade you at any
time? This type of invasion signifies worth. It says you're worthy of
invading. If you don't defend yourself, you may be dethroned. People
will no longer see you, they'll see irony and iambic pentameter. They'll
see you seeing a dog peeing in your yard. They'll find it to be a satisfying
social commentary.

The poetry must sleep.

And what do people have against bad poetry anyway?

Bad poetry is the truest poetry.

This heart writes bad poetry. Sometimes I attempt to change but most times I am lazy and statistical. I wouldn't know good poetry if it slapped me across the face. I do know what comes across the junior-high gym and asks me sweetly to dance. I see braces and my cheeks fill up to my eyes, red and sweaty.

Luke 8:19-21

Obedience to God's word is extremely important to Jesus. I've always stumbled through this passage. Does family mean nothing versus the mission, or is putting God's words into practice so important that it makes you family?

Luke 8:22-25

I had a thought this morning after a particularly fitful night of sleep: Why is it always a revelation that we are going to die some day? There are always those thoughts that just kind of make you dizzy or thought drunk. They kind of make the things you emphasize meaningless. They kind of show you the limitation of your brain. Hard drive overloaded; restart or upgrade needed. It was a good day today, however. I got a great deal of work done. I came home. I ate a great dinner of ham broccoli bake, a new recipe—a success. I read to my kids. I tucked them in. I came upstairs to write. Did you ever notice that writers describe every part of their day minus the time they are writing? It must be a writer-school axiom, but I think I need proof. I think if I am spending a significant portion of my day writing, it's worth writing about. The movie of my life (staring David Arquette in his defining role) would require some shots in front of my computer. I'm sure David will look fabulous in his underwear, which will be an unrealistic portrayal.

Meanwhile, Jesus and his disciples are crossing a lake. Jesus sleeps, while a storm rages. The danger grows. The boat is being swamped by the squall. The disciples wake Jesus to tell him they are drowning.

What peace.

Jesus rebukes the storm first, and then the disciples. Where is your faith?

I feel this story inside. I feel rebuked. Where is my faith? In times of trouble my prayer life increases, but my faith decreases.

The disciples marvel, with a mixture of fear and awe. Who is this, they ask, who commands the winds and waters, and they are obedient?

How long has he been here?

I've heard many a person berate the disciples, asking how long have they been with him and don't know him? I see from today's perspective how they might sink to this. We have the benefit of context and the big picture—they did not. Also, and I emphasize this for my own benefit, it's one thing to read about someone commanding the storm, and a whole different animal to watch it. No matter what has been done prior, you're not prepared.

If I just would have been there, I want to say. But I'm not sure that's true. First-hand experience doesn't guarantee belief, faith, and trust. Not everyone who saw and heard believed. I bet it didn't hurt though. What does it take then? What's the secret ingredient?

When I think of what a giant leap it is to believe all of this, I feel as though I am in a storm. But to not believe, to distrust what you feel and even want inside, well that's pretty crazy too, especially with all that's at stake.

Do I write different animal too much?

Luke 8:26-33

I'm back to my old doubting self. It's that easy. Have you ever had a dream? Have you ever wanted something so badly that you were willing to schedule and plan and reschedule time to pursue it? Did you ever accomplish that dream, but it didn't turn out the way you thought it would? Did you ever sit in front of your computer in a lonely office and watch the cursor blink? I'm not sure if anything lives up to how you feel when you read a great book. Even then—and this is just a wild guess—you might be disappointed that it's finished or that you didn't write it or that you will never read all the great books that are out there because you just can't find them. Wouldn't you like to search and search and search by car, plane, boat? Bookshop by bookshop. People might know you by name. Honk when you drive by. Throw books at you on the street. The days would rush by. Your family would be there. You'd eat at fancy restaurants. Your kids would always be happy. You'd woo your spouse and those great romantic moments would be all moments. Wouldn't you like that? Wouldn't your life be just corny and wonderful?

Jesus and his disciples were sailing the Galilee; it must be an adventure. Of course, Jesus is met at shore by a demon-possessed man, who lives in the tombs. This man has been chained up and kept under guard, but even the chains and guards can't hold him. The demon is too strong. Isn't this like your life? It's more like a horror film I probably wouldn't watch. The man sees Jesus and falls to the ground. He shouts, what do you want with me Jesus, son of the Most High God? I'm begging, don't torture me!

Him torture you?

So the demon-possessed recognize him. Why the demon-possessed? Why is his identity so clear to them? It makes you think recognition isn't enough.

Jesus commands the evil spirit to leave the man. Commands. What is your name, Jesus asks.

"Legion."

Luke notes that this name signifies that many demons were in this man. They beg Jesus not to order them into the Abyss. They recognize his authority over them. Demons recognize who he is and his power.

The demons see pigs feeding on the hillside and beg that Jesus allow them to go into them. Jesus gives his permission. So the demons go out of the man and enter the pigs, which rush down the bank, drop into the lake, and drown.

The story seems familiar. I might just gloss over it. I might just ask myself, so what? But then, I don't want to think about demons. I can't relate to demons. I can imagine pigs.

So I try again. Demons. It's not a story I would tell my children. It's not a story for which I can quickly find an effective application for my own life. What then? What does it amount to? Jesus isn't afraid; in fact, he's in control. The demons fear him. They drown before him. I fear unfulfillment. I fear believing in something that might not be true. I fear buying into a lifestyle that might mean standing up and facing major challenges and the ridicule of others. I fear committing to a religion that might call me to face real or imagined demons. I also fear having to wrestle those tough ideas that separate rather than unify people. My demons are those issues—you know which ones I'm speaking of without me naming them—that bring up questions of faith and belief and are all too often argued in the political realm, which seems the wrong house. We all love freedom and democracy until we face people that believe differently, then we just want to change their mind by finding any way or means necessary. Isn't The Way and The Truth and The Life supposed to unite rather than create a battleground? Isn't truth its own argument? Why prove it by any means if it's true? Aren't Christians to be known by their love? Or is it their superior moral code? I'm on unsteady ground now, so how am I to decide? How does one writer figure out the mysteries of the world when everything mixes with everything else? How would I react if I met this Jesus face to face? I don't even want to ask the question. I don't want to be made to choose sides. Everything isn't relative, but it's not all the same either. We all have our own shoes. We all have our own issues. We all have our soapboxes. I don't have to deal with everything every other individual must. It's easy for me to have opinions about scenarios I will never face. Who then will I trust for my opinions? If not by experience, then I must give another the authority in my life, to tell me how it is when you face tragedy or victory or moral decisions that pull at the fabric of your beliefs. I can believe anything if that belief is never tested. I must trust others and history (who's history?) in helping me form my world view. What if you hear the same stories and come to completely different conclusions? What if there is a dominant school of thought based on the stories and you disagree or differ in how you believe that truth should be applied to life? What if you only know the outcomes rather than the story itself? What if at times the followers don't seem to match the message? What if you find yourself not acting according to what you decided you believe? What if everything turned so complicated even when it sometimes seemed so simple? There's a great man, God. There's a great collection of stories. There's another man at his computer so confused he's asking a storm of questions and he doesn't know if the hurricane is productive or reverent or that which will undo him? My shoes. My responsibility. My storm. Fear. What next?

I should let you know that I just made a note to myself to reread and edit this section. I'm not sure if I can share all of this. There's a battle inside, where there used to be excitement. There's turmoil, where fun used to hang out. This isn't so fun anymore. This doesn't feel like testing ideas anymore. I was pretending before. I was putting my best foot forward. I have to admit I'm praying now. I feel out of control. This was supposed to be just an exercise. Why this fear inside? If I ask one more question, I might just give it all up. Enough for now. I said I wouldn't edit, but I'm reading it. I can't help but revise as I write this passage. I can't help but rethink because I can't just throw this out and not think about where it will land. If a bad feeling is a demon... horror film!

Luke 8:34-39

I reread what I've written and can't even remember why I felt the way I felt. I was afraid and now it doesn't even seem real. I want my words to be as authentic as possible, but how am I to revise without the person I have become changing the person I was? I will never be the man I was yesterday ever again. I know too much now. I've been through it and I can't go back. Aren't my unedited thoughts more important than grammar and the imperfect editor inside?

Meanwhile, those people who were there tending the pigs saw it all. They ran off and reported it to everyone they could reach. People came to the spot, so they might experience it too. When they encountered Jesus, they saw the man who had the demons sitting at his feet. He was dressed and in his right mind, which made them afraid. When they learned what Jesus had done, they asked him to leave. They were too afraid. So Jesus left.

However, the man who had been cured begged to go with Jesus. Jesus sent him away. He told the man to return home and tell the people all that God had done for him. So the man went away and told all about what Jesus had done.

The people were afraid of Jesus, but the man who had been demon-possessed wasn't. He wanted to follow. According to the story though, Jesus seemed to think he was more needed among his people. Jesus left, but the man stayed. This was a chess move. The people might see how he had been cured by God. This man might be able to tell about the great thing Jesus had done to the very people who knew him. Jesus sent him home. He sent him to a place where he himself wasn't welcome. This man was a messenger; he was a minister. Imagine God sending someone else to tell about him, to a place where God had been asked to leave.

My phone rings. A friend from college, and the connection is fuzzy. We talk about kids and remember our college days. We can't believe how much has changed, how distance has spread between us. Crackle, crackle. We don't want to hang up, but we do.

I sit down to type again.

I remember the story. I wonder if I will have a testimony someday that might benefit people. I wonder if doubt might be the ingredient to a good story.

You might watch a man grow up and sit in ruin. You know him. You know his parents. You speak about him in hushed tones. You use him as a good bad example. For years, you make up jokes. You fear him when you see him in the grocery store. You know he deserves to be feared. You know he is capable of just about anything. Years more. One day a story reaches you about how he has dramatically changed. You go see about it. You encounter a crowd. You encounter something foreign and shun it. The man you once feared tells you a story. You can't ask the story to leave.

Luke 8:40-56

Why didn't Jesus just heal everyone? Why did he want some stories told and some kept quiet? I have no doubt how wonderful this Jesus is, but I do sometimes find myself considering, or even questioning, his methodology.

How the story of the dead girl and sick woman intermingle is just amazing. They mix together to form something completely new. One healing is because of a petition, and one is because of faith in action. How many more people must have wanted something from Jesus, but these two succeeded. Why?

Jesus was being swallowed by a crowd. Jairus, who was a ruler in the synagogue, came and fell at Jesus's feet because his twelve-year-old daughter was terribly sick. Rulers don't often fall at a man's feet. For a dying daughter, a man might do anything, but they won't do it before just anyone. And they certainly wouldn't want to do it before a crowd. Desperate times, extreme measures—extreme faith.

Jesus follows Jairus toward his house, but is swarmed by more and more people. A woman sick from bleeding—a malady that no doctor had been able to heal and that had tormented her for twelve years—touched the edge of Jesus's cloak and was healed. Jesus felt something so he asked who it was. No one answered. Peter was baffled. There are too many people to know, he said. In a somewhat strange moment, Jesus says he felt the power go out of him. It's a moment where we get a glance behind the curtain. There's a power Jesus releases that heals. I don't know how else to put it, but it almost reminds you of X-Men. I feel uncomfortable even saying it, but it's the only frame of reference I have.

The woman speaks up because she has no other choice. Jesus says it was her faith that healed her and she can go in peace. The woman is bold. She believes and she puts that belief in action. Jesus blesses her; tells her to go in peace. It makes me imagine that she may have been overwhelmed, and even afraid, of what had happened. She knew something would happen if she could just reach out for Jesus, but who could be prepared for what she received? I pray for healing—I do. I pray for family and friends, sometimes boldly, sometimes only in my heart, and I always wonder what to expect. I can't say that I've seen a miracle healing, and I can't say that I've ever expected one, or acted on the belief that the healing would happen. Do I lack the faith? Do I only believe that God will heal who he already planned to heal? What do I learn? How does it change me?

Friends of Jairus interrupt this tender moment. They tell Jairus not to bother Jesus any further because his daughter is dead. Immediately Jesus tells Jairus not to be afraid, but just to believe, and she will be healed. Belief is a part of healing?

So they arrive at Jairus's house. A select few are chosen to go in with Jesus: Peter, John, James, and Jairus and his wife. Jesus tells the others they can stop mourning because the child is only sleeping. They laugh at him. They know she is dead.

Inside, Jesus takes her by the hand and tells her to get up. Luke tells us that her spirit returns and she stands up. Jesus gives her something to eat. The parents are "astonished," but Jesus orders them to not tell anyone what has happened.

One healing is seen by all, one is kept quiet. Jesus heals, but he also credit's a woman's faith and a man's belief. All are overwhelmed. Even the faith and belief that is enough to assist in healing is not enough to comprehend such power.

People laugh.

The mourning may have been contrived but the laughter is real.

I want to believe in such things, but experience can sometimes contradict. I've stood by as those close to me have passed away. I've prayed. I've written in secret about such experiences because I've thought it might help with my grief. I've never for a moment believed those who claim to heal. What then do I believe? Am I outside God's select because of my resistance to such supernatural possibilities? Am I wrong to believe that God heals who he heals? Isn't it at least something that I believe God is in control even if it doesn't lead to front-page news? Even the most faithful have died. Everyone dies. Even those who were healed by Jesus at some point died. Maybe, and I admit I'm just one man with one theory, it's not this type of death that Jesus is most concerned about. Maybe God's plans are beyond our understanding, our world. Maybe if we admit our lack of understanding, our unbelief, our lack of control, we might just be filled up with something new. Maybe believing in a God we might not always understand is more powerful than claiming to understand. I have only one frame of reference: I don't always understand why my wife does the things she does. I do believe that she does them out of love and the belief she is doing what is best. How much more can this be applied to a God that knows all, rules all, loves all, controls all? It's a leap, no doubt, and I say this with all sincerity: What's the harm in taking this kind of faith for a test drive and if we find it has merit, then applying the gas?

nine

I can't help but review it. It was only a few nights ago that I was afraid of my own words. It was only a handful of hours past that I was doubting everything because of the politics and opinions of others who surround me like a mountain range. Yet—days later I am full of high ideals. Yet—hours later I am at the edge looking in, knowing I can dance here forever, knowing I can test the waters for only so long. Is it really as much like poker as it feels? All in or fold?

Luke 9:1-2

Jesus sends his disciples out with a few tricks. He must think they are ready now. One man teaches twelve, which teach 144, which teach a lot more than that. It's pretty strategic. So how does he prepare them? with new powers and some simple instructions. First, he gives them power and authority over demons and diseases. Then he gives them a ministry plan: to preach and heal. The two most important tenants of the Jesus Ministry Plan are to tell them about the kingdom of God and then to show them, by healing the sick. His simple plan makes me ask this question: What else is there that is more important than the good news and health? Go out. Offer people what they need. I am a little overcome with the simplicity, and yet it's everything. I know there must be someone out there with a good argument about how people are being preached at in order to be healed or that the healings will just enable people or make them lazy. I'm sure on another day I might have a cynical attitude, but not today. Today I feel the need to be healed, and I'm not able to belittle it. It's real. It's hopeful. It's simple, well, except for the part about power and authority over demons and diseases. So not simple. That makes it a bit more supernatural, than say, practical.

Luke 9:3-6

Jesus also tells his disciples not to bring anything for the journey, not a staff, bag, bread, money, or even an extra tunic. Enter only one house and stay there until you leave the town, he says. If you're not welcome, shake the dust off your feet and leave as a testimony against them. Luke reports that they went out, preaching and healing.

It must have been difficult to just go out on faith, depending on the generosity of others. Jesus anticipated resistance to the message. He told his disciples to not linger, but to move on. I just can't imagine what it would take not to bring backup. Would I do it? Would I receive traveling preachers with a new message into my home for an undetermined amount of time? I can't say that I definitely would. I might; I might not. But I might.

In college, I went to another country to help with building an orphanage and to do Vacation Bible School. Let me tell you, I was uncomfortable and I brought backup. I received more than I gave. It was as easy as that. I didn't do much, but I was given much. I didn't heal. I didn't preach. I was just there. It was difficult, but afterward, I went home and sadly forgot many of the lessons I had learned. No recreation possible. I can't think of anything else worthwhile to say. I don't go anywhere without money and water, maybe a buffet of food and emotions. It took a faith I can't even imagine. Living simply, and on faith, has many lessons, but they are easily forgotten and replaced by comfort and a TV series.

I feel tired and pulled in every direction. I am sure these verses deserve more consideration.

Faith. No backup.

Preach. Heal. Move on.

Luke 9:7-8

These things that were going on were significant on a national level as well as a personal one. Even Herod the tetrarch was hearing rumors and becoming a step above curious. He was feeling guilty. The reports were borderline ridiculous. They were saying John or another profit had been raised from the dead or even that Elijah had appeared. But Herod was nervous because he had beheaded John and wanted to know who he was hearing such stories about. So Herod attempted to see Jesus, so he could find out what was going on.

How quickly did this little band of preachers and healers create national news for their leader? How much power is there in a message that even makes the tetrarch nervous before he's even met the players? It almost puts you in the mind of Moses, or The Beatles, with their long hair full of revolutionary rock. My uncle might be proud of that example, but prouder still if I would have used The Rolling Stones as an example instead.

Luke 9:10-11

So us again, sitting here you and I. The computer and I are doing some kind of dance. I write these things only to say that dinner is finished and the dishes are in the dishwasher. My desire is to write something new, so I'll try. I'll give it my best.

The disciples return with reports for Jesus. They attempt to withdraw to Bethsaida, but the crowds follow, so Jesus welcomes them. He tells them of the kingdom of God, and he heals.

Jesus is never too busy. Isn't this one of those great compliments that you could live on for years? You know that Ink he is never too busy. You can never overdraw on his generosity. Yeah. I like the sound of that.

My day goes like this: I interview people. I write articles. I sneak in moments of poetry and a novel I am working on. I complain to my wife. I go to a community meeting. I eat dinner. I worry about my kids. I play a game on the Wii with them. I tuck them in. I worry. I write a little, read a little. I watch some TV. I plan for the next day. I lay in bed and read and worry and wish I was already asleep, yet once you go to sleep, the next thing you do is get up and do it again. All these words, what's the point really? I would have to say it's to be a better person and give back to the literary world, which has given so much.

My wife peeks in on me. She wonders how it's all going. I read her a few lines I am particularly proud of and they don't sound as good as I remember. I wonder if I will ever figure this thing out. I look at her and I wonder if when she thinks of me, when she boils down the last 12 years we have spent together both dating and married, if she thinks I am basically a good guy, a loveable man. I know she does, but I still wonder what exactly she thinks of me. I wonder what it is about me that she likes best and least. I wonder which days are her favorite. I wonder if I still romance her with the way I spend my days. If days really are a currency, then am I thought of as a good and faithful steward? I look at her so long, she says what with a smile. Oh nothing, I say. I'm just thinking, I say. She tells me about how she's planning to use the office as a nursery when the new baby comes. She laughs. Do you have to type while we talk? No, I say.

Luke 9:12-17

This story has always been one of my favorites. It's just so impossible and wonderful. It's one of those stories that no matter how much you try, you can't explain or forget.

The disciples attempt to tell Jesus what to do. They say send the crowds away because it's late and they need to find food and a place to sleep. It's as if they think Jesus doesn't have the people's wellbeing in mind, or that he is so focused on the kingdom of God that he has forgotten their basic needs.

Jesus says, you feed them.

They say, there's five thousand and we only have five loaves and two fish, unless we go buy more.

Jesus had them sit down. He gave thanks up to heaven and broke the bread and fish. The disciples gave food to the people and they ate and were satisfied. Twelve baskets were filled with leftovers.

He takes a little and he makes a lot.

Each disciple had a basket of leftovers, new faith.

Luke 9:18-21

Back again. Feeling distracted. Can't even write complete sentences apparently. Lazy. Distracted. Talking to myself. Outside is melting snow. Muddy. Mushy. Wet. Distracting.

Jesus was praying in his own space, but his disciples were there. It was a pivotal moment that I haven't given much thought. I'm considering it now though. He asks his disciples who the people say he is. John the Baptist, Elijah, a prophet from the past who has come back to life, they say. It's quite a list. People believe he is beyond the norm, beyond the farm. He, his teachings, beckon back to a time when prophets spoke directly to God on behalf of the people. They name the giants of faith. It's not to be taken lightly. But who do you say that I am, Jesus asks. Peter says, you're more. You're the Christ. You're God. Jesus strongly, emphatically warns them to tell no one.

And there it is. Doesn't all depend on this fact? He's God or just some guy?

Can I, at this point in my life, decide what to believe? I want to say in truth that I believe he is none other than the one true God, but it's not something to just say. I would tell anyone that asked that this is what I believe, but when it comes down to it, it's too difficult to just claim. Where's the evidence? John the Baptist asked through his followers if this was so or if he should look for another, and Jesus said tell him what I do. These people, the most religious among them, were waiting for a Messiah. Some said yes, it is he. Some said no. Yet, I wasn't waiting for a Messiah. I wasn't waiting for a savior. But I'm reading about Jesus and there he is messing with my life through the words that Luke has written. Before I read, I could have gone on without making a decision. Now I can't. Reading and responding has become my burden.

Before I had kids I didn't have to worry about being a parent. Before I was married, I didn't need to act like a good or adequate husband. There is a burden. There is a decision to be made. It's not like choosing a church or a friend. It's choosing, or buying into, investing in, something that will change everything, which will impact everything that makes up your day. Yet, it's not something you can just figure out. Is logic enough? Does the Bible have the authority, the word on Jesus? I can think with my head. I can think with my heart. I can see how the words have made my life more than chasing one desire after another. Can I give away my kingdom? I rule my life. I am able to think through my day. I am able to use logic and come up with the best solution, or work off instinct. I am able to make good and bad decisions. This would change all that. This would change more. Why this man? Why a man? Either he is God or not. It's as easy and complicated as that.

I already try to emulate his life, but to give him the glory, the worship of my day, it's selling your birthright. Do you receive a kingdom for such faith or a bowl of soup?

What is beautiful is what you wash your
heart with. What is burdensome is what
you wash your day with. You put these
words together and attempt a meaning that
is servant to truth or music or something else.

All words have their masters. You tell them
what to do, what to wash, how to walk. You
line them up and dress them down. The words
never follow your orders. They do what they
want to do. They have a way that is all their own,
these wonton words.

They're moving too fast now. They've jumped
a train heading out west. It's freedom they seek.

They never wanted this life. They wanted to run

through the hills and valleys. They wanted an
adventure story. They explore your mind and
want their freedom.

One word, their spokesperson, asks is this what
they were created for, only this? A small word
asks, who made you boss?

They tire of your insecurity. They tire of standing
next to words that have sprung up in nature. They
plead for you to hit the delete button. We belong
somewhere else, they say. You never planned to
force words where they didn't want to go.

You dust them off. You bathe them. You ask them
to forget. You look around, check under your bed,
for all the words that are trying to hide, trying to get
away. You want to get away, get out of this somehow,
but it's too much. You run away with the words and
grant them their freedom. You unchain the question
mark. You forfeit your rights, your ownership. You promise you won't
do it again. Promise is the only word that stays with
you, sleeping soundly in the bed you've made for it.

When all else fails, I reach out and turn the computer off, or I mean I
plan to once I finish typing this. Words. Haste. Distraction. Snow. Melt.
Move on.

Luke 9:22

Jesus tells them what makes some sense now, but couldn't have then.
The Son of Man must suffer, he says. The Son of Man will be rejected by
the elders and chief priests and teachers of the law. The Son of Man
must be killed and on the third day be raised to life.

Must? Did you notice the must? He must die. He must rise again. And there it is, all of it. There's the reason he came. See, these are the type of destinies that make believing a burden. He must die. He must rise again. Belief is no small thing. We make it easy because most people we know casually believe. What is casual about this belief? Either it is fantastically real, true, or it is something like a myth or fairytale or something. Something. Something. Both are useful, but their usefulness is very different.

If you attempt to be thoughtful about the whole thing it isn't easy. It's something you really have to decide for yourself. My parents believe. My brothers believe. Do I believe? Do I risk my life on it? Do my kids after me?

Luke 9:23

Does this sound easy to you? Jesus says if anyone should follow me they must deny themselves and take up the cross daily. The cross. Not the one around your neck, the one you hang on. The burdensome cross that somehow, someway maybe takes away the burdens. Somehow, someway it releases your burdens, your guilt. Deny yourself. I've always indulged myself, encouraged myself.

Luke 9:24-25

There's more: Those who want to save their life, must lose it in order to save it. Jesus asks, what good is it if you gain the whole world, but lose your very self?

This doesn't sound anything like the gospel I hear day by day. Do good, people tell me. Follow the rules, people say. Deny yourself and pick up a cross? Who says that?

Luke 9:26-27

These are a couple of troublesome verses for me. I'm just not feeling it today, but I am writing anyway because I said I would.

Jesus says if anyone is ashamed of me and my words, then I will be ashamed of him when he "comes in his glory and in the glory of the Father and of the holy angels."

First, I am not sure I entirely understand the part between the quotes, but I am going to boil it down to when you face God (Jesus) in all his glory, or even maybe once you die, if you are ashamed of him then he is ashamed of you? With all due respect don't we expect more from God than this? With a little bit of fear of my own heart and being irreverent, I ask why what I do is so important to God? Does it matter to him how I talk about him or think about him? This is way beyond a God out there; this is a God here and now, involved in our conversations, impacted by how we treat his words, his pronouncements. How differently does this seem than the free gift of eternal life? How we talk about God has consequences. Don't use his name in vain. Don't be ashamed that God expects much of us. I'll admit it: I have a difficult time discussing what Jesus says with others. Everyone has preconceived notions. Many call it being preached at. No one listens to anyone anymore, if they ever did. Also, the name of Jesus has power today. If you mention Jesus, the whole conversation changes. There are rules about religion and politics. It's not polite. It's not seen as loving people; most times, it's seen as judging. And as if that wasn't enough, I can't always claim to understand everything that Jesus has to say. I can't claim that I have the insider's story to everything Jesus said or did. I believe in absolutes so strongly that I am not going to claim that I am absolutely sure that everything is clear to me. I do try though. I read and I take the words seriously. I don't pick and choose. If I disagree or am confused, I keep wrestling. What I can say is that I try to measure what Jesus says against everything else he says, and come to it with a full perspective not an individual quote. I look at context. I attempt to keep my mind wide open. I listen to people I trust. I'm not ashamed, but I am careful. I try to be thoughtful and respectful. I don't try to convince everyone of everything. I try to be truthful. I try to be honest and truthful. I try to figure out who God is and act accordingly. I try to understand, and even be loving toward my audience, my friends. It's never enough. I still hurt people's feelings even though that is the last thing I want. I don't say the right things all the time (who does?) no matter how I try. I can't say I pick up the cross daily, but I am aware of the cross. I am aware these matters have weight. I try to let his words speak for themselves instead of making my life, and my words, the focus. It's not easy today. It never was easy. I'm always disillusioned when someone makes it too easy.

Jesus says, I tell you the truth, some who are standing here will not taste death before they see the kingdom of God. Is this a prophesy? What exactly is the kingdom of God? I think of eternal life and of the kingdom of God here on earth. I wonder, did some of these see the kingdom of God? Isn't that what Jesus promised? Am I so bold as to claim this in my own life? Don't such promises go beyond Jesus being a good man? I think we have been down this road before. Jesus speaks in absolutes because he has the authority, but do I? Can I tell people this is what Jesus means or only this is what Jesus says? Isn't this something we must figure out individually, even if we discuss as a group? I don't want anyone to figure it out for me so why would I figure it out for anyone else? All we can do—in my mind (that dangerous gameshow) anyway—is point someone in what we feel is the right direction, but we can't take it lightly. It's no small thing, I tell my kids. It's no small thing.

I come back to one final thought: What is our motivation? Is it to unify, to love, or to separate, saying one person is right or one person is wrong? Do we come to these words with an open mind or do we come to them with ideas already formed, which we are only attempting to justify? Whether atheist or religious (Christian or otherwise) or somewhere in-between, isn't this a valid question? Can we be convinced of anything if we hold tightly to yesterday's faith, eyes, ears? Isn't today's faith always different than yesterday's?

Luke 9:28-36

Here is one of those moments beyond explanation. I might read over it quickly because I've heard it before, not think about how crazy it would be if I were to believe it really happened. How can you read this and not think of Jesus differently? Did that sound like a challenge?

About eight days later, Jesus took Peter, John, and James with him to a mountain to pray. As Jesus prayed, his face changed and his clothes shown bright like a flash of lightening. Moses and Elijah appeared and talked to Jesus. They told about how he would leave, something that would come to be, soon after, in Jerusalem. Although the disciples had been half asleep, it is reported that they were now fully awakened by how Jesus had changed; he was with the two prophets of old, speaking. Peter thought this moment needed to be remembered by three monuments, one for each man, but Luke said he didn't know what he was saying. Then a cloud enveloped them and they were afraid. There was a voice, it said, *this is my son, whom I've chosen, you should listen to him*. Afterward, Jesus was alone. The disciples kept all this to themselves.

It's like a living resume. Moses and Elijah were character witnesses, and if that wasn't enough, a voice, which must have been God, called Jesus his son, the chosen one.

What else can I say? These disciples seem bewildered. I feel a bit bewildered myself when I really think about it.

Might we just believe that this is but a legend, a myth that came after Jesus? Might we comfortably explain it as such?

Luke 9:37-43

Yet another demon possession. It's just something I have to face. I don't like thinking of demons as real. I don't like it at all. It doesn't seem real at all to me, and I am glad of that.

It was the next day after the transfiguration. They came off the mountain and a crowd met them. One man asked Jesus to look at his son because he had a spirit that would make him scream out, throw him to the ground in convulsions, and cause him to foam at the mouth. The disciples weren't able to do anything. Jesus makes a somewhat strange aside: He proclaims this generation perverse and unbelieving. How long will I stay with and put up with you, he asks. He asks the man to bring his son forward, but even while the boy approaches the spirit throws him to the ground and he convulses. Jesus rebukes the evil spirit and the boy is healed. He gives the healed boy back to his father. Everyone marvels about the greatness and power of God. They are amazed at what they have seen.

So that's the story. The more I read, the less I am able to call Jesus just a good man. Such stories restrain me from easy answers. Such stories take me to a place I have never known. No experience can explain this to me. Why do we mix Jesus with magic? Or is it true?

But this isn't what I discuss with my friends. They want to know how I can follow such debilitating rules, those the church teaches, represents. They want to know why I don't use logic. They argue politics and the strong, unloving stances that the Christian Right takes. They wonder how I deal with all the guilt. They wonder why I don't want to have fun and accumulate goods. I wonder what is happiness anyway, or contentment for that matter. I've never seen wealth equal happiness. Freedom equals happiness. Doing good equals happiness. Family equals happiness. Health equals happiness. That's what I've seen.

I admit, I worry all the time. I bully happiness out of my life with worry and insecurity. I have a loving, lovely, understanding, pregnant wife and two great children who have turned my life upside down and inside out. I enjoy what I do most of the time. I have no demons, but what I bring into my life. I believe there are consequences to my actions. I believe in absolutes. I don't believe in using those absolutes to exclude or judge.

I write things because I am not able to not write things. I love people because I am not able to not love them. I pray because I am not able to not pray. I read Luke because I am now not able to not read Luke. I know what happens. I've heard the stories. I am surprised with every verse. The today me sees differently than the yesterday me. I sit here at my computer, instead of say watching the baseball game or going to the park because I feel something missing, and this in its imperfect way fills that void. I am a better person once I spend time writing and thinking and even praying some. Not a lot really, but some.

You must see the demons all
around you, balanced in you,
a battle being staged.

Leave your conclusions at the door.

You wonder what to do with such
writing on the wall. You wonder what
such open ocean might mean, change.

You can't imagine without the music. You
can't have these words forced upon you.

Your mind must be free.

Every good has an equal and opposite bad.
You don't believe it. You eat it.

You can't begin again. There's nothing but
birth and death. You hope. You wouldn't have
made it like this—not now, not ever.

You can't even set yourself upon such a
stage. You're no actor. You haven't any
prepared lines.

You swim the entire open, through blue, as
if it were sky. You hit the concrete and sky
away, I meant shy away.

You are never seen again. You don't believe
in demons. You don't believe.

I know there is nothing of worth in this hurried poem. Sometimes in abstract thinking, I come to concrete thinking, but not this time. Sometimes I read existential writing and fill in the gaps with my own meaning. An argument against can sometimes be the best argument for. But not this time. Not this time. This time it's just writing. This time it's just what it is, good or bad. This time it's just the process, a process that might come to something someday. That's me, I guess. Nothing great, but something all the same. Isn't it beautiful? Something not so good, attempting to be great? I write a poem I want to be something it will never be. Isn't that life?

Luke 9:44-45

Afterward, Jesus said, listen carefully, the Son of Man will be betrayed into the hands of men. The disciples didn't understand. The meaning was hidden from them, and because they were afraid, they didn't ask him about it.

Of course, we know that is just what happened. Why was the meaning hidden from them? Why were they afraid to ask?

Everything Jesus foretells comes to pass. We know that now. But then. Then, they weren't sure what he meant. Why is he going through with this if he knows how it will end? they might have asked themselves or each other. It's strange that a man would submit to such a fate. We often wonder why there is suffering, yet Jesus doesn't attempt to avoid it himself. Is his goal longer term? Or do they even understand he is speaking of himself? So many questions. What we know for certain is that Jesus knew what was going to come about, and he submitted to it.

Maybe this is so obvious there is no need to write it down, but I write things down, obvious or not, because I do. Because I need to write it down and read it and swallow it whole like bitter herbs or Jonah. The fact is that I avoid discomfort and especially pain whenever possible. I am afraid to give myself over completely to any one thing because it is putting too much faith in a single idea, a solitary pursuit. I want to diversify like my life is a stock portfolio. Jesus didn't live his life that way. Whose life is more successful, profitable? Who cares?

Luke 9:46-48

Such a strange, even crazy, thing for the disciples to be arguing about. Funny that Luke wrote it down too. It's like something my son might argue about at school. Jesus, the way he does, knows they are arguing about who is the greatest. He shows them a child. He says whomever welcomes a child such as this in my name welcomes me, and welcoming me is welcoming God. Who is least among you, is the greatest.

Easy as that. It's the upside-down hierarchy of Jesus. I can't add to it. I don't wish to subtract from it.

Luke 9:49-50

Nothing about my day was all that interesting. I got a haircut. I thought about writing. I wrote. I ate dinner. I ate way too much dinner. I read. I danced with the kids. Something else, I can't remember now since I was typing the other stuff. I ran downstairs. I ran upstairs. I did push-ups. I ate breakfast and lunch. I worried about my weight and a recent doctor's appointment, which felt more like a trip to the principal. I know it's spelled like that rather than principle because the principal is my pal.

John has seen a man they don't know driving out demons in Jesus's name. He tried to stop him because he wasn't one of the 12. Jesus says don't stop him. Who is not against us is for us. Inclusivity! Solidarity!

How was this new religion spreading beyond even who the disciples knew? Why was that threatening to John? I see a bit of today in that. We think because we don't know them, or they don't go to our church or sing the same hymns or run the veer offense, they're not on the same team, but aren't they?

Luke 9:51-56

My Bible calls it Samaritan Opposition. It says that as the time was approaching for Jesus to be taken up to heaven, he set out earnestly for Jerusalem. He sent messengers ahead into a Samaritan town to prepare, but the people were not welcoming because he was headed for Jerusalem. James and John thought they might call down fire from heaven to destroy them; instead, Jesus rebuked them and went to another village.

Again, we see how Jesus approaches opposition differently. Instead of destruction, he moves on from those who aren't receptive. Why didn't he attempt to change their mind? It must have something to do with his time nearing as the passage suggests. He had a clear mission, but he wasn't bent on thwarting those not with him, only in accomplishing what he set out to do. I wish politics worked like this. It's not about who's against you, or even who's for you—it's about <u>who you are for</u> and what you're about and how you go about it.

What is to be learned then? Pick your battles? Know when and where?

I get the feeling Jesus was concerned with what he was concerned with, which was fulfillment of what he was called to do. He also wasn't one to destroy. If he was, he wouldn't have laid down his life the way he did.

Sounding a bit like I have it all figured out, which is certainly not my intension. He brought a sword, which is a hard fact to deny or make congruent with what I just said.

Luke 9:57-62

Try these words on for size. Out of left field, Luke tells of many people wanting to follow Jesus. Jesus warns of the cost. It's a tough suit to wear.

One man on the road says he will follow Jesus wherever he is going. Jesus says that while foxes have holes, and birds nests, the Son of

Man has no place to lay his head. No word on the man's response.

Jesus asks another man to follow. This man says let me bury my father first. Jesus replies, let the dead bury their own dead, but you go and tell about the kingdom of God. No response?

Another man says he will follow, but first he much go see his family and say goodbye. Jesus says no one who puts his hand to the plow and looks back is fit for service in the kingdom of God. Did he follow?

Harsh. Cold. Unfeeling?

Was Jesus rebuking because they were flippant about this call to follow? Did one wish only to follow for what he could obtain? One was not committed to the urgency of the call? And maybe the third was already looking back to what he might be giving up and having second thoughts?

I'm uncomfortable even commenting. I could get it all wrong. I might be looking for an easy way out that will please readers. It reminds me of exuberant volunteers that are sure to shirk when the full commitment comes due. Is that it? Is Jesus saying that unless you know what you are getting into from the first step, you won't complete the journey? Is he saying that the journey is more important than an earthly destination and creature comfort; a father's funeral; saying goodbye to loved ones?

The first I can somewhat understand, but the next two? Leaving my family unkissed or my father unburied seems unthinkable. Were they but excuses? Or was Jesus really saying what they were about was more pressing and important?

I have pictures of my kids, my wife, my siblings, and my parents right here at my desk. I look at them often. An emotion wells up in me that is unequaled in any part of my life. I feel invincible with love and motivation to give. Nothing is impossible. Could I believe in something so strongly that I could follow, leave? Is this a calling specific to then or one for right now as well? Isn't my place here?

All this reminds me of nothing. I can't relate it to any experience I've ever had. There's no simile, no baseball metaphor. It's really a call that seems to supersede any other and even any comparison. Jesus calls people to be good husbands, mothers, workers, friends, neighbors, and also to follow forsaking all else. I can't make it work. I can't unwind it and produce some comfortable, easy truth. It's too difficult. It's too much. Is this writing my plow, and I am now looking back? Could that be it?

Is there time to decide?

Love/forsake all.

Sounds more like a Shakespeare play. A *Measure for Measure*.

ten

Luke 10:1-4

The Lord appointed 72 others to go ahead of him to every town. He said the harvest is plentiful, but there are few workers. Ask then, the Lord of the harvest to send out the workers to the harvest field. Go, he said. I'm sending you out like lambs among the wolves. Don't take your belongings or greet those on the road.

Again, there's a sense of urgency in Jesus's words. He sends them out with a clear mission: Attend to the harvest, and the harvest only; but he also says they are lambs among wolves. There is danger in what they are doing. Why? Who are these wolves and why are the 72 like lambs? What shepherd sends out his lambs among the wolves?

It's strange to think back to how Jesus always had time for people along the way. Have the circumstances changed or is he making a point based on past experiences? Should I integrate this thinking into my own life or recognize the times these instructions were made. Probably both.

Luke 10:5-7

Jesus has further instructions about peace and room & board. He says enter a house with peace on your lips. If a person receives, the peace will rest upon them; otherwise, the peace will return to you. Stay at that house and eat or drink what you are given; the worker deserves his wages.

The first is a little more abstract: offer peace. It will only be received by those who are of peace. The second is more practical: eat and drink what you are given, this is your pay. Also, stay in the home where you are received. Have a relationship, enjoying peace and drink. Is there a message of not scrutinizing what you are offered? Offer peace, build relationships, give and receive. This is how you build the kingdom of God, tend the harvest.

Luke 10:8-12

My eldest son has had a difficult time at school lately. It's a major weight on me. I can't seem to separate my thoughts from it. Just yesterday, he cheated at a game, lied about it, and had a "major" argument with another student, the teacher told me. She stopped me as I picked him up. I discussed it for half an hour with my son. He didn't seem to understand. He walked away maybe 20 times and I had to call him back. I took away video games and movies. I told him if he didn't shape up, we would have to get rid of the video-game system all together. He said OK. He said, can I play Lego Star Wars? I yelled: Are you even listening to me? He wasn't. He made good arguments. He said he tries to be good. He's good most of the time. I said, how about all the time? I said, you just don't understand. I'm disappointed. I expect more. My wife walked into the room. She was patient. She explained things more calmly. He got it. He said he would try harder. I went into my room, laid on my bed, and read the same paragraph a hundred times. I felt worthless. I wanted him to show self-control. I wanted to show self-control. Worthless. Not up to the task. I try so hard in big sweeps and struggle with the day-to-day details.

While I am at it, another thing has been bothering me. I no longer see needs and hurts, I see political motivations. Someone tells me about how the economy is putting them in a headlock and I wait for their defense of one political faction or another. I look for opportunities to take the opposite viewpoint. What a mess I have become. It's no longer how can I help, it's how can I make us more thoughtful? How can I attack disillusionment or political belief without basis? I've noticed that I've become the person I've disliked so well. Does being a Republican or a Democrat mean anything anymore? Is the Bible my authority or something I've read, seen on TV, or heard on the radio? So quickly I get caught up in public policy rather than relationship. Be thoughtful, I tell myself, but be loving. Belief should be with the head and the heart, I say. How can I argue what I have no experience with? How do I have such strong opinions on matters that have never impacted me? When's the last time I was in the military, dealt with an unwanted pregnancy, or was in a relationship that challenged the fabric of my faith or the law— when did I become a scientist?—yet I seem to think I know best about all of these. I think of them only because it's a part of the national conversation, not because I have a stake in them. I'm a fake, or if not a fake, even worse, a know-it-all. Having beliefs I don't understand, or haven't thought through, can be just as destructive as having no beliefs at all.

I don't know. Now that's the truth. I feel confident about that.

How can I help?

Jesus says to his 72, if you are welcomed, eat what you are offered. Heal the sick and tell them about how the kingdom of God is near them. However, when you aren't welcome, go into the streets and kick the dust off, saying even the dust has been wiped off against you, but still tell them the kingdom of God is near. Jesus says it is more bearable on that day for Sodom than for that town.

The message is that the kingdom of God is near. Be aware. Watch for it. Are you for it or against it? Excitement or destruction is ahead.

Is it really as easy as that?

Luke 10:13-16

Jesus says woe to the cities that reject the message; on judgment day it will go bad for you, worse than cities such as Tyre and Sidon. Much has been said about Tyre and Sidon in the books of the prophets. I seem to remember judgment against them, destruction of their cities, the wiping out of the Philistines, or I guess I remember now that I looked it up. I guess they will be, or were, destroyed; not sure of the timeline. Jesus goes on to say that he who listens to the disciples, listens to him; but those who don't listen reject Jesus, and God who sent him.

I guess it was time to choose a side, God's or the other. It seems more like a challenge than a loving request. It sounds like the speech of a conqueror, rather than that of a nonviolent leader. What then should we believe? Does Jesus have many motivations—faces—or is he consistent? He loves. He heals. He gathers together. He warns of things to come. He says decide now which side you are on. He tells his disciples to be decisive. He's telling everyone of the kingdom of God and what will happen if one accepts or doesn't.

I have to admit the message is troubling. My first reaction is to get on the side of God. It seems easy enough. But... I'm not comfortable with the message of destruction. Should I be? Is this what I should be telling others? I like the message of love much better. I like the good promises. Can there be one without the other? Is it okay to be confused?

Luke 10:17-20

The disciples came back to report. They were amazed that even the demons were submitting to them. Jesus says he has seen Satan fall "like lightning from heaven." He explains that he has given the authority for them to trample on snakes and scorpions and overcome the enemy. Nothing will harm them, he says. But he also tells them not to rejoice about their power over spirits, but only that their names are written in heaven.

What a great power. What an interesting circumstance with a battle going on beyond my understanding or experience. But we've been there before. What seems more telling is that Jesus seems unconcerned with a battle he says is already won. What he says is more important is the disciples' reserved seating in heaven. Rejoice about that, he says. That's what you should emphasize. There is where you should live.

Luke 10:21

Jesus was full of joy through the Holy Spirit. Jesus praises his Father, who he calls Lord of heaven and earth, because he has chosen to hide things from the wise and knowledgeable, but reveal the truth to little children. This was the Father's good pleasure, Jesus says.

Instead of the confusion of a complicated walk, even hike, these are the verses that inspire a reader, even amidst confusion. Jesus is filled with joy. He thanks God, his Father, that he has bestowed the truth of his kingdom to the lowly and the young, rather than the wise and the rich. God is in favor of those the world passes by. He works where he is welcomed rather than in those who claim to have it all figured out and have no need for help. What an amazing father you are, Jesus says, and I have to agree. This is why I would sign up. This is why I would risk something. These are the verses I can't ignore even as I become more and more cynical.

Luke 10:22-24

Jesus says all things have been committed to him by his Father, and that the Son only knows the Father and the Father the Son, but for those who the Son chooses to reveal the Father to. Aside to his disciples, Jesus then says, you are blessed because of what you see. Many prophets and kings have wanted to see what you see and hear what you hear, but do not.

Jesus has revealed all of this to those he has chosen. Why were they chosen? It seems to me those who were willing and empty were filled. Jesus chose his disciples based on his own criteria and it seems to have nothing to do with the criteria we might use.

Luke 10:25-37

My wife is getting very large with child. It rules my thoughts and is pregnant in every call or deep breath she takes. We have had many close calls. We are packed and ready. In her words: She is ready to pop at any moment. Nothing else really matters, as they say.

Here is another of the great stories, where the ruling class is put to shame by those known as outsiders or peasants. An expert in the law asks Jesus how to obtain eternal life. Jesus asks him what he thinks in a return volley. The expert says to love God with all of your heart, soul, strength, and mind, and also your neighbor as yourself. Jesus says yes, do this. But also, Jesus asks, who is my neighbor?

Jesus then tells about a man who is headed to Jericho from Jerusalem, but he meets a band of robbers, which beat him, take his clothes, and leave him half dead. Both a priest and a Levite come upon the man and pass on the other side of the road, but a Samaritan takes pity on him. The Samaritan, not of the "chosen" people, bandages him, cleans his wounds with wine and oil, and takes him to an inn. He pays for his stay, and says he will pay further upon his return, if more expenses are incurred.

So, Jesus asks who was the neighbor to this man? The expert says, and you can almost hear the gritting of his teeth, the one who had mercy, maybe not even able to verbalize the Samaritan. Jesus says, go and do likewise.

It is amazing that even with the free gift Jesus offers, he also expects that the free gift will have the power to change, to regift. This gift—this love of God, this kingdom of God inside—will make you into the type of neighbor you've always wanted—needed—fence or no fence.

My mom calls to say that Dad's procedure went well. She says he's asked me not to write about the details because he knows I will if he doesn't. I let out a breath I wasn't aware I was holding so tightly. I am not sure if my prayers have worked or if this is the way it was supposed to be. No matter. I rejoice. I smile. I write it down. I make some calls of my own to share the news with brothers and sisters and close friends. I forget about writing for long, powerful moments.

Luke 10:38-41

Mary and Martha. We know the story. You can almost split the entire ocean of humanity into Marys and Marthas. You would think, even after reading the passage a thousand times, that Martha would be the hero.

Martha opens her home to Jesus and his disciples. Mary, the sister, sits at his feet and listens to everything Jesus says. Martha makes all the preparations and is distracted by them. In her frustration, she goes to Jesus and says, Lord don't you care that my sister has left me to do all the work? Tell her to help me!

Martha… Martha…, Jesus answers, you are worried—upset even— about many things, but only one thing is needed (*City Slickers*?). Mary has chosen what is better, and it will not be taken away from her.

eleven

A girl. A more qualified writer than me will have to explain what it's all like. It's terrible and wonderful. Birth more than any other event makes a person have faith, I think I've said that many times before. It's no accident. She was eight pounds even. A big girl. Our girl. I can't imagine anything more painful that brings about more joy. You forget the pain almost immediately, my wife tells me, and I love her all the more. She is perfect. Beautiful, sweaty, exhausted, nearer to the brink than any other time I can remember, and perfect, she is.

I watched as the gray animal breathed life into herself. Sometimes it takes time to fall in love; sometimes it takes only a few breathes. I held her last night. I tried to rest with her in my arms. I thanked God without any doubts or questions. I knew our family was complete. We named her Adeline Ruth. Adeline for one grandma on my side and Ruth for one on my wife's. I call her Addie. I thanked God aloud and was surprised when the doctor added an enthusiastic amen.

Luke 11:1-4

It is difficult for me to approach the topic of prayer. I can see how the act is worthwhile for those who pray. Prayer changes people, no doubt. Meditation is good for you like spinach or downward-facing dog. Quiet is cathartic, challenging, and sometimes scary. Quieting your mind is a

164

dragon holding your credit-card bill. Being alone with your inner thoughts can be as scary as a Stephen King novel. You have to decide who it is you are praying to and how that being responds to your prayer. Who does prayer impact most, at all?

Jesus prayed a great deal according to accounts. He went boldly before God. His disciples wanted to be taught how to pray. Other teachers, such as John, taught their disciples after all. There is something different about how you pray, they seem to be saying. Prayer is natural. Prayer is a learned practice. Prayer is difficult and easy.

Jesus says WHEN you pray, say Father your name is holy. Let your kingdom come. Give us our daily food and forgive us our sins as we forgive those who sin against us. Lead us not into temptation.

You wouldn't pray this prayer unless you were serious. This is no lightweight prayer. God you're holy. I want and trust that you offer everything I need, which includes your kingdom, which you have prepared for me and can bring about in me even now. You can provide for even my most basic needs both physical and spiritual. I want, need, and trust your food and forgiveness. I know I sin. I require your forgiveness because you are the lord of my life. Yours is a kingdom. Forgive me as I forgive others. Forgive me so that I can forgive others. Forgive me because I know I need it and because I know I need to forgive others and myself. Forgive me for not forgiving the way I should. Forgive me because I need your forgiveness in order to be the forgiver you would have me be. Does the world run on forgiveness like a car on gas or our body on water? Will I really ask God to forgive, knowing that forgiveness is also required of me? And don't lead me into temptation. I know there is much temptation to not live according to the high calling that this prayer maps. Keep me away from what I can't withstand. Guide my ship away from the waters I want to travel, but can't handle. Steer me away from the storm I will no doubt sail toward.

This is not a simple prayer. This is a prayer of faith and of practicality. This is not a prayer of confusion. It is a prayer that asks a great deal from God. This is a prayer that assumes much, expects much, and requires much. This prayer offers love, affection, worship, and bequeaths ownership. I trade me for a kingdom.

Luke 11:5-13

Jesus follows up with a story about praying. He says, so you have this friend, and you go to him in the middle of the night for bread, to feed some unexpected company that is passing through. We have nothing for them, you say, please help us out. The friend says don't bother us we've already went to bed. However, even if your friendship isn't enough, your boldness will be more than enough to get him out of bed to give what is needed.

Jesus goes on to say, ask and it will be given, seek and find, knock and the door will be opened. Everyone who asks receives.

If a father is asked for a fish, will he give his son a snake? Or give a scorpion rather than an egg? So even though you are evil, you know how to give good gifts to your children, how much more will your Father in heaven give the Holy Spirit to those who ask?

If I am to summarize, I would say it like this: God will give what is good for you, notwithstanding even himself. Come boldly and ask. Pray often. Ask much. Much will be given. God is your father. Your father is a great giver of gifts. He will give what is good.

This story makes it seem ridiculous not to pray. God, you are holy. God, you are my father. God, you are a giver. God, I need. These may be difficult to admit, but once admitted, so easy. This reaches my head, but is a much greater trick to win over my heart. Does everyone really get all they ask for, or only what they ask when it is good for them? Why are there so many stories of unanswered prayer? Why do I disbelieve or explain away every story of answered prayer?

Luke 11:14-23

I am not even sure why I am sitting here. Thoughts play pinball. I'm even pursuing an idea about my own literary magazine, just because I want to do something worthwhile and have ownership in it. What good am I if I don't? Why can't I have dreams just because dreams don't often work out? This has been my dream, so it's about time I do something about it and see if I am even in the ballpark.

Jesus drives out a demon from a mute man. It's become somewhat commonplace in his stories. I never thought that would be. The previously mute man speaks. Is muteness often a spiritual circumstance? I can't even begin to answer that question. Some of the people around think Jesus drives out demons by the devil. Others ask for a sign from heaven. At least other people are confused too.

Knowing their thoughts, Jesus responds that a kingdom or house divided against itself will fall (Lincoln?). If Satan was divided against himself, how can his kingdom stand? You figure I drive out demons by their king, but what of your own who drive them out, let them be your judges concerning this. Let those with applicable experience—rather than a bag of theories only—speak (Thank you!). That is how I read it anyhow; it's a bit tricky. However, Jesus continues, if I drive out demons by the finger of God, then his kingdom has come to you. There's your sign if you need one. Do you see it? (I inferred that last bit.)

Jesus goes on to say that when a strong man guards his own house it is safe unless someone stronger attacks and overpowers him. This stronger man will divide the spoils. He concludes, he who is not with me is against me; he who doesn't gather with me, scatters.

Again Jesus points to strong dividing lines. For those of us who want—need—a middle ground, he leaves none. We can take his words, ignore them, or defy them—unless we simply give them no authority. I see no other choices. However, I also believe there is a danger in dividing his words up for sound bites that further our own agenda. We must, in my mind anyway, weigh all of Jesus's words together in order to see a full picture. There are many canonized writings for a reason. I have no real authority more than anyone else for a reason. I have less than many for a reason. I am responsible for myself for a reason. I don't like talk of demons, not one bit, but I can't just dismiss these passages because they make me uncomfortable. There's more to say on the subject I am sure, but for once words have run away and hidden themselves behind the structures that my insecurities have built for protection. A stronger person must come and break them down.

Luke 11:24-26

Jesus goes on to teach more about demons or is it more about protecting yourself? Or could it be that Jesus is warning that if you commit to the kingdom and drive out your demons, whatever they may be, more will come? Frankly and honestly and bluntly and straightforwardly, I'm not sure what it means. I'm not sure why he says it now other than that he has been speaking about a strong man protecting a home and how a stronger man might come, and that it's all about under who's authority a demon is driven out. Maybe that's it. Maybe if your demons are driven out for the wrong reasons, under the wrong person's authority, then you will be worse in the end. Maybe that's it. See what you think:

Jesus says that when a spirit comes out of a person, it roams around seeking rest but can't find it. The spirit goes back to the house he came from, but finds it clean and in order. So he goes and gets seven of his worst buddies and goes back to live. In the end, the man is worse off than before.

See by the final result who is the strongest man, who has the greatest authority. It's not enough to clean house, you must then fill it. *I'll also say I've forgotten what it's like to have a newborn around the house. There's crying, but there is also great joy. You can sit quietly for hours. You can forget about everything else in your life for the longest periods imaginable. People come to visit. They bring food. People slap you on the back, hug you. They hold your new daughter. They look you in the eyes with awe. No one argues about politics or the existence of God. No one argues at all. Everyone recognizes the season. Some even surprise you with their optimism or their unabashed praise of God. It's not commonplace no matter how often it happens.*

Luke 11:27-28

A woman called out from the crowd, blessed is your mother, who gave you birth and nursed you. Jesus replies, blessed rather are those who hear the word of God and obey it.

It seems at many different times, and in many circumstances, Jesus changes the focus from his family to those who hear the message of God and are obedient to his kingdom—those, apparently, are his family. He gives all glory to God. He focuses his blessings on those who respond to his message. It's that simple; it's that difficult. In the end, it seems, it's not just a birthright—it's a birthright and a calling. Those who take ownership in what they are offered, and give their life to the kingdom of God, are blessed. It's easy, all are offered membership. Membership requirements are simple, but not without their difficulties. All is required. Your whole life is required. It can be annoying though, let's just admit it. When you praise for the best of intentions, maybe even oversell it just to make someone happy, and the person responds by bringing out a whole new meaning—something you didn't even consider. Your words are twisted. You even hear a bit of mockery. Can't Jesus just say thank you? Is everything a teaching opportunity? We know there's a better way. There's pretty much always a better way. Jesus is focused, driven, and comes off as a bit snarky. His tone is as hard to read as a sarcastic text. Why can't he just smile and nod his head, maybe give a hug? I'll tell you why. And here it comes: Jesus cares too much to be flippant. This wasn't his close buddy, this was a crowd of followers who were still wrestling with his message. It wasn't a time for a hug, it was time for clarification. But it does sound snarky.

Do you ever feel like if you become a full-time Christian you'll just walk about speaking widely unintelligible Christian-eze, talkin' about God this and God that and God, God, God? God told me this... God helped me to see that he wanted me to be rich. God God God. I'm just waiting on God. He'll show me. He wants me on this couch. It's a TV-watching ministry, a pizza-eating ministry, a chewing-tobacco ministry, a beer ministry (I, by the way, would get involved with all of these ministries). God can get you in or out of anything. It's God's will (the Christian get-out-of-jail-free card). He told me. It's not so much that I'm being a jerk, I'm suffering for the kingdom. We'll have easy conversations, "God God God God... God God God." You respond, "God God God God, God God." We say everything, and we say nothing. To paraphrase for my own amusement, Montana poet Richard Hugo said something like be faithful to your feelings and don't let truth push music around. If this makes you afraid of what you might say, then examine your heart not your writing. Emotions are more powerful than facts.

Quit hiding behind your Godspeak.

The enemy of excellent is good enough, but perfect is the enemy of good.

Don't let church get in the way of your relationship with God; don't let your Godspeak affect your friendships/authenticity; and don't let your friendships/authenticity keep you from church.

And especially, be true and musical and kind.

And this is yet another reason I don't say much on Facebook.

Luke 11:29-32

It was a bad day with the kids. I was too hard on them. I'm not always the man I want to be, but that's obvious.

Jesus called them a wicked generation, asking for a miraculous sign. He said none would be given besides Jonah, who was the sign to the Ninevites, so also is the son of man to this generation. The Queen of the South will rise at judgment and condemn this generation, he said. She traveled to the ends of the earth to listen to Solomon, and now one is here who is greater than Solomon. Jesus also noted that Nineveh repented because of Jonah, and they will also stand up at the judgment, but now one is here who is greater than Jonah.

The message is the same: repent. We look for signs even while we disregard, or attempt to discredit, the signs we are seeing. We've heard the stories of Jonah and Solomon, but ask for more. We hear Jesus's words, but ask for more. There is no more. There is what there is, and it should be enough. We say what it might take to make us believe, yet more has been given and still we (I) waffle. What will it really take? What do I really want? Have I even opened my eyes?

Luke 11:33-36

The body is a lamp. *This coffee has an alcoholic disguise. I'm more optimistic than a moose. I'm laughing at myself and it feels good. So much for the business of my mind. So much for stress. I don't need this. It's the first time in months I've tackled more than one passage in a single day. I don't have the emotional fortitude. But today, today, I have it. Today, I have the ambition and hope and what's that word I'm thinking of, it's not cockiness, but more along the lines of where you can't feel the insecurities that so often snake you. Do you know this word? Are you laughing because I can't come up with it? I was reading just moments ago with Luke staring at me, accusing me of writing and then wandering off into another life or world. It's tough to follow through on anything. I enjoy words. They are my party guests and my party favors. It's the Superbowl and words are throwing touchdowns. Words are avoiding defensive lineman and throwing 70 yards down field. Words as Randall Cunningham?*

You don't put a lamp under wraps; you put light on a stand so it can be seen, utilized. Your eye is the lamp of your body. When your eyes are good, your whole body is full of light; when bad, you are full of darkness. See to it then, says Jesus, that you are full of light rather than darkness.

Be full of light. Let this light wrap itself around you like a family blanket. Let the light engulf you. Say no to darkness, yes to light.

Luke 11:37-54

A Pharisee invited Jesus over for dinner, but was surprised when Jesus didn't wash his hands before he ate. Jesus said to him, you Pharisees wash the outside of the cup and dish, but inside you are full of greed and wickedness. You're foolish and not like a trout. The same person makes the inside and the outside. Give what is inside the dish to the poor, and everything will be clean.

Jesus wasn't one for appearances or rituals for rituals' sake. He is about the heart. He is about the poor. He calls people foolish. He speaks strongly. He expects much from the experts. Does it appear to be clean or is it clean?

But Jesus isn't finished with that. He has more to say to the Pharisees. He knows hearts, Luke reports over and over. He didn't let his friends get away with being falsely faithful. He says woe to you Pharisees:

You give a tenth of your goods, but neglect justice
and the love of God. Practice both. You love important seats
and good greetings. You are like unmarked
graves, which are trampled.

One expert in the law says, teacher, you're insulting us also by saying these things.

Woe to you experts also. You load people with
burdens and then won't help with the load. You build
tombs for prophets and forefathers, even though it
was your forefathers who killed the prophets. God declares
he will send prophets and apostles, some will be killed and some
persecuted. This generation will be responsible for the blood
shed since the beginning of the world—the blood
of Abel to the blood of Zechariah. For all the blood. You experts
have also taken away the key to knowledge. You have not entered
and you hinder those who are entering.

Then Jesus left. The Pharisees and teachers of the law began to oppose him fiercely. They questioned him like it was a battle and waited for any slip up that could be used to their advantage. It was a war now.

Jesus didn't hold back. He knew he would see either repentance or opposition. He left no middle ground. This isn't what I think of when Jesus enters a conversation. Jesus is all about love, above this. I know this to be true. He also loves enough to tell people how it is even when it's not popular, you might say. It's not simple: This blood is on your hands. You want me to wash the dust off of mine when yours are blood red. Either your blood or my blood will pay the price... manners or meaning.

twelve

Luke 12:1-3

I actually enjoy pointing out hypocrisy (from the safety of my own computer, of course). I contradict myself with word and action, but I don't always enjoy pointing to it like a lizard in the road. However, hypocrisy is everywhere. It's as plentiful as the common rock or a starling, but I still see it, watch it hide or fly by, and record it. I tell my wife about it. I think of it as being thoughtful or seeing below the surface, but really it's just being critical. I think that sometimes incongruences are a passion of mine. Which of these things doesn't go together? I'm not saying it's right. I'm not saying it's healthy as salmon, but I do it. I do it without even thinking about it.

My wife says, knock it off.

There was a crowd of many thousands, trampling each other like a rock concert or soccer match. Jesus spoke to his disciples. Be on guard against the hypocrisy—the yeast—of the Pharisees. Nothing can be concealed or hidden. It will be made known. What is said in the dark will be heard in the daylight, and what is whispered will be shouted.

Nothing will be hidden. All will be transparent.

Luke 12:4-7

Don't fear; you're known, loved, and cared for.

Jesus says, friends, don't fear those who can only kill the body. You should fear him who, after killing the body, can throw you into hell. Yes, fear him.

I'll admit, I'm sometimes afraid—for myself, but even more for my children and parents and brothers and sisters. Especially my children. But there's more:

Sparrows are cheap, but God does not forget a one. He even knows every hair on your head. Don't be afraid, Jesus concludes, because you are worth much more.

Don't fear any but God, and don't fear God because he knows and loves you.

It's easier said than done, but it can be done, and there is peace.

My kids find a wounded baby bird. They cry. I do what I can, which is not much.

The morning is upon me before I even know it's there. I react to the morning, rather than waking ahead of it and ordering it around. If I'm not prepared, it's out of control. Anything that breaks routine becomes dangerous. Any call, at any time, can usher in bad news and change my life. Is this call about work, a new publication, or the health of my Grandpa? Will I fear or will I hope?

We chase the baby bird to the bushes away from our dogs, who are more than interested. We see a cat. We chase it away.

We also chase away tears with popsicles.

Luke 12:8-10

My heart is just not in it this morning. I write because I told myself I would. Got a call last night from a college friend. We were once close as brothers, now we talk every few months and bombard each other with just about everything. We still share details we wouldn't speak to others. His son died. He was only a few months old. We were planning a trip to see them, the new baby, Joshua. I'm not sure whether to cancel or accelerate plans. I wasn't sure what to say. He didn't cry. The silence went on for several minutes. I tried to understand. He asked me to pray for them. I have been. All the things I had been worrying about seem so small now, insignificant, petty. I can't even make myself imagine. We had joked that our kids could be married one day, we relatives. The last call we had was one of utter joy. He said his son was with God now. Before we said goodbye, he asked me, why? I didn't have an answer. I didn't feel like a very good friend. I can't make myself do anything today.

I don't know if I'll have much to say today, but Jesus says those who acknowledge me, I'll acknowledge them before the angels of God. However, he who disowns me before men, I will disown. Everyone who speaks a word against me will be forgiven, but those who blaspheme against the Holy Spirit will not be forgiven. What does it mean to blaspheme against the Holy Spirit? Who cares? Watch out.

I have no answers today. No new thoughts. I trust that things are not out of control, happening without any rhyme or reason, but I'm not sure why all things happen when they happen. Someday I might know, but surely not today. I thought there was no sin that was unforgiveable. Was I wrong? How does slandering the Holy Spirit cross the line? I know that God, according to the Bible, has often acted swiftly when people hamper the spread of his kingdom, but I haven't often heard such definitive wording. My world has entered the tumble cycle. A child?

It's all way bigger than me.
Why shouldn't it be?
I wouldn't have it any other way.
If I'm the biggest, we're in trouble.
Why a child? My kids are treasure.
This life sucks. My friend. His son.
I can't even imagine. This sucks.

Luke 12:11-12

Don't worry how you will defend yourselves, the Holy Spirit will teach you at the time what you shall say. Is it a given that the disciples will be defending themselves? What is it like when the Holy Spirit teaches you? Do you sound more profound than you ever should?

I distrust anyone who claims to have it all figured out.

I pray for my friend. I plead for my friend. For sleep and peace and answers. How could this happen? It didn't even happen to me and I am having a crisis of faith over the whole thing. What must he feel like?

He is saying now is not a good time to visit, and although I'm hurt a little now that he says it, I'm also a little relieved. Who knows how I would react once I was there. He needs to be with his family. I said I would pray, and it has been one of the few times that I have followed through. I even asked the Holy Spirit to pray prayers that I wouldn't think of, fill needs that I wouldn't even know or understand.

Have you ever really tried to think about who God is really? Why is it that I always come up with an idea of how he must be and then try to fit him into that idea? Why can't I just let God be beyond my understanding?

There's only so much I can understand, right? If I keep my eyes open, maybe I will see more, know more, be changed for the better. Who cares?

Tears.

My friend. His son.

This life. What worth is it anyway? It goes on.

Luke 12:13-15

Finally a verse I understand. I know greed. I see greed fully grown all around me like a forest. The Redwoods.

A person in the crowd says to Jesus: Teacher, tell my brother to divide the inheritance with me. Jesus replies, who appointed me arbiter between you? He says to be on guard against all brands of greed. Life is not made up of the abundance of one's possessions. That I can absolutely agree with. I may even say the less possessions, the more peace. That has been my experience, yet still possessions I want. Books and buildings, I feel I need. Two-hundred channels a must.

Luke 12:16-21

Jesus told a parable. The ground of a rich man produced a good crop, but the man didn't have enough storage space. He tore down his barns and built bigger ones to store his goods. Then he figured he would have many years of storage. It was time to take it easy, to eat, drink, and be merry. But God says, you fool. This night your life will be demanded. How prepared will you be?

This could be anyone who stores up for himself, but is not rich toward God.

Your standing with God is what matters. Anything can happen at any time, I know this right now. I know that we can plan for the future, but we have no idea what the future will bring. I know some people have their head in heaven and care nothing for this world. Each day they ask for Jesus to come again. I can't say that's me. I think of the future. I plan for things to come. Being responsible is important to me. I think of retirement. I put money in a retirement program. I plan for a new literary magazine. I expect to see my kids grow up. I look at the day before me and many others besides. My focus is ahead. I think of my friend. He must have imagined his son growing old as well. How will it all turn out? I have no idea, but I think God is a pretty good bet. I'm not a model Christian, but I can't think of a better stock to invest in. In hard times it's the account I count on. That much I know to be true.

Luke 12:22-26

I do worry, there is no doubt about that. Listen to what Jesus says to his disciples:

Don't worry about your life, what you will eat or wear. Life is more than food, the body more than clothes. He says consider the ravens, who don't sow or reap or store, yet God feeds them. You're a great deal more valuable to God than birds! Anyway, who can add a single hour to his or her life by worrying? Since you can't do this tiny thing, why worry about the rest?

I believe this wholeheartedly, but still I worry. How can I get this great perspective, faith?

Luke 12:27-31

It's been a few days and it's been a few days. I went to church on Sunday and thought hard during the sermon. I thought that a belief in God is an earth-shattering belief. Nothing is the same. It changes your whole view on every decision and every look at the stars. Are you the center of the universe or are you an insignificant speck? The stars are out and they are beautiful beyond just about any other thing. Nothing can be said, or written down, that will outlast or outshine those stars. Try to describe them. Try to outdo their patterns displayed across the dark sky. Outthink those stars. Ignore them. Try. Try. Try.

Lilies grow without labor, yet are clothed better than Solomon, Jesus says. God clothes the grass of the field, which is here now and gone to the fire in but moments; how much more does he cloth you, who have such little faith? Your heart should not be set on what you will eat or drink or any other worry. A pagan world runs on such a focus, but your father knows what you need. Seek God's kingdom and all these things will be given to you as well.

This is simple; this, I can explain. Stay close to God and he will provide for all of your needs. It's an easy concept. Have faith that God provides and he is all you will ever need. What does a life look like that is focused on God? Is this person annoying, his or her head stuck in heaven, feet on earth? Or might this person be so consumed by an eternal perspective that they live a worry-free life? Might they be full of joy able to believe in infinite resources? Focus on God and need not. Give and you will never need. Although this is a perspective, a lifestyle, I might desire, how do I practically wash my day-to-day business with it? Wouldn't it be something like selling myself empty in order to be filled up with something I can't even see? What could I expect then?

Luke 12:32-34

I sincerely thought that a new mission—my literary magazine, the dream of it anyway—and the loss of a few pounds from running all over town, would make a difference. As I relieve stress, new stresses attack me. Why is nothing simple? Why does a friend lose his son so easily? Why does the wind blow my day away like some lazy bomb? Why do I still worry sleep away? No decisions, only this: Life is difficult. I distrust anything in absolutes. Without absolutes I wander through a maze never finding a comfortable chair or a barn that holds all I've done before.

Today really is like any other day. It's not romantic or heroic. I flinch at even using the words. It's so easy to write about. I go for a run and ache and come back the same, if not tired. A sprint. A marathon. End. Begin. End. Begin.

Don't be afraid little flock, God is pleased to give you the kingdom, Jesus says. Sell your stuff and give to the poor. Pursue treasure that will not be wore out or stolen. This treasure can never be exhausted. Believe in forever. Spend with an infinite mind. For where your treasure is, right there is where your heart will be also.

What you do, how you live, what you store up is who you are, what you will be. Everything passes away like so much wind, but there is treasure, a kingdom, that will not pass away. Live with eternity in mind.

There's nothing new today, but should there be? Can we put our trust in something that is always changing? Is it okay to put your trust in something that is old? Can you discover, uncover an old thing and it will be new every morning without changing at all? Is a secret discovered, even if it is ancient, beyond time?

Luke 12:35-40

Be ready, Jesus says. Dress appropriately. Have your lamp burning like one waiting. Sit and hope for your master to return from a wedding so when he knocks, you can immediately open the door. He will come and serve while you recline. He may come in the middle of the night, be ready. If the owner of the house knew when the thief was coming, he would be on guard. So should you be ready because the son of man will come at any hour, when you least expect. God as a burglar?

She has an exact date in her mind, a
calendar loose in the back pocket
of those old jeans you bought.

You've loved her and the bright sea
since the flood. At night, you stargaze and
small lights are burned into your eyes.

You love those jeans, time promises. There's
more and more and more. She asks you for
a coat or a family blanket crocheted by lamplight.

Another log burns salty. It's your idea. You stay
up through lightening and cold rain. You wait. You
wake up a mystery that's been sleeping everywhere.

You wait, up at the fitful dawn. She knocks only
in those words you wrote, only you didn't write them,
afraid the night would usher in day, sorrow, end.

You wait. You hope.

No poem ever gets it quite right, you know this. You write them anyway. Hasty, practiced, or prolonged, they still come out the same. You resolve to quit writing about yourself in the second person. Sometimes you do anyway.

Luke 12:41-48

Peter asked are you telling us this parable only, or is it for everyone?

Jesus replied, it is good for the wise and faithful manager, who the master returns to find taking good care of his possessions and the other servants. The master will put him in charge of everything, because he is trustworthy. Wise, faithful, and trustworthy. However, if a servant goes wild with his master away, maybe beating the other servants in his drunken fits, the master on the very day he comes home will cut the servant to pieces and throw him in with the unbelievers. Any servant who knows the master's will and doesn't do it will be beaten with many blows, but one who doesn't know better will be beaten with only a few blows. Those who are given much, much will be expected; those trusted, much will be asked.

Cut to pieces? Beaten? Much is expected if you know better? What else can I say? Jesus promises that punishment and reward is ahead. In answer to Peter: The message is for everyone, but much more is expected of you. Hear it, and respond. It's difficult to hear and impossible to ignore. You may be beaten or cut to pieces. Justice?

Luke 12:49-53

This is one of those difficult passages to read. I wish it were easier, but it just isn't. There isn't much for me to say today besides what the passage says.

Jesus exclaims: I have come to bring fire on the earth, and how I wished it was already lit! I have a baptism to undergo and I am distressed until the day it is completed! Do you think I came to bring peace? No, I came to divide. From here on there will be even division among families, including father against son and mother against daughter, even father-in-law versus son-in-law and so forth. In a family of five, two may be against the other three.

I did think Jesus came for peace and unity. He says in this instance he came to divide. It's a hard thing to take. I don't wish for division, so something must be wrong with my understanding. I don't, apparently, grasp the whole of Jesus's mission. I haven't fully digested the message or kingdom of God as shown in Luke. Am I the only one? What is the source of my resistance, understanding? Am I too nice for truth? Is truth not nice?

Luke 12:54-56

I rushed through yesterday's passage because it was such a difficult message. I wrote as quickly as I could because I couldn't make sense of it. It isn't, however, for me to make sense of as much as it is for me to digest and decide if I will apply it to my life. Should I just agree or should I wrestle? We have my niece and two nephews staying with us this week. I'm not sure how much time I will be spending on writing. I have a few free moments while they play video games or watch movies with our kids. Sometimes I struggle with spending time writing when I could be with my family. It's a constant struggle, two forces pulling at me. Sometimes writing focuses me, other times it is just an escape. Writing can pull me away from reality, which is good and bad depending on the season and the purpose. Does this make any sense at all?

Jesus says you can read the clouds and the wind to know when it will rain or be hot. You are hypocrites if you know how to interpret the earth and sky, but not the present time.

Watch and see what is coming. What better to befriend than the sun and the wind and the acts of men?

Luke 12:57-59

I've stepped into a funk. This whole thing is dragging out longer than I expected. I envisioned a ferocious couple of days or weeks, not months. This has turned into a marathon rather than a sprint. Have I said that before? Am I repeating myself? I've also lost track of the excitement. I write every day because I've committed to it; I've scheduled it. It's all a puzzle. I take it too seriously. I'm not serious enough. I'm almost there, a million miles.

Jesus asks why they don't judge for themselves what is right. Reconcile before you are drug off to a judge and thrown in prison. You won't get out, he says, until every last penny is paid.

Reconcile now before it goes any further.

thirteen

Luke 13:1-5

A question has been in my head: Does it get any better than this? Will circumstances change my attitude at all? We've been traveling to see family. I've seen my parents and my in-laws and my niece and nephews. I didn't think about much while traveling. I just was. I just talked and swam in pools and went out to dinners. I just listened and I talked. I made promises about visiting more often. I listened to the radio as I made the long trip home. I didn't plan anything. I didn't worry about money. These matters were a flood at my doorstep. Happiness is an idea.

I'm not sure of the setting as some told Jesus about the Galileans, whose blood Pilate had mixed with their sacrifices. Jesus asks them if they are of the opinion that these specific Galileans were worse sinners because they suffered in this manner. This is an unfamiliar passage to me. Jesus answers himself. He emphatically says no. He also asks if the 18 who died in the destruction of the tower in Siloam were more guilty than all in Jerusalem. Again, he says no. He says repent or you will all perish.

In a time of war and other wars and earthquakes and revolutions and acts of violence and violent talk and violence, and violent theatre, and violence, these words hit you where you live. No person is more guilty before God than the next. Repentance is the only cure. We're all

185

dying. We're all offered life. Do we believe this? Is it a comfort?
    A friend.
    A son.

Four boys enter with trouble in their coats. You might
think guns. You might think parties, slurs. You might think
nothing at all. You might carry your own troubles and
wish you were ultimately young and stone yellow. The
water falls; the road runs. The motel you rent is traveling
south in your mind. Four boys enter. Four boys look around
for trouble and a mighty kiss that thieves leave behind. Questions
grow old like classmates. A reunion is planned. You
plan to attend and fall silent before the night goes dim. The
birds are stuck in the wall. They scratch and scratch. You show
up, no coat. No coat at all. It's summer. The sun is out looking
for a foreclosure. No coat. No coat at all. Four boys enter with
trouble around their necks. You've been four. You've been
nothing at all. Questions grow old and young, wither night.

Luke 13:6-9

Afterward, Jesus tells a story to solidify his point. A landowner has a certain fig tree in his vineyard that hasn't bore fruit for three years. He's disappointed with the progress and takes up the matter with the head of the vineyard. Why should this tree take up soil? he asks. Cut it down, he says. I don't even want to look at it anymore. Isn't this soil too precious to waste on a barren tree?

    The master of the vineyard replies: Let's leave it for one more year. I'll dig around it and fertilize it. We'll give it one more chance to bear fruit; if it doesn't, then we'll cut it down.

    The fig tree receives more years to produce than it deserves. It's easy to see the correlation. You haven't accomplished much yet, but I will give you all you need to succeed, but the time is coming soon when the matter will come to a close. Bear fruit or be cut down. Here are the resources and more chances than you deserve. Is it a challenge or a sign of a loving master of the vineyard? Both?

What have I accomplished in 30 years? I find hope, but I also feel worthless. Another chance! What can I do differently?

Luke 13:10-17

A car pulls up beside me. I recognize the car and the girl who is waving me over. I get out. The sky is blue. The wind is light and warm. She rolls down the window with her left hand. She smiles. I put my hand where the window has just escaped. It's a moment that feels all wrong. Her car is red and revs angry or it's just my imagination.

"How long've you been back in town?" she asks.

"Hours," I say.

"Easter?" she asks.

"Easter," I say.

There's a pause. We've been here before.

She touches my right hand, which is still shy on her door. She switches the engine off.

I look at her. Too long.

"Walk?" She asks.

So we walk down Main Street and more doors seem to be closed than open. My heart says no to me, but I don't listen.

Are you really going through with all this?

She tells me about Seattle. She tells me about computers. She's practical. She's planning something. I walk and listen. There are cars driving by. There are choices in the Idaho sky.

"Pizza," I ask, and a romance begins. Three children later, I miss those moments of indecision and unknown. I'll marry this girl, but at that moment everything was details and chance and everything.

Her dress was yellow.

Cheesecake.

I take my wife for granted.

I forget these moments. I remember. I write.

It was the Sabbath day when Jesus was teaching in one of the synagogues. A woman who had been crippled for 18 years, bent by a spirit, was before him. When Jesus saw her, he called her forward and freed her from her infirmity by putting his hands on her. Immediately she straightened up and praised God. She would never forget that moment.

The synagogue ruler was indignant. He said to the people, "Six days are for work, come and be healed on those days, not the Sabbath."

Jesus called them hypocrites. "Don't you untie your ox or donkey from the stall and lead it out to give it water? Then shouldn't this woman, a daughter of Abraham who Satan has kept bound for 18 long years, also be unbound—freed—on the Sabbath day?"

His opponents were humiliated. The people rejoiced at the wonderful things Jesus was doing.

Why can't we see beyond ourselves when something good has been done for another? Do we hold so tightly to our traditions when the master of tradition is before us? Do we rejoice or become indignant about the rules? Are we healed or do we miss the moment? I don't always understand the traditions or motivations, but I can see how we get so wrapped up in our own day that we get so far in front of ourselves. The Sabbath is extremely important, there is no doubt, but not more important than the people it's for. It's a difficult lesson. It can't be ascertained only by rules. A set of rules can be a comfort, but also a confinement for love and charity. Each circumstance has its own solution. Each person has their own need. People are important. Hasn't it been said that the Sabbath is for the people not the other way around?

It's confusing, all of this, I don't want it to seem otherwise. The Sabbath is not an ideal I've taken as seriously as I could, I admit. Caring for people is not my every thought. I'm selfish. I'm self-absorbed. I'm no different. The answer is rest. The answer is healing. The answer is in the original text not in my ramshackle retelling. I get in the way. Jesus heals. I rejoice. I ask for healing. I keep my head up for once. *I look out and remember the Idaho sky and even the people around me. I walk around my office and think it over. I get another coffee, while holding my new baby in my arms. She looks up at me. I can't think of anything to tell her. I hold her close and wonder what to make of it all. I don't feel equipped. I quit for the day.*

Luke 13:18-21

I'm back to writing in italics. The door to my office opens. It's a friend from church. He's worried about me because I haven't been showing up. I wonder if my face betrays my annoyance. I shake hands. I sit back down. He looks over at my computer and asks what I am working on, what's been keeping me busy, and if there's another cup of coffee available anywhere in the universe.

I laugh.

Kip has been a good friend for a while now. We're both confessors so it works out fine. Kip may or may not be his real name as if that matters. He's exhausted he tells me. He takes his hat off and runs his hands through his hair. I look around my office/nursery as if for the first time. Chips are scattered. Evidence of gluttony I'm afraid. It's funny, I'm in a cheerful mood. I'm now glad he's come by so I have something to write about. He says quit typing.

"Yes, you can read some," I say, although I don't really want him to. I've told practically no one about all this. I print some random pages. I try not to watch him read, but I watch.

He laughs.

"You're writing little sermons?"

"Well, not exactly." Absolutely not. That is exactly what I am hoping not to write. This isn't about preaching is it?

"I'm just reacting to the text, to Jesus's words really."

"Oh. I see. I guess." I don't think he does.

"I'm writing and fictionalizing it a bit. I've even put a fictionalized self in there with a fictionalized family. It's fiction. It's true too. I just don't think I take the Bible as seriously as I could. It's been good to look at Luke through the eyes of a character I created. Many of the emotions

are real. The doubts are sometimes true. The faith is hardly ever true. I don't know. It's a lot of work and I don't know what I'll do with it when I'm finished, but it's been good for me if nothing else."

"It sounds pretty cool. I'm not a writer or much of a reader really myself."

He takes a drink of the coffee I got him. Kip builds houses. He hasn't had much work lately. He's worried about his finances. It's not a unique story these days. Our town is losing businesses by the block. The recession is on the boom.

"The times," I say.

"Obama," he says.

Geez. I couldn't disagree more. It's not one thing. It's not one guy. We can't even blame it all on big-box retailers or those others.

So we sit there.

Quiet.

"Sorry. I know you disagree. I forget sometimes. I'm not used to having liberal friends."

"I'm not a liberal," I say, but, I guess, around here, maybe I am.

"Yeah," he says.

We talk for more than an hour. My annoyance has gone out the French doors and into the yard. Kip is a great guy. He's genuine, what better can be said? He says he better get going. His coffee is gone and his cell is ringing. I walk out into the front yard. He's in his truck now.

"Thanks for the coffee. I'll see you Sunday maybe?"

"You bet," I say.

He starts to pull away, then stops. "I'll be praying for you and your work," he says.

"Thanks," I say.

Jesus asks, and it sounds a bit like a Shakespeare sonnet,

What is the kingdom of God like? What
shall I compare it to? It's like a mustard
seed that a man plants in his garden. It grows

into a formidable tree on which the birds of the
air perch.

To what shall I compare the kingdom of God? It's
like yeast that a woman mixes into a large mound
of flour until it is worked throughout the dough.

The kingdom of God is a growing and living entity like the constitution
or sourdough. The more it is added to, the more it grows and mixes. The
kingdom of God is a mustard seed, yeast. The kingdom of God is a
catalyst. The kingdom of God is inside, is everywhere.

Luke 13:22-30

Jesus taught as he moved through villages on his way to Jerusalem. A
person asked him if only a few people would be saved. Jesus said, do all
that you can to enter through the narrow door, because many will try to
enter, but will not be able to. Once the owner of the house gets up and
closes the door, he continued, you will knock and plead, but the owner
will not know you or where you have come from. You might say, but we
ate and drank with you and you taught in our streets. He will reply again
that he doesn't know you or where you came from. He will conclude, *go
away, all you evil doers*!

At this time there will be weeping and gnashing of teeth. You will
see Abraham, Isaac, and Jacob, and all the prophets in the kingdom of
God, but you will be thrown out. Furthermore, people will come from
the east and west and north and south, and will take their places at the
feast in the kingdom of God. Indeed there are those who are last who
will be first, and first who will be last.

Come through the narrow door while it remains open. Don't be
late. People you expect, and those you don't expect, will be saved, make
sure you are among them. People from everywhere will enjoy the
kingdom of God, but some who aren't among them might surprise you.
It doesn't matter if you are first or last, only that you enter in time by

the narrow door that at some point will apparently be shut and not opened for you again. It's a difficult teaching, no doubt. No one is in automatically. No cultural or regional or political distinction is enough, only that you enter by the narrow door at the appointed time.

Luke 13:31-35

Jesus receives a threat or a warning... I'm not sure which. It's difficult to unravel what is meant by every comment in this interchange, but what is maybe clear is that Jesus won't be put off point and Jerusalem is a killing field, one claims.

Several Pharisees seek out Jesus for a word. Go now, they say, Herod is after your head. Jesus says, tell that fox I'll be driving out demons and healing people today, tomorrow, and a third day to reach my goal. No prophet can die outside of Jerusalem!

Jerusalem, Jerusalem, Jesus continues, you who kill the prophets and stone those sent to you, I've wanted for so long to gather your children together as a hen gathers her chicks under her wings in a fire, but you are not willing! Your house is desolate. You will not see me again, until you're saying, blessed is he who comes in the name of the Lord. He ends with a Psalm. He never wavers from his purpose even when the threat comes from the highest on earth. Here I am, he says, out in the open. Who can say the same? Who can be so sure of what they are doing, what they are about?

A hen will burn up protecting her chicks in a fire.

fourteen

Luke 14:1-6

It was the Sabbath, and it feels a bit like a review of an earlier scene. Jesus is eating at the house of a prominent Pharisee. Jesus must have known that he was being watched carefully, but he accepted the invitation anyhow. My guess is that he cared enough to eat with the Pharisee, and those looking on, even though he knows he will be heavily scrutinized. We might run, hide. Among them was a man suffering from dropsy. To refresh my memory on dropsy, I look it up on an Internet dictionary. I know it's caused by bacteria, but also learn it is infectious and causes swelling and spongy skin along with scales. Scales. It's scary and not to be fooled with apparently. It's infectious. I take a moment to consider the scene and how I might react. My initial reaction is embarrassing. I'm ashamed of my own secret thoughts. It's a wonder this man is even at the dinner, much less close enough to be considered by the group. With the man in mind, Jesus asks the Pharisee, and other local experts in the law, if the law would allow healing on the Sabbath. Silence. Jesus takes hold of the man, heals him and sends him away. It seems no small thing that Jesus takes the man in a healing embrace. No doubt it had probably been a great while since the man had been touched, shown tenderness and care. To be there, the man must have known that such a moment was possible, why else would he have risked being present? Nothing less than amazing if you really think about it.

Jesus then asks again, breaking the silence, If you had a son or even an ox that had fallen into a well on the Sabbath, would you not immediately pull him out? Silence. What could you say? The heart knows what the heart feels. In silence at least people can only guess you a fool. I know my heart is nothing but foolish.

Luke 14:7-11

I'm watching a Dodgers-Giants game. I'm supposed to be writing, so I'm writing, but I'm also watching the game. Pick-off play. Curveball. Hit and run turns into a FC 6-3. Man on second, one down. Baseball is such a great game. Not for everyone like chess. I can't get enough. I just came home from the high-school game, now here I am typing in front of the TV. I guess that kind of devotion is strange. I never claimed to be otherwise. Well, enough of this.

I love writing but it has been work lately. Ever feel like that? Has a passionate love ever become hard work, a struggle? Has it ever not? I feel so unoriginal. Taxes, mortgages, potty training, and a whole stew of others, always battle optimism, contentment. It's not poetic. I sit here at my computer doing what I love, watching what I love, married to who I love beyond imagination, with kids who are sleeping, and yet my mood is blah. I'm spinning my wheels, running in place.

My friends speak of the sin of pride. I can't always relate. I see the opposite in myself. My pride is born of insecurity. After all, aren't they the same? Both pride and insecurity put self in the center. Anyway.

Jesus, meanwhile, notices that the guests picked the places of honor at the table, so he said this: When invited to a wedding feast, don't choose the place of honor for yourself because someone more distinguished than you may show up afterward. The host, who invited both, may ask you to give up your seat. Humiliated, you'll end up in the least important seat. So, when you're invited, take the lowest place and allow the host to move you to a better spot. Then you will be honored rather than demoted. For everyone who exalts himself will be humbled and he who humbles himself will be exalted.

This isn't always the way of the world; self-promotion often works for other people. If you tell everyone you are great, people often believe. You can bluff people, but God knows. In his kingdom, justice reigns, humility—not false humility—is honored. Not so on the ball field, but the kingdom of heaven isn't a baseball game no matter how often I believe it to be.

My mom calls to ask the score of the Dodger game.
I can answer.

Luke 14:12-24

Jesus turns his attention to the host. He says, when you have a dinner party, don't invite your friends or relatives or the rich neighbors. If you do, they'll pay you back with a return invite. Instead, invite the poor, crippled, and blind, and you will be blessed. Although they can't repay you, you will be repaid at the resurrection of the righteous. Where else is this being taught?

One at the table said, blessed is he who will eat at the feast in the kingdom of God.

Jesus replies with yet another story. There was a man who was preparing a great banquet. He had invited many guests but at the appointed time, when all was ready, everyone came up with excuses. One had bought a field and said he would be going to see it; one had bought five yoke of oxen and wanted to try them out; and one had just been married and said he couldn't come. The owner of the house become angry and sent out his servant into the streets and alleys of the town to bring the poor, crippled, blind, and lame, but still there was more room. He sent out the servant again into the roads and country lanes to bring people in so the house would be full. He concluded, not one of those men who were originally invited will taste of my banquet.

An invitation isn't as important as showing up. The first last; the last first. While excuses are sometimes valid, family shows up.

Luke 14:25-27

In college, a close friend of mine, an outspoken Christian, even a fanatic to some, became utterly disillusioned after reading these verses and was never the same.

Jesus says to the large crowds following him: If anyone comes to me and does not hate his father and mother, wife and children, brothers and sisters, and even his own life, he can't be my disciple. To be my disciple, you must carry your cross and follow me.

Would anyone foresee Jesus carrying his own cross?

Justifications immediately come to mind. These seem like easy ways out of a difficult calling. It was only for that time. This wasn't meant for me. Those he was speaking to weren't really following him, so he was scaring them off or shocking them back. Following Jesus now is different. He only means hate in comparison to how you love him. I find no comfort in these excuses. Jesus said what he said, how will I respond? In other places, he is adamant about loving your parents and children, brothers and sisters. He says love your wife as he loves the church. Is this a contradiction? Jesus isn't supposed to contradict himself. Who can stand among such a calling? I can see hating myself compared to others and my God, but not my family. I love my family. I love my wife, children, parents, brothers and sisters. What does this hate mean? What does it look like? I have no answers...

I wish I could come up with such an original concept that I would even impress myself. I wish I could explain this passage in a way that would justify myself and even Jesus (I had to keep it as I wrote it no matter how much I wanted to change that statement). I want to be comfortable. I want it all to make sense to me. Why would Jesus say such a thing? Is it hyperbole? Is it literal? Is God's hate better than our love? I don't think I can answer any of these questions until I've been through the whole book. I will say that I think the truth is somewhere in the idea of what or who will you forsake first if it comes to choosing... but why do we have to choose? Why doesn't the calling to follow Jesus include loving your family with everything you have? How can you love your neighbor as yourself if you hate yourself? I feel ill-equipped, severely so. Who am I to say? Do others look at this set of verses and immediately know their meaning? Is it because I am a doubter that I can't wrap my mind around this hard saying? Who can I ask? Who can I trust? How can this be in the Bible and not be more fully explained? Where is the conclusion? Where is Luke's explanation?

If you're reading this, whoever you are, please figure it out for yourself. Don't take my opinion too seriously. If you figure it out, let me know.

I'm tired of hearing my own voice in this gumball dispenser.

Is hate a divinely inspired word? Must be a translation problem. Sarcasm won't help.

All I can say is eternal life must be so much more than what we see here on earth that we can't even see Jesus's perspective because we are blocking our own view.

God, my prayer is for understanding... I feel like a hypocrite asking for this so late in the process. I hate the word hate.

Luke 14:28-33

The previous passage has been on the tip of my tongue. I've spoken with my wife and friends and sister. We've all taken a shot at attacking the words and defending the words. My wife said read on. She said it's not the last word. She said there's more context to come. I've taken her advice because that's what I do. She's smarter than me. She's more faithful than me. I'm not kidding. She's beautiful.

Jesus goes on to say if someone is building a tower, won't he first sit down and estimate the cost so he knows he has enough resources to finish the tower? If not, he'll lay the foundation and might not be able to finish. Everyone who sees it will ridicule him because he began what he was unable to finish.

Furthermore, what if a king is going to war against another kingdom, won't he first sit down and consider whether he is able with his 10,000 men to oppose the kingdom, which has 20,000 on the offense? If he can't win, he'll certainly send a delegation while he is still a long way off and ask for peace. In the same manner, if you don't give up everything you have, you can't be my disciple. I don't get the connection between tower building, waging war, and divesting. I guess they are the expense line items in the company budget that is our life.

So Jesus asks for everything up front. He says there are no secrets. Here's what I demand, make sure you are up for it. Sit down now and consider what is required to follow me. No secrets. A religion without secrets? This doesn't seem like it would be a successful recruiting campaign. Usually only the good foot comes forward, and that foot is quick and utterly convincing. Usually the bad news is saved for last, in the fine print, after you've signed the contract. (Where's my lawyer and team of accountants?) However, there's nothing hidden—there's no fine print. It's all on the table. What are the terms? Everything. With an eternal perspective, it seems different. Everything for so much more than everything. Can you do it? Can I do it? I guess that's the question. At least the right questions have been asked. All of them.

Let's not forget the word hate. Let's not forget giving up everything.

When I was finishing up high-school baseball, there weren't a lot of recruiters, but there were a few. A couple said they could make all my dreams come true. Some said days on the bench would pay off. No one said divest all your dreams, hate baseball and your family, and trust me beyond everything. No one said count the costs for there are many. I didn't count the cost. I made an emotional decision. It turned out somewhat well because of my writing degree, not because of my glove, definitely not because of my bat. I miss baseball and easy decisions.

I consider the costs. I read on. I hate the word hate.

The truth is I relate more to the building a tower than to going to war, yet it feels more like a war than a tower. I'd rather be ridiculed than be the cause of an unwinnable war (or any war, for that matter). I would plan, however, in either case. I wouldn't go into it blind. So often it's difficult to see what the future might bring. We'd like someone to tell us what we can expect. With the pipe dream of starting my own literary magazine, I'd like someone to tell me exactly what I might expect. I'd love it very much. The unknown is difficult, but knowing, I suppose, doesn't always make it easier. There's no adventure, but who needs adventure when the gamble is your whole life, and not just your whole life, but how tightly you will hold the treasures in your life, and love in your life, compared to your God? Might it be too much to ask? I can't believe so many have made the plunge. Would my family understand? Could I make the commitment and follow through? Might I be ridiculed, or attacked, no matter what I do? It's unimaginable to even think of anyone reading such things.

I still want to believe I'm missing something. I still want to believe that in all of Jesus's honesty about what it will take to be his disciple the word hate is either a mistake, a translation problem, or simply my uninspired ears. The immediate listeners are silent. Jesus—a peaceful, inspired leader, even the son of God to many—has truly captured my attention and even more than that, he's made me reconsider it all. Being one who believes I've done so before, it's humbling, and even humiliating, to think it all feels new again. I wish I could claim an epiphany, but I can't. For now, I'll leave it at that, and as my wife has suggested, I'll keep reading and keep running.

Words run the world over like an unorganized army. They don't get stuck, they march on.

Luke 14:34-35

It's far from over. Words have failed me and surely will again, but I keep at it.

Amidst it all, thousands of miles and years away, Jesus says, salt is good, but if it loses that saltiness—it's only purpose—how will it regain its saltiness? If the salt, then, is neither fit for soil or compost, you chuck it. He who has ears to hear, let him hear.

I've seen a billboard where a church apologizes for losing its saltiness.

I salt nearly all my food. My doctor says slow down, but I'm not sure that has much to do with it.

Salt that isn't salty, I would compare to words that don't say anything. Enter the pen of an editor.

Jesus is a man of words and stories. He's a man of love and healing and sacrifice, isn't he?

I'm confused. First time you've heard that.

The salt is certainly salty.

A man is worth or not worth his salt, some have said.

What about the food? Why is no one considering the food? I can make anything taste good with a little Johnny's Seasoning Salt.

fifteen

I'm in a funk, but I'm glad to at least be back on the subject of love rather than hate, gathering rather than scattering. I feel a funny excitement, a strange optimism.

Jesus is surrounded by tax collectors and those known as sinners. Pharisees and law experts alike are muttering to each other that Jesus welcomes sinners, and even eats with them! So Jesus tells another story. Consider a man who has 100 sheep and loses one of them, he says. Doesn't he leave the 99 for the one lost? When he finds the one, he'll joyfully put it on his shoulders and go home. Then he calls his friends and neighbors to rejoice with him. He cheers, I've found my lost sheep! In this same manner, there will be more rejoicing in heaven over one sinner who repents than over 99 righteous, who do not need repentance. Or it might be better said those who claim they don't need repentance.

The message is one of hope. Heaven rejoices over the one. Also a message for those who resist repentance—could be the Pharisees and experts or you and me—Jesus would rather eat with so-called sinners and tax collectors because they embrace repentance, than those who see no need for Jesus, even see him as a nuisance, or worse, an opposition. Some will always sit aside and criticize. Some will be inspired and run with it. Jesus seeks out those who know they need him. He invites all to his dinner feast, searches them out, and rejoices when they come to eat no matter what has been their former title. Hope rather than hate. There's a banquet and we're invited.

Luke 15:8-10

Again a story of hope. Consider a woman, Jesus says, who has ten silver coins, but loses one. Won't she turn on the light, sweep the entire house, and search carefully until it is found? When she finds it, she'll call her friends and neighbors to rejoice with her. I've found my lost coin, she'll exclaim. Likewise, there is rejoicing among the angels of God over one sinner who repents.

The angels rejoice. Hope. Plus, now her house is clean.

Luke 15:11-24

It gets even better. We're on the upward swing again, a crescendo, like a great concert. This has always been one of my favorite stories. Hope.

Jesus says a man had two sons. The younger asks for his father to give him his share of the estate *now*. So the man divides his property. Just like that. Imagine asking for your inheritance while your father is still alive. It could be construed as: I wish you were dead so I could have my money. Living inheritance, you are. I like that boat a lot by the way, just sayin'. When I see you, I see a big fat wallet. So. It starts with a slap.

The younger son pooled his resources and left the country. I'm outta here. I'm not leaving town. I'm leaving the country. He squandered his wealth in wild living. After it was all gone, famine hit. The younger son was forced to get some work feeding pigs. He quickly longed to eat what the pigs ate, but no one gave him anything. He was no one. Have you ever heard a testimony like this: 20 minutes about "wild living," people laugh, are on the edge of their seat, and then, I got desperate, was saved, and became boring.

He came to his senses. His father's hired hands have food to spare, he thought, while I'm starving to death. So he went back, admitting his sin against his dad and even heaven. I'm no longer worthy to be your son, but make me like one of your hired men. No one can say what he was thinking on the trip back, but he was desperate. He wouldn't have gone back unless he absolutely had to. He expected severe punishment. He expected an angry father. He expected to be in the dirt. He could be walking to his own humiliation, death, but it was better than starvation. He deserved it. He would rather face it than die. Maybe he even learned he needed his family, but a little too late now. He must have been that byword to his town. A rumor. A lesson told. No one wants to return home empty, dreams lost, and have to face family, sweethearts, and high-school buddies.

With this in his head, he may have even reconsidered. "But while he was still a long way off," his father was filled with compassion. He ran to his son and threw his arms around him. There was no room for retreat. He kissed him. I read once that patriarchs at this time did not often run. The boy was hugged and kissed. He was run to.

The son began his prepared speech. He'd sinned. He was no longer worthy. His father interrupted him, yelling to his servants to quickly bring his best robe and put it on the son, along with a ring and sandals. Bring also a fattened calf for our celebration, for my son was dead but is now alive again; he was lost and is now found. So they celebrated. The father valued his son beyond anything else, even how much the son valued him. Love. It was worth it. I've redeemed my son from the pawnshop. Hope.

Luke 15:25-32

But there was another son. The eldest was out in the field at the time. When he came near the house, he heard music and saw dancing. He asks, what's happening? A servant tells him that his brother has come home and his father has killed a fattened calf because he's back safe. The older brother becomes angry and refuses to go into the house. His father comes out and pleads with him. He tells his father, all these years I've been like a slave to you and never disobeyed, but you haven't celebrated with me. But now when this son of yours, who has squandered your money on prostitutes comes home, you celebrate with him?

The father answers, my son, you've always been with me and everything I have is yours. This, however, is a time for celebration: Your brother was dead and is now alive in our presence. He was lost, but now is found.

Isn't this our attitude? We don't rejoice, we ask where our portion is. We feel neglected, taken for granted. Life is unfair, we say. We walk away. It's the Christmas Eve service and people are excited to see your brother has come to church. You grumble as you usher. You make jokes about the ceiling falling in.

sixteen

Luke 16:1-12

I spent some time in prayer today. I prayed for wisdom and understanding. It was pretty simple. I couldn't wait to write about how I felt. I was thinking, planning what I would write. I didn't hear anything in return, but I did feel peaceful. I did feel right with the world. I don't feel it so much anymore. Concerns have snuck back in, making themselves at home. They are eating my nachos. I feel uncomfortable reporting about my prayers and inner thoughts.

I also went to church this morning. I usually feel the inspiration to write after going to church. It typically brings up topics to think over and write over, but honestly, today, I feel inept. The pastor had so much more insight and obvious Biblical knowledge that I'm not sure I should be the one writing all of this. What's it worth anyway? I'm no authority. I'm just reading or rereading. Sometimes it feels like old hat, and sometimes I'm surprised. Sometimes I rant an agenda and sometimes I'm fully humbled. I'm a jumble. I'm different every day. I'm changing and turning and seasonal. Who really has the understanding and experience to teach? I'm no teacher. I have no story to tell. I don't have an agenda. I am who I am and the words are the words.

It's not my story. And that's not a disclaimer; that's a feeling I'm explaining. I'm attempting objectivity if there is such a thing in a first-person narrative about another narrative. Well then, let's get on with it now that I've gotten all that off my chest.

The Dodgers are down by nine by the way; that's not helping my attitude at all.

Jesus takes an aside with his disciples while I type away across time and space. He says there was a rich man whose manager was being accused of wasting his accounts. The rich man pulls in his manager to hear it from the source. Am I hearing the truth, he asks. Tell me about your management because you can't be my manager any more. The manager takes stock of his situation. I'm out of work. I'm not equipped to dig. I'm too proud to beg. He comes up with an idea of how to survive once his job is over. He needs to make friends who will welcome him into their home. So in his last days he calls up all his master's debtors and asks what they owe. One owed 800 gallons of olive oil, but the manager made it 400. Another owed 1,000 bushels of wheat, but the manager made it 800.

Afterward, surprisingly (to me) the master commends his dishonest manager for his shrewdness. Jesus says the people of the world are more shrewd in dealing with their own than are the people of light. Worldly wealth can be used to gain friends, so that when it is gone, you will be welcomed into eternal dwellings. Furthermore, those who can be trusted with very little can also be trusted with much. However, those who are dishonest with very little will also be dishonest with much. Being trustworthy with worldly wealth translates to true riches. The truth is if you're not trustworthy with someone else's property, who will give you their property?

Practical thinking. Practical teaching. It's not really how you handle money that's the issue as much as it is a testimony of your character; therefore, it's extremely important. You can be shrewd. You can be honest. There's a difference. There's a difference in perspective. Where does your honor belong? Is it in the world or in eternal dwellings, as Jesus puts it? Actually it's simpler than that. Forgiveness is more powerful than fortune. Even a dishonest manager can win with forgiveness.

Dodgers still down by 9.

Luke 16:13-15

Jesus has more to say about money, as you might imagine. He says no servant can follow two masters. The truth is he will either hate the one and love the other, or be devoted to the one and despise the other. Therefore, no one can serve both God and money. Couldn't say it better. With two contradictory masters, one must be forsaken. Choose God or money; there's no other way. The Pharisees heard all this and distained Jesus because they loved money, Luke reports. So Jesus said to them, you justify yourselves with the eyes of men, but God knows your heart. What is important to people is detestable to God. Who doesn't love money? I'm committed to only liking it.

Luke 16:16-18

Another trip to the local church lets me know that my insights are minor and pedestrian compared to a pastor (as they should be), yet here I am writing again. Here I am treading through the verses like anyone else. I'll see it through because I'm caught up, but not because I feel qualified. I write because I want to be a writer not because I feel like a writer every day.

Amidst my insecurities, Jesus is teaching that the Law and Prophets have been proclaimed until John came to preach the good news of the kingdom of God. Everyone is forcing their way into it, Jesus says, but it's easier for heaven and earth to disappear than for the least stroke of a pen to drop out of the Law.

Jesus seems to say the Law is forever as is the kingdom of God. No contradictions. Nothing's changed. The Law hasn't lost its power. A new messenger hasn't changed the message, only the delivery system.

Then in an abrupt transition, Jesus says anyone who divorces and marries another woman commits adultery as does the man who marries the divorced woman.

I guess he really is battling contradictions. No one is blameless, not the followers of John (or Jesus) or those of the Law and Prophets, or likewise the man or the woman. I imagine the men weren't being held to as high a level of accountability as the woman were. And accountability is probably the wrong word when the punishment was so severe. How can one be blameless and the other labeled a sinner? Is this the message? Don't throw out the Law because John is clarifying the good news. Is this also the message?

Life is full of contradictions. Those rich, and full of political power, seem to have a get-out-of-jail-free card in the Monopoly-type world we live, while the poor, and less powerful, are held accountable for everything. Isn't this the way of the world? Don't we chase wholeheartedly after the newfangled only to forsake the truths we've held so strongly to in the past? We use new and old teachings to justify ourselves rather than to unify.

I can only guess at the totality of these words—notice I don't argue the moral implications of the teachings themselves, only the contradictions they uncover, because I don't feel qualified nor do I wish to be a moral policymaker for others, but only to search out the teachings and respond with my life as the canvas. What a coward I have become. Jesus seems to say no one is blameless. I don't count myself among the blameless. I count myself among those in need of understanding. Teachings on divorce, or any other part of the Law and Prophets, are not my areas of expertise (what is? you might ask), but that doesn't mean I won't read them, consider them, and compare them to how I go about playing out my days. That doesn't mean Jesus doesn't have definitive words on these topics, nor should it. It's not a question of the words, it's a question of the authority and context you give them. Should we give them the power of derision, unification, or purification? I won't force my way into it. I won't give myself the authority. I will, however, not dismiss willy-nilly to make this whole thing more comfortable. I'm not comfortable and no one is throwing me a couch.

Luke 16:19-31

There're just some memories you'll never get rid of no matter how hard you try to kick them out. I rode my bike today and was singing to myself a song from a movie we had watched the night before. It was cool out. A few people waved to me. I had gloves on and was rewriting in my head, which might not sound like much, but it meant the bully was taking a sick day. Wham. I'm sixteen. I volunteer to sing a solo in front of the church. I know there's no way I can do it in my own voice, strength. I'm depending on God for this. A leap of faith, I think. I had a girlfriend at the time—way out of my league and leagues really mattered—she was backing me up on the piano. One of my brother's best friends was out in the crowd looking like he'd been stung by a bee. I feel like sushi. Heather keeps playing the intro over and over again. Her shoulders are up and she pounds the note I'm supposed to come in on. She mouths the words. Where are you God?

This passage is chilling. We always think we have more time, more options, but a time will come when it's too late, Jesus says; it's a deadline, he points toward. Does it have to seem like a threat? Is it really good news? It's not about time, because God is beyond time, it's about when it is finished, because there is a finish line.

Jesus tells a story of a rich man and Lazarus. Although I resist the label of rich man because of my seeming middleclass status, I know I am more akin to the rich man than Lazarus. There are few like Lazarus that I know. America is a rich man.

This rich man Jesus tells about is clothed in his treasures—a ring, a robe—and lives in luxury each day, while Lazarus lays at the gate begging and the dogs lick his sores, which cover his whole body. Lazarus longs to eat what has fallen from the rich man's table. He longs for what is even left over. He longs for comfort and a half-empty stomach. We call him lazy. He would eat like a dog if he could.

When Lazarus dies angels carry him to Abraham's side; meanwhile, the rich man is buried. In hell, the rich man sits in torment. He looks far off and can see Abraham with Lazarus by his side. The roles have reversed. The rich man calls out, Father Abraham, have pity on me and send Lazarus to me, if he could but dip the tip of his pinky in water and cool my tongue, I would be comforted because I am surrounded by this fire. It doesn't seem like a ridiculous request, but Abraham tells him, son, remember your life of luxury in the face of Lazarus's suffering; he is now comforted while you are in agony. There is a sense of justice. We only want justice when we are on the right side of it. Where's the mercy on this and that side of the grave? We have excuses for why we've been the way we were. It was a special case. We have reasons. Abraham continues, even if we wanted to there is a great chasm before us, which no one can cross either this way or that. Hell is separation from comfort. There's a hell on earth and a hell for all eternity, the passage seems to say. You can see heaven from hell and hell from heaven?

Thinking not just of himself, in what seems like true repentance, the rich man responds, then I beg you, father (again terms of endearment are used), send Lazarus to warn my father's house, for I have five brothers who are living the same as I have. I don't want them to come to this place of torment. Not only is this request far from ridiculous, it's selfless. If it's too late for me, at least save the others I love. How could Abraham refuse such a desperate plea? After all, isn't this story a warning to us, just as Lazarus would be to his brothers?

Abraham replies, this is why Moses and the Prophets have been sent into the world with the good news and a warning to all. They will hear it. Let them listen. No, father, the rich man says, it's not enough for them, but a man back from the dead would convince them to repent (Jesus?). Abraham replies, if they don't listen to Moses and the Prophets *or their writings* (my addition), then they will not be convinced even if someone rises from the dead. It's only over because there is no more hope, your mind is no longer open—it's not a matter of timing. We've waited out the clock. We've given you every chance. That's why the game has lasted this long.

We often ask if God has made it plain enough for us. If someone would just tell it to us straight, show us, reveal the right evidence, then we would all believe. If God would only give us an irrefutable sign— these words echo through the entire Bible, yet it's made clear that even then, we would not repent. Why is such a specific faith required? What would it really take to convince?

Reading this it seems so clear. Reading this no answer but one makes sense. But. But first I must believe, internalize, eternalize, what I read. How many trustworthy reports are out there? Can I believe an old book, I might ask. There are many religious texts. There are many religions. There are many divisions. Is this really all that persuasive? Am I really willing to gamble with my life? My luxuries? Do I even believe in a hell? Show me hell now and it might make a difference, one might say. The rich man said it. A glimpse of hell would be enough, he says. A glimpse of heaven too. Is this story not throwing back the curtain? Reading, I would say yes, but my life is not only this reading. Even Jesus says you have to give all to get even more. I have everything right here in my hands. What will I do with it?

The words are plain, no doubt. The question then is only if I give them authority in my life.

If I look out into the world through the eye of each day, many paths seem adequate to me; some better than others in my estimation, but still many. Just put your faith in something, several say. Church, the Bible, does people good whether it's true or not. We're all cowards. I've noticed recently that when God does speak directly in the Bible, in passages such as those found in the later chapters of Job or in Isaiah or in Jeremiah or elsewhere, that he uses the natural order of the world, it's animals and the earth itself, it's obvious design, to show how they point to him and his ways, his authority, his power. Even man's lack of power over the earth is evidence. The world is where you see me, God seems to say. So I look out to the world. I see the trees and the whales and the manner of horses and lions. I see the evidence. I see fingerprints. When I take time to consider where I walk and run and swim and bike and eat and sleep, I spy something. When I'm quiet, I become prayerful. I hear whispers. I hear shouts. No one hears or sees it for me. Busyness chokes it out. Quiet breathes it back. We choke the world. We kick out the evidence like it is an unpaid, unkempt renter. Here is all the evidence you need. Could it be that the very things we see that convince us otherwise are the carriers of the message we so badly hope for? Isn't it that the days sprint by and we reach for anything that will comfort us? Isn't it the very water that could cleanse and refresh all that we keep for ourselves, and pollute whenever possible? The most beautiful field full of flower and food causes ownership disputes, is paved, and becomes a parking lot, a storage unit for the treasures we might need, but don't have room for in our cluttered house. Two cars, three TVs, 10 computers, 18 self-help books, 25 old photo albums, 32 appliances, 44 boxes of clothes, 53 baseball cards, 68 trophies, 74 magazines, 89 novels, 92 scrapbooks, 100 I-don't-know-whats, and not a single solitary concrete commitment to what might be called an absolute truth because absolute truths are not evil in and of themselves, but how they have been used throughout time has been repulsive and reprehensible, I'm sure you will agree no matter your viewpoint. A message of love. A message of meaning. A message of warning. I might argue those have been hidden between the trees and under rocks. They swim the streams to ocean. They power the wings of birds. They direct the instincts of the smallest to the largest of animals. They bounce around and fire the engine of your mind. I would argue that it only takes a moment to recognize them and less than a moment to choke them out. The point isn't the law—whether it be the natural law or the law of the prophets—the point is what is illuminated, what is whispered, what is glued. The point is not discovering some new truth. The point is the magic that powers it all. The cause. Does it all—all of nature, all of these words, all of days—point to God or should we be looking for something else?

seventeen

Luke 17:1-4

It's been a rough week. The whole house has been sick. First my sons and wife, then the daughter, now me. The flu makes you reexamine your existence. You look from the inside out. Sleep is a commodity. I'm writing through a cloud.

Jesus says to his disciples that it's impossible for no offenses to come, but woe to him through who they come. It would be better for a rock to be hung around his neck and be thrown into the sea, than to offend one of these young ones. Jesus must be pointing to the children around him. Don't be a negative influence. Sin is more than just sin; it can be an infectious disease, a sickness. Don't be the cause. The consequences are dire.

Jesus also says take stock of yourselves. Forgive. Rebuke a brother who sins, but if he repents, forgive. Even if he sins against you seven times a day and seven times repents, forgive. Forgiveness is the antidote.

Be a good influence and forgive. We're all dying, that's the truth. Time is always short. Live rightly and forgive. That's what you can control. Health is precious, but can easily be taken for granted. Children, brothers, are precious, but can easily be overlooked. Live rightly and forgive. A son? A sister? A life without entanglements?

Luke 17:5-10

If you can believe it, I've signed a lease on some office space. I've gathered a couple of friends and we are going to give this literary journal a shot. We're doing it as a co-op in our off hours. I can't believe it myself. We have plans for our first issue. We're still thinking of a name, but I like our most simple, The Rattlesnake. *To be honest, the office space is old, and even a little rundown, but no one seems to care all that much. It's a family affair. We're all getting involved. Kids are running the two rooms as we make plans and argue and dream big. It feels like a step forward. We're all way too optimistic, way too happy. I'm waiting for the ceiling to cave in. Who cares if the electrical is from the 1950s? We have laptops and optimism and are on our way to a business license. We're way ahead of ourselves, and the stress level is sometimes high. It's the best time I've had in forever. We're wound up in a big ball of cheese.*

The apostles must have been feeling a similar type of optimism when they asked the Lord to increase their faith. Luke records that the Lord responded: If you have faith of a tiny mustard seed, you can say to this mulberry tree, be pulled up by the roots, and be planted in the sea, and it will obey. What faith that must be. A little faith has much power.

Moreover, the Lord declares, if any of you have a servant plowing or tending sheep, will you say to him or her upon returning from the field, come at once to sit down and eat? Rather you might say prepare something for my supper, afterward you can eat and drink. Do you thank that servant because he did what was commanded? I don't think so. Likewise, when you have done all that you have been commanded, say we are unprofitable servants. We have done only our duty.

The message seems that with faith one can do amazing things. However, the life of a servant is not one full of thanks. Be thankful, but don't be confused. Be humble. Do your duty because it was commanded not because you expect to be thanked for doing what you were supposed to do in the first place.

It's not an easy lesson. We expect to be rewarded for our work, yet Jesus compares his apostles to servants. Servants do what they are told.

This isn't exactly what we wanted to hear. We want praise. We don't want marching orders and expectations. We don't want to admit we are unprofitable servants. This is what is expected of those that follow Jesus? It puts us in our place if this is the place we choose. The apostles ask for faith. Jesus praises faith, but also explains duty. Don't confuse faith and duty, he seems to say. He never seems to say what you expect. He exalts faith beyond even our highest accomplishments, but then reminds the apostles of their place, their duty. It feels like a reprimand. Know yourself; know your limitations; know what is expected of you. What else can be added? I feel humbled and I wasn't even there. Isn't what the apostles asked for a good thing? Did they have the wrong motive, only looking to elevate themselves rather than searching for real faith? Given how Jesus responds, I might suggest Jesus was telling them faith is gained by fulfilling their duty, learning their place, and giving the glory. Only faith well placed is faith at all, he might be saying. Faith at its roots is reaching out beyond yourself to someone worth putting your faith in, not reaching inward, is this his message? Faith is duty? Duty is faith? Maybe I am a bit confused. Never a dull moment.

Luke 17:11-19

Tonight I'm in my new office. There's a chair, a table, a laptop, no Internet, and a happy, overweight writer. I have my own space. The Dodgers are playing but I can't see them. Sacrifices. One light. A bird's nest somewhere in the ceiling, I can't tell where, but I hear the baby birds. Those glorious birds, so hungry. I've walked around the block wondering if anyone knows the crescendo I'm on. Literature is being produced just down the block. On the corner is a coffee shop—perfect. Everything is perfect. A stocking cap. A group of teens. Everything is a trigger. Enough, I'm sure you're saying. I can't help the details from running the streets. Life should be like this. I thank God.

Jesus was on a walk himself. He was on his way to Jerusalem, passing through Samaria and Galilee. When he entered another village, he met ten lepers, who stood off in the distance. They yelled to him,

Jesus, master, have mercy on us. Jesus replied, go, show yourselves to the priests. So they went and were cleansed. One of them—a Samaritan—when he was healed, returned to Jesus and glorified God with a shout. He fell on his face at Jesus's feet, giving thanks. A Samaritan? A leper? some in the crowd must have been thinking, a nobody. Who cares?

So Jesus says, were not ten healed? Where are the other nine? Only this foreigner has returned to give glory to God? Go, Jesus says, your faith has made you well. Faith. Stepping out in faith when your race, your lack of status, your disease could hold you back, has made you well. God deserves the glory. Only you have understood. Go on your way, you are well. It was a social travesty to some. It was a new world order to others. It was upside down. It was a miracle. Faith and nothing else mattered. Faith pointed to authority.

But does this stuff really happen?

Luke 17:20-21

I've been working on the submission guidelines today. It's still unbelievable. We're actually doing it. We're excited. We're researching publishers and publishing rules and bookkeeping and buying second-hand furniture. We're painting the walls with our new ambition. As silly as it sounds, it's true. To be a literary journal, you must act like a literary journal. The only rule of starting your own literary journal is to start one. It's the only requirement. An idea is just an idea, whether it's good or bad, but a literary journal begun is a literary journal. It infiltrates your life. We're an editorial committee because we're doing it.

The Pharisees asked Jesus when the kingdom of God would come. Jesus said the kingdom of God will not come with observation. You can't say it's here or see it there, for the kingdom of God is within you.

We expect the kingdom of God to be ushered in like a new military regime, a coup d'état, but Jesus said it is all around. It is in you. It is in others. The kingdom of God is more than what can be seen, it is God. It is God invited into your heart. The kingdom of God can be eternalized, personalized. It's in a person. It's in a community of those who accept it and live it. The kingdom of God isn't something that can be put in a box, it's here now and it is to come. Who can explain this kingdom of God? You live the kingdom of God. It goes before you, with you, after you.

Writing like this makes me uneasy. It's not literary writing. It's not a new best seller. It's an explanation outside my own understanding. But I feel the spirit of it. I can't get over the idea that the kingdom of God is something that can live inside you, change you, develop you. This description puts me in the mind of music. Music is just music until an audience hears it, is influenced by it, inspired by it. A concert can change your outlook. A song can attach itself to you. You can't get the tune out of your head. You sing as you change diapers. You dance as you do the dishes. You invent a duet with the lead singer. The song becomes a part of your day. It may be the best part. The kingdom of God is the art you can't help but become a part of—a painting, a novel, a song, a sculpture, a poem, a picture, everything. As crazy as the description becomes, the artist knows. Being an artist is creating art. Being an artist is allowing the art to come to the surface. The art was already there. You're a silly conduit. You don't go anywhere introducing the song, no matter what your ego tells you, you only discover that you're singing the same song as everyone else.

Luke 17:22-37

My wife was reading pages, the sneak. She had one note for me left on a print out: more dialogue. I thought about it all morning, went through a collection of emotions. There's no one's opinion I respect more. On the way into my office, I had this conversation:

"Nice day," I said.

"Cheep, cheep."

"Hungry?"

"Cheep, cheep, cheep, cheep, cheep."

"I can't do anything for you guys, wish I could. Wish I could make sense of the world."

"Cheep, cheep, cheep."

"You ever try to make your dream come true? You ever try to do what you've always said you could do?"

"Cheep, cheep, cheep, doubts? Cheep? Cheep?"

"Right. You're all right."

" Cheep cheep."

"You're mother's coming. Don't worry."

"Cheep, cheep."

The birds kept chatting, maybe screaming, as I walked through the door and up the steep stairs. I thought of a poem, but forgot the first line on the steps. When I arrived at the computer it was gone. That's my dialogue so far today. No way my wife is proud of that. I could be home discussing it with her, but instead here I am with my doubts. My doubts make themselves comfortable, drink coffee. The day is just a day. Typing away. Typing away. Cheep. Cheep.

While I talk to the birds of my mind, Jesus says to his disciples, the day is near when you will desire to see one of the days of the Son of Man, and you will not see it even though others will say look here or look there, but don't listen, don't follow them. The lightening that flashes on one part under heaven shines on the other part, so also the Son of Man will be in his day.

I ask, only some will see the lightening? You have to see it for yourself? Otherwise, you'll face the lightening?

Lightening can be seen from all directions, not just by one.

But first, Jesus says, the Son of Man must suffer many things and be rejected by this generation. There's the sign. Readers know it's true.

Jesus continues—he reaches back in time for his examples—with Noah it was the same, people were eating, drinking, buying, selling, planting, and building when Noah entered the ark and the flood came and destroyed them all. The flood is coming, he says. The ark or tsunami are your only choices. I think of the Philippines and know the truth.

Also, the day when Lot left Sodom, fire and brimstone rained from heaven and all were destroyed who remained. The same is the day when the Son of Man is revealed. In that day, one is on the housetop and his treasure is in his house, but he shouldn't come down to take it away. If one is out in the field, let him not turn back. Remember how Lot's wife turned back. You know the stories. You know how it happened. It will happen again.

Jesus explains, those who want to save their life, will lose it; and he who loses his life will save it. It makes you rethink what it means to save or lose a life. Saving this life, Jesus seems to say, is not worth losing the next. Holding to what is important now will only ensure you lose what is eternally important. How difficult is it to transition to an eternal perspective? Only now seems real. Who can reevaluate? Who can trade the now—the rock of the day—for the idea of tomorrow? Where's the evidence? It's in the stories. It's in the lessons. Are stories containers for power? If I, if you, buy into this perspective, there's no going back. There's no fitting into the crowd any longer. Every word I read takes me further away from my couch. My couch is the comfort of today. Life lessons used to feel like better citizenship. This is a flood. This is fire from heaven. This is separation from everything you hold tightly.

Who can see beyond the materials of today?

Billboards spell it out: eat, drink, be merry, buy, look like this, be loved like this.

There's more. In this night, Jesus says, there will be two men in bed, one is taken and the other left. Two women work side by side; one is taken, the other left. Two men are in the field—one taken, one left. The day of the Son of Man is the last day. It's decision day. There are two sides, not three or four.

Way back 100 days ago or more, maybe close to a year, I thought of this idea. I was reading the Bible in a hotel room. It was more interesting than I ever thought it could be. I thought what better journalistic exercise than to report on the life of Jesus. It would be fun. It would be interesting. I could study the cultural implications of a cultural text. It shouldn't be difficult; after all, I already know the text. No surprises. Only there are a million surprises. It's a text that I am unable to take lightly. It asks too much. Most of my friends are Christians. I thought I was a Christian. Christians believe the Bible is the authority. Christians believe that the Bible is true and literal. But. But the book of Luke—the whole Bible—is no book of easy life lessons. It says choose a side. It says a day will come when everything important to you will become unimportant. It says only one thing matters. Imagine bringing that up at a dinner party. Imagine discussing these words with your friends. It won't be an exciting social exercise. It will create divisions. It will set up a dichotomy of right and wrong, truth, absolutes. Throughout time, among friends, it has created derision. I guess I'm too worried about being well liked, respected, loving. Some say loving is telling the truth, but even the truth can be misused. Remember the desert. But do I want to be taken or left? That's not a journalistic question. What questions are important? Is taking the words of Jesus seriously the same as becoming an abrasive religious fanatic? The world is a strange place. Many ideas swim across my desk, I had to choose the idea that would make life more complicated. A simple truth? A simple truth complicates everything. One taken, one left. I never wanted to usher this idea into my life. It seems I can't go back. Do you understand that I never meant it to come to this? Did we ever think that reading the Bible—a nice, religious book—could be so dangerous. Some say whether it's true or not it makes better people—does it? What will I tell my family, my friends, the boys and girls asking for a book to be signed or a free copy of the next journal?

Why take it so seriously? Isn't it just a book? Why does it feel so real? Once you read it, there's only two choices, reject or accept. How did it come to this? I want another assignment. Another article. Back away from the city, the flood, the ark. Just a story? Maybe. How can you read it casually? Why won't I stop typing? Each word is another step up and across the plank. If you get this wrong, are the consequences real? Why offer an opinion on something so central to all of life? Why not write about something that culminates in a small change, not a full change? Stop typing. Stop making yourself more and more unlikeable! Where did the easygoing persona disappear to all of the sudden? At least it's not me. It's the writer. He did it. He's the thief. Blame him.

I was at a family gathering just moments ago. Beer and wine and interesting stories. There was jealousy. Someone had lost weight. A nephew joined a band. A cousin made the college soccer team. The world went in all directions. Moments later there was a funeral. More beer and wine. Scotch for the mighty. A factory shuts down. Big ideas discussed. The economy. Politics. Racism. People mocked. Moments later trout fishing, video games, a softball tournament. A long drive to a huge canyon. I sit peacefully and consider everything and nothing. I try to live life like a poet. Moments later a short conversation. Buzzing in my ears as I seek the right words. A meeting. A discussion about a new book, a new movie. I try to live life like a poet. Moments later, a work day runs long. I argue with my wife. I change a diaper. I finish another article, two, three. I search the want ads to feel better about my situation. I write more. I try to listen more. I kiss my wife. I say I'm sorry. A poet because I write poems. I look for small answers. I try to live rightly. I don't want to be like everyone else. I don't want to live a fictitious life. I don't want to pretend to be this or that. I want to be genuine. I go to church. I read the Bible. I read words that shake the foundations. Hasn't everyone read this book? Am I the only one to see the world shaking? Everyone has an opinion. I don't want to stand out. I don't want an old idea or a new idea. I don't want to discover anything that will make me like him or her. I don't want to be offensive or take sides. I try to be thoughtful like those who I respect, those I look up to. Thoughtfulness takes me to a mountaintop, promises a valley. Thoughtfulness is the highest calling. Be thoughtful. There is thoughtfulness on both sides. With thoughtfulness, two sides are discovered. I'm not attempting to convince anyone. I wasn't attempting to do anything. There's no dialogue, my wife says. She's right. She's wonderful. She's so, so beautiful. Life is a cube. There's a riddle. It's not an exercise anymore. This is the worst article I've ever written. I can't separate myself from my words. It's a flood. Does it sound as tumultuous as it feels? I bet not. Stop typing.

Two asleep. Two thoughtful. One taken, one left.

"Don't enter your own story," the professor says.

I keep writing.

The disciples ask, "Where, Lord?" Jesus says, "Wherever the body is, there the eagles will be gathered together."

Dialogue.

Eagles around a carcass?

eighteen

Luke 18:1-8

Not a lot of sleep last night. Worry is an enemy. The heart beats rapidly. It could power a motorcycle, maybe a Harley. I walked home from a friend's house. We had been talking literary journal most of the night. The worry followed me home. I did a sweep of the house, checking on the kids. My wife was up feeding my daughter. She gave me a tired smile. I turned on the lamp and read a while. I prayed some and realized for the thousandth time I only pray when I'm worried. I don't know how to pray. I just ask out of frustration or panic. I tried to pretend it's natural. The desire is instinctual, but I'm out of practice. I felt like a fake. I felt like the night was utterly different than the day. I feel in control during the day. I feel worthless at night. I couldn't think of any reason to feel this way. That worried me more. No reason. I was outside myself. The night me is unreasonable, unthoughtful. I hide the night me from the rest of the world. My wife leaves the room, comes back. She rolls over. I stay up in my little spotlight. I'm not reading. I'm not entirely asleep. The ice falls in the fridge.

Showered and newly shaved, I'm back to the day. Jesus is talking over my thoughts. He says to pray and don't lose heart. He says there was a judge in a certain city. He was known not to fear God or even regard man. There was a widow who needed help, and she asked the judge for justice against her adversary. He ignored her, but she continued to ask. He wouldn't help her for fear of God or regard of men, but because she is persistent, troubling him day after day, he helps to get rid of her. She's become annoying.

This is what an unjust judge does, Jesus continues, how much more will God avenge his own, who cry out to him day and night, though his patience is long? I tell you now that God will avenge speedily. However, when the Son of Man comes, will he really find faith on the earth?

Keep praying, he says. Be persistent. See if God won't be faithful. Will God find you faithful?

Honestly, I can't say I've seen a direct answer to any of my prayers, but there's nothing disproving it either. Things go the way they go without my direct knowledge of why. Life, however, only rarely seems unfair. But. It does at times. A car wreck. A disease. A lost child. Prayer does help, there's no doubt. But. The effect is not always what I intended, after all I don't answer prayers. I'm committing to pray more and not just when I'm really desperate. Maybe it's a test. Maybe. But. It seems like the right thing to do. Sometimes it changes me. My attitude is susceptible to prayer. All else is outside my hands. Prayer should seem supernatural. Maybe it's a test. Even my most pessimistic self says prayer doesn't hurt anyone, but that's not convincing enough, it's just a starting line for more inquiry. Persistence. Need. Looking beyond. It's a funny thing that comes to mind, belief in prayer doesn't always mean a belief in God. I believe in both. I'm wondering where that belief will take me.

Luke 18:9-14

A journalist has an agenda, a thesis, and a crew of questions. It's about time I get back to them. I've taken notes all day. Here's what I've come up with:

1. Do Jesus's words, reported by Luke, make the reader feel big or small? In the scheme of things, I feel small. The world is big, God bigger—huge. However, so often when people grasp a truth it

puffs them up like a balloon. Truth humbles rather than elevates. So, why isn't this true through experience? According to this text, God big, man small.

2. Is the focus celebrating good works, forgiveness, love, and the mercy and provision of a mighty God, or enjoying how easy it is to point out how evil the world is and how weak a foe? Again, the answer seems easy, but more time seems to be spent on how fallen the world is rather than celebrating right living and the words of a great man, even the son of God.

3. Should there be an adversarial relationship between art and religion? Is art the reflection or the enemy of God? A mix of the two depending on the art? Creation reflects a creator, yet art continues to throw punches in the world where it is both celebrated and despised.

4. Is Luke to be read literal, figurative, hyperbolic, didactic, or as an intellectual or cultural exercise?

5. Do we all—even this writer—have a secret agenda?

These questions are on my mind as I read the next of Jesus's parables. Luke reports Jesus is speaking to a group of people who believe in their own righteousness so that they despise others. Jesus says two men are at the temple for prayer. One is a Pharisee while the other is a tax collector—one honored, one despised. The Pharisee's prayer is Thank you God that I am not like other men: extortionists, unjust, adulterers, or even like this tax collector. I've fasted twice this week and I tithe. How great am I? Meanwhile, the tax collector hides himself, his eyes down, not worthy of heaven. He beats his chest and says, God, be merciful. I'm a terrible sinner!

Jesus notes the latter man was justified rather than the first. Those who exalt themselves are humbled, he claims, and those who humble themselves will be exalted.

The questions, as numerous as they are, aren't about the person of God, but about the response of the followers.

Luke 18:15-17

The insecurities that have been hiding for quite a few days under papers, or in dusty desk drawers, are out again slowing my fingers on the keys. There's a complete lack of gumption behind my words today; to say, distractions everywhere. It's a Sunday and the sermon is still warm. The pastor says so much more than I could ever write, but I do believe reading, even inexperienced reading, is important. Research is important. Writing can be important, medicinal, a love affair. Now I've gone too far again. I read. I write. I do so when it's easy and when it's a job. Isn't that life? I could be doing a number of other things beside this. My son is in the backyard. He wants to play catch. I'll be back.

Children were being brought to Jesus so that he could touch them, bless them, but the disciples were rebuking people. They were out of sync. Jesus says, let the little ones come to me, for this is the kingdom of God. Whoever doesn't receive the kingdom of God as a little child will not enter.

Many believe, or don't believe, with their mind, while their heart remains unattended. Faith comes from the heart and the head. Children model true faith. It's a difficult lesson, I think as the ball goes back and forth. Don't snap at the ball, I say, let it come to you. Use soft hands. Don't be afraid of the ball. I make it too complicated. I choke out fun with rules. I throw a fly ball. He dives for it. I laugh. I haven't really dove for a ball in years.

Luke 18:18-23

I have learned one thing today: Be expectant. Why only react to life, when you could expect to see the good that is hiding out all around you? Attitude changes what you see. I can give it a try.

A ruler in these parts came to Jesus saying, you are a good teacher, tell me what I can do to inherit eternal life? Finally, someone asks it straightforwardly. Isn't this what they were all asking?

Jesus says, why do you call me good? Only God is good. You know the commandments, don't commit adultery, murder, steal, or bear false witness. Also, honor your father and mother. It seems like common sense. We would all probably agree with these. Is that it? Just a set of rules?

The ruler says, yes, I've done all these since my youth.

Jesus says, then you lack only one thing, to sell all that you have and give it to the poor. You will have stored up treasure in heaven. Afterward, come and follow me.

At this hard saying, the man left with sorrow. He was a rich man.

Two masters.

Again Jesus says, live a good life. This makes sense. But then he says let go of what you hold most tightly, what holds tightly to you, and follow me instead. This is no easy task. This isn't hedging your bets. This isn't diversifying your portfolio. This is betting it all. This is risking it all. This is the commitment Jesus asks for. Jesus says, you don't need it, you need me. In church, I might nod my head, but not elsewhere. Maybe my riches would be my self-worth or my writing credentials. Give them up. Sorrow. A set of rules or faith? What can I possibly add to this?

Every time we think we have it all figured out, that we're in control, the clock strikes worthless. A safety net is our real comfort. Sure, it makes sense in theory. Sure, we'd like to pretend such faith. Sure, at church we make such commitments, but we live outside those doors.

However, there is another simple truth, the more we get rid of the less we are shackled to. Simple is good, less worrisome. But. There's more to it than that, I'm sure you'll agree. Riches isn't the problem here, it's the love of riches, the faith in riches. The embrace of riches. Eternal life isn't a finish line it's a life change, a lifestyle, it begins now. Living forever doesn't have a starting line, it's from now until, well, forever. Isn't that eternal life? Isn't God the God of the living?

It's easy to say. This isn't an end around. The only way around your problems is straight through them—*Fifteen*.

One more question: Is faith an argument won or something else completely?

This isn't new, this is old:

An Attempt on My Life

It must begin somewhere, this thing. Why
not in a new, twelve-emotion town? It's
as easy as telling yourself and the history
all around you that you're here now until
you're not here anymore. It may sound
simple like raising kids on a domestic
plateau, but it's not, it's not, it's not.

Tell yourself to get angry, to dig yourself
in and throw off your former occupation,
which is holding yourself down in this
composite dirt. It's just a place, and you're
just an easy idea. It's easy to be you and
invent names and misuse words like
wind and dream and magical migrating mythology, and here we go
again

Look out there, is there someone standing
on a cliff or at the water's edge? Are there
leaves being blown about by death? Can you
even see a painter out in your tall grass making
this moment as magnificent as the words you've
thrown together in haste? Say no to all of it for goodness sake.

This moment is just a moment out of a thousand
moments, except for your hand moving systematically
across what might be described as a piano if you're
a liar. So it's new. So it's unsteady. Everything is
new the first time you play it or hit it with a
bat. The slider will stretch on for miles. Is that

really what you want?

You can only force yourself to see the colors. So
force yourself. Destroy the old you. Use violence or
envy if you must. An angry car crash would work;
it might change the world or make for better news. It's
your town too. The
shapes are stretching out like an old woman who misses
her husband, the sky, the heavens. Why has the woman
aged at all? Why this talk of heaven from left field? Why
can't we finish this over coffee and those
Mexican doughnuts you love so well?

Luke 18:24-30

At tee-ball practice, balls flew everywhere. My son looked skyward. He ran the bases with reckless abandon. Afterward, he stripped down and ran through the sprinklers. My youngest daughter said dah dah, and I pretended she was talking to me. Hot dogs, a novel. A debate over whether tie goes to the runner. My son in his Dodger pajamas. A Star Wars graphic novel. Another debate over home runs versus bunts, defense versus everything else. Some sleep. Some crying. A shower.

Jesus says, How difficult is it for those who have great riches to enter the kingdom of God! It's easier for a camel to go through the eye of a needle.

The crowd around him wonders, who then can be saved?

What's impossible for men, Jesus says, is possible with God.

Peter responds, we've left all and followed you.

There is no one who has left house or parents or brothers or wife or children, seeking the kingdom of God, who will not receive many times more than they sacrificed. In the age to come eternal life is theirs.

Such sacrifice does seem impossible. Jesus says faith in, and commitment to, the kingdom of God trumps all. The rich man left, the disciples sacrificed all for a greater treasure, even life ever after.

However, fairytale or not, I don't know how to respond to the possible leaving of family—riches, yes; wife and children, NO! Was this only for the time while Jesus was on earth or now too? How can Peter be so bold? How can too much, or too little, be sacrificed? Count the costs, Jesus has said, and the costs are high. It's not an easy commitment. It's an ultimate ordering of priorities. I go back and forth every day. I walk around it like a deep pond. I dip a toe. I imagine diving in. I don't pretend. It all seems counter to the daily run. Books all around me. Words in the sky like light clouds. A leap in the horizon. A world compartmentalized. Is the argument about authority or authenticity or interpretation or willingness? Is it one man's journalistic exercise or something so much more important that this is the wrong venue? I keep writing because it's words on a couch. My life, however, is not a couch. I push these words and my life closer and closer together, but they won't mix any more than the pasta, sauce, and vegetables on my son's plate. I run around the track while a young player runs an exciting touchdown on the field that lies between.

It has nothing to do with popularity, likeability. It has nothing to do with success or personal achievement. It has nothing to do with a double play in the ninth or a novel bestseller. It has nothing to do with a prestigious literary journal. It has nothing to do with romance, childcare. It has everything to do with everything.

A blind man. A disease and its cure. An earthquake. The infield late in the game, one out. A seeing-eye groundball. No authority. I'm learning an easy answer can have the most difficult consequences. Knowing an easy answer offers no options. Freedom only grows in commitment. Commitment either chokes out or feeds freedom. A good man or a fanatic? I've never been decisive. That's not a last line.

One more thought: If it's only an insurance policy we're looking for, it's not worth it.

I pray and I'm the one who changes.

It takes courage, all of it.

Remember, many tried to stone Jesus for the things he said and did. Ultimately, he was killed. What is more serious and dangerous than that? An uncomplicated, nice, good man? Many didn't think so. Only time has smoothed it over, like water on rock, like a river carving out a canyon. It may be slow and smooth, but it's still a coup d'état.

Luke 18:31-34

Aside, Jesus tells his disciples, we're headed to Jerusalem where all that the prophets have written about me will come to fruition. The Son of Man will be delivered to the Gentiles; he'll be mocked, insulted, spit upon, and killed. On the third day he will rise again. But they didn't understand.

Luke 18:35-43

A man sat begging on the road. What crowd passes by? he asks. Jesus of Nazareth, they say. He yells, Jesus, Son of David, have mercy on me. His boldness echoes.

Shut up, they tell him, but he yells all the more, Son of David, have mercy on me.

Jesus stops. Jesus calls him near. What do you need? he asks. Lord, I need sight, he says. Jesus says, receive your sight; you're faith has made you well. Immediately, he sees. Immediately he follows. Immediately he glorifies God. All who saw, in fact, praise God.

nineteen

Luke 19:1-10

I sneak back into the story. The original text and my own journalist instincts, such as they are, keep elbowing me out. I don't mind it. I respect the need for it. I smell. I get in the way. I feel defensive. I give explanations when none are needed.

I've been married ten years today. I've been reviewing, of course. I've made more mistakes than I've expected. I've taken my wife for granted. I've written out of compulsion. Thankfully, my wife is patient, amazingly so. We had a nice dinner after the kids were tucked. We spent time telling each other our favorite moments. She named my least favorite characteristics. I'm surprised. I'm unimaginative, but overwhelmed. I can't believe how many times she uses the word respect. I can't believe she thinks I'm a good father. I wonder if selfish is my defining word, maybe attitude, maybe inconsistent. Pork tenderloin. Chips & salsa. A strange mix of our favorites. A movie paused over and over to air additional thoughts. I try to put it into words. I try again and again. We both fall asleep prematurely. We laugh about it, let the dogs out, and climb into bed. It's beautiful, more real than any description. The AC kicks. Peace. Later, I hear the baby crying. I get up and find my wife is already there. She waves me off, but I sit up with her. I try again. Tired words. Why don't you wake me up, I ask. Who could, she answers.

Jesus passes through Jericho. There was a rich tax collector there named Zacchaeus. He was a short man and couldn't see through the crowd that had assembled. Zacchaeus runs ahead and climbs a sycamore tree. Jesus looks up and sees him. There's a long beat, I imagine. Nothing significant. Then Jesus says, Zacchaeus, come down, I'll stay at your house.

Me? I'm nobody. I'm a bird.

Imagine a rich man running ahead and climbing a tree. Not for anyone.

Zacchaeus hurries down. He's excited.

Others grumble. Jesus wants to be a guest at a sinner's house? What is going on? How do they know each other?

Zacchaeus says, I'll give half of my riches to the poor. If I've taken anything from someone under false pretenses, I'll restore it fourfold. Just the presence of Jesus changes Zacchaeus completely. He didn't need anyone to tell him what was needed, he knew. He volunteers. Jesus says he's worthy to be his host and Zacchaeus immediately goes about being the man Jesus seems to know he can be. Isn't that so often the case? We want to be different but we need a catalyst. We hold tightly to some comfortable, regrettable, eternal struggle—in this case the love of money and the corruption that grows, eating you from the inside—and when we begin to release it, it releases us. How can we ever change? We're trapped. We run and climb a tree. We climb down to freedom. We finally listen to our heart. Don't miss, however, how Jesus stopped. How Jesus invited him down. How Jesus invited him into a new life. Zacchaeus embraces the opportunity without pause. A new life. A vocal heart.

Jesus concludes: Salvation has come to this house because he also is a son of Abraham, a part of the long-declared promise. The Son of Man has come to seek and save that which was lost.

Luke 19:11-27

I went to a concert with a few friends from high school last night. It threw a fit in the middle of my schedule. I loosened up. The music was great. It was a small bar with an Irish band. We laughed about base-running blunders in old baseball games. We created new legends. We argued about politics and religion. We quoted our kids. There was a moment when I watched the journalists taking pictures and notes. I imagined their lives. I sat back and listened to the lyrics. Jealousy was in every seat, even on stage. I couldn't reengage. I wondered what difference it all makes. I wondered if words not set to music made people other than me feel like this. I wished I could set my life to music. Optimism doesn't cut it, but it's close. Music is inspiration? Music takes you outside yourself. It was a moment frozen. I imagined a better version of myself. I couldn't wait to get back here to write about it. I drove home. I fell asleep. No matter what song I try, I can't revisit that moment. I can't bring it back. So there it is in the past, losing its power every moment I push it back. It's not so sad. I imagine all the preparation and unexceptional practice that came together in that moment. I don't want a stage other than my house and streets. I don't want an audience other than the one in my mind. I see them reading this and I edit based on how they might react. Writing is never a solitary concert no matter how emphatically I try. I look over at the treadmill. I could use more exercise in my life. Later.

Amidst it all, Jesus continues a parable and someone is there who tells someone, who writes it down. Luke says the parable is directed to those with Jesus, who being near Jerusalem are expecting the kingdom of God to appear at any moment. Jesus says there was a nobleman who went to a far country to receive a kingdom and then return. He called together his ten servants and gives them $10,000 a piece (I changed the money so I might have a better feel for the implications, it was 10 minas; mina was apparently about three month's wage). He said do business until I come back, but his citizens hated him, sending a delegation after him to report that they would not allow this man's reign any longer. Upon his return, after receiving the kingdom, he gathered the servants back to him, to see how they had managed his resources. The first reported turning his $10,000 into $100,000. Well done, the nobleman said, because you were faithful in a little task, I give you authority over ten cities. Likewise, the second earned $50,000 and was given five cities. The third said I have kept your $10,000 in my pocket because of my fear for you. It is known that you collect what you did not deposit and reap what you did not sow. The nobleman responded, I judge you by your own words and wickedness. You knew me well yet you did not even bank my money, that I might collect interest. He took his money and gave it to the servant who had made him $100,000. Why give more to the man who already has so much, many asked. The nobleman said, everyone who has, will be given more, and from him who does not have, even what he has, will be taken away. Bring to me my enemies, so that I might reign over them and have them killed. Killed?

No matter how long I sit in front of this computer, I can't come up with an interpretation or run from the word killed. Who is the nobleman in this parable? Who are the servants? Servants of an austere ruler follow commands or pay the consequences. What if the ruler was fair and loving? The ruler will return at any time, Jesus seems to say, what will he find you busy with? Will he know you at all? Jesus is going away to claim the kingdom he was promised.

Luke 19:28-36

Sometimes I think my wife and I couldn't be more different. She's patient and kind. She's level headed. She believes the best of people. She's beautiful and fair, a champion of what is right. I sit and write, while she raises children, makes friends, cooks meals for those who need it, all while working as many hours as me. I sit and write, while she impacts people's lives. Someone stopped me in the store to tell me how much she loves my last novel. I looked down. My wife goes to see a friend who has just had a baby. She's brought a broccoli braid. She hugs the mom and holds the new child. There are tears. Her meal was made of hours. I see its impact, and I feel worthless. I'm jealous. My wife says you helped. My wife says you were a part of it. My children rush me at the door. "Daddy, daddy." We're different. She's amazing. I write because it's what I do. I arrange words over and over again and pretend it makes a difference. What am I if not a writer, an arranger of words?

Jesus nears Jerusalem, while I sit in front of this computer. He sends two of his disciples into a village to find a colt. He says loose it and bring it here. If the owners ask, tell them the Lord is in need of it. The disciples find the colt exactly where Jesus said it would be. Why are you taking my colt? the owners ask. The Lord needs it, they say. They send the disciples on their way. The disciples throw their clothes on the colt. Jesus rides the colt, and many more spread their clothes on the road.

So many are swept up—disciples willing to go; owners of a colt who have no objections despite the strange circumstances; and the audience who honor, worship him, with their clothes thrown in the road reminiscent of a classic romantic moment. Not the triumphant entry that one might expect. A colt. Clothes. Charity. A king without his own colt, steed. A spirit sweeping through without resistance.

Imagine it now. Imagine a humble march, a borrowed colt, clothes thrown down. Even the parades through town celebrating a district championship for the local baseball team have more firepower. A fire truck leads them, not a colt. A king. A triumphant entry. Humility on display. They give what they have. They offer it freely. A king lowers himself enough to except. He is a king because he acts like a king, he's heralded like a king, just no king we've ever known.

Luke 19:37-40

As Jesus neared the top of the Mount of Olives, all of his disciples began rejoicing and praising God loudly for all the "mighty works" they had seen. "Blessed is the King who comes in the name of the Lord! Peace in heaven and glory in the highest!" Now, some of the Pharisees called Jesus to rebuke his disciples, but he says if they were to keep silent, the stones would immediately cry out.

Luke 19:41-44

I was discussing it all with a good friend. It was a phone conversation. He said you can make a load of resolutions or learn life lessons or you can seek to meet the person of Jesus. At first I thought it was just Christianeze, but I could tell he really meant it. I said I'd try. I don't always expect. I certainly don't expect miracles, or for a savior to jump off the page. I don't expect much. I try to stop gliding through my day.

Jesus saw the city and wept. Certainly no gliding. He wept for the city. I can see his shoulders slump and bounce slightly. His fingers are up into his eyes. In almost a whisper maybe, Jesus says, if you had only known, even you my child, on this your day, what would bring you peace! But you have hidden it all from your eyes. The days will come upon you when your enemies will surround you, and level you, and even the children within your borders. Not a stone will be untumbled because you did not know the day or time you would be visited. You missed it all until it toppled you. What could have been peace has now become destruction: your future.

Luke 19:45-48

I have come to believe that writer's block is nothing more than a reflection of the writer's life. You can live writing, pondering it all day long, taking notes. You steal or borrow from your own life. Or you can leave writing to its appointed time and find nothing at all to write about. Writing is not a closet or a compartment. Writing is just another facet of what you are already doing. Writing is a continuation of the day, not a piece. It's nothing new; it's a song remembered. The more frustrated I get with the materials of my day, the more I force words, push them around. The more I read, think, pay attention, the more rapidly I click the keys, dance, sing. It's more of putting down what is already there. It's difficult to be comfortable in your own blanket of words. I pause only when I don't understand myself. I'm Ink. Writer's block is too much fatty foods built up over a lifetime. Writer's block is lack of exercise. Writer's block is a sleepless night. Writer's block is ignoring what's right there under the surface. Writer's block is lack of participation. You can't catch it from a plant or a friend or a certain food. You can catch it anytime, anywhere, even though it doesn't really exist.

That's what I brought to the table this morning, mixed in with my oatmeal, while Jesus was in the temple driving out those who were running it like a business. He says, as it has been written, "My house is a house of prayer," but you've made it a "den of thieves."

Jesus was teaching daily in the temple but the chief priests, scribes, and leaders sought to destroy him. They, Luke reports, were unable to do anything because all the people were so attentive to his words.

twenty

Luke 20:1-8

He was a king; she was a peasant, or maybe she was the queen and he a peasant. They run off together, forsaking all for each other, the greatest of stories. Do they ever have second thoughts? Does the fairytale always end well?

But Jesus was about his business, preaching the gospel in the temple. Of course the chief priest and scribes and elders were confronting him, saying by what authority do you say such things? Who gives you the right? You're not my dad. You're not the boss of me.

Jesus answers with a question. I will answer you, if you will first answer me truthfully, he says, asking, was the baptism of John from heaven or men?

They huddled together thinking if they say it is from heaven, then Jesus will ask us why we didn't believe, but if we say from men, the people will stone us for they think John is a prophet. So they said they didn't know—the safe, rather than the honest, route.

Jesus responds, neither will I tell you by what authority I do these things.

An honest conversation is not always easy to come by. Jesus doesn't seem like one to argue just to argue. I imagine he would tell anyone who genuinely wants to know. But I am just here imagining.

Luke 20:9-19

Who can describe the ocean? It was many years ago when I sat before it and the wind. It was cold and it was Oregon. The ocean was vast. I sat with a book, but read the same sentence over and over again. Dogs were chasing their owners and vice versa. It was morning. It was cold. The ocean defied. I had ocean in mind. I sat down, the book on my lap. The waves came in, one following another. My shoes were off, my pants rolled up. The ocean was brilliant. I can't get it quite right. Who can describe peace? Who knows the words to say about taking a brief aside from your life? The words were scattered across the ocean. Nothing seems so huge as the ocean. You miss your children. You miss your wife, who is only a matter of feet away, still asleep. They are all asleep. The air smells of salt. You're small and your words are on the waves. You quit trying so hard and listen.

The ocean was just a small memory, a peaceful moment, as Jesus was telling another parable. A man planted a vineyard, leasing it to his vinedressers when he left to a faraway country for a long while. At vintage-time, he sent a servant to the vinedressers expecting some of the fruit of his vineyard, but the vinedressers beat the servant and sent him back without. The owner sent another servant, who was also beaten and shamed. With the third it was the same. Surprisingly, the owner next sent his son, his beloved, thinking they would at least respect him. However, the vinedressers saw an opportunity to seize the inheritance by killing the son. So the owner came and destroyed the vinedressers and gave the vineyard to others.

Many shout, certainly not! But Jesus looked at them saying, it has been written, the stone which the builders rejected has become the chief cornerstone. Those who fall on that stone will be broken, but on those whom it falls, it will grind them to powder.

The chief priests and scribes knew the parable was about them. Luke writes they sought to lay hands on Jesus, but feared the people.

A threat? Why did the owner send his beloved son to his death? Why did the vinedressers get so greedy with the owner away? Is God giving his blessing to another people?

There are waves. There is the ocean. There are words. There are words. There are words, waves.

Luke 20:20-26

I apologize. It's cold season. I'm writing from a cloud again. Nothing makes sense, not for a while anyway. Everything takes extra effort. So. I'm sorry. I'm sorry for the narrator I am and the one I almost am and the one I am far from being. I write sick. I write tired. I write distracted. I bomb words from a cloud.

I make no promises.

One man wrestles truth and the world all around him. It's no match.

Who's made it this far?

Wow. Mom, are you still reading?

Where's the laughter? Where are the tears.

I watched a program last night where people of many religions argued over the world. Each had truth in their pockets, just as each had blood. People were angry. People were tired. People forced smiles. No community, only kind verbal wars. But pain. But suffering. It unites us. There is no religion in a hospital room with a sick child; there is only God.

Words from a cloud.

The chief priests and scribes and elders were getting more anxious, and with anxiety, came strategy. They watched Jesus. They sent spies who pretended to believe. They seized his words, imprisoned them, looked for the opportunity to deliver him to the authorities, to the governor. If not violence, then the law.

They ask him, teacher, we know your teaching is right without favoritism, but teach us the way of God in truth... is it lawful to pay taxes to Caesar?

A slick trap.

Jesus knew their craftiness, Luke reports. He answers, why test me? Show me a denarius. Whose image and inscription do you see?

They answer Caesar.

Then render unto Caesar that which is Caesar's and to God what is God's.

So they could not catch him in his words. They marveled. They were silent. It was probably the best strategy.

Luke 20:27-40

I fade from my own writing because the story has a life of its own. The story is the story, not my life. I fade as I deconstruct myself. I fade. I'm out of here like a disgruntled teenager in their own imaginings. If my parents (the stories) do one more thing, I'm gone. Smoke.

Dreams are made of patience.

I'm an editor of my own co-op lit magazine, but nothing happens. It all takes time. I run ahead, too far ahead. We dream of submissions. We work behind the scenes. The journal is only an idea. An idea has no feet. We research. We plan. We construct feet. We have nothing to show for it, but the thought that there will be in the year or years to come, feet. Experts say make estimates, then double them. That is the mathematic logic of new ventures. So we are doubling our timeline. We are extending our expectations. We are sitting on our hands while we construct what could be feet or something close.

Why are we such an optimistic people by trade?

More came with tests. The Sadducees, who Luke reports "deny" that there is a resurrection, came to see Jesus. They had their own riddle. Teacher, they say, Moses wrote that if a man's brother dies having a wife but without children, then his brother should take his wife and raise up children for his brother. (Still an odd concept to me.)

Now it gets more interesting. They use the over-proportioned example of politicians. The slippery slope. There are seven brothers. The first took a wife and died without children. The second took her for his wife and also died childless, and the third and all seven. Later the wife also dies. In the resurrection, whose wife is she?

Jesus answers directly (a change?), the sons of this age marry and are given in marriage, but those worthy to attain that age and the resurrection, neither marry nor are given in marriage, nor can they die anymore. They are equal to the angels and are sons of God and sons of the resurrection. Even Moses showed in the burning bush passage that the dead are raised when he called the Lord the God of Abraham, Isaac, and Jacob. For he is not the God of the dead, but of the living. All are alive to him.

Some of the scribes respond, teacher, you have spoken well. Afterward, they dared to question him no more. I'm sure theologians would have a field day. I say the resurrection is more of a mystery than this riddle gives it credit. Jesus promises eternal life, sonship and daughtership, and we whittle it down to scenarios we can argue over. We split. We segregate. New churches. We can't imagine mysteries. We can believe in God only if all can be explained. I'm not saying it's easy, I'm saying it seems strange that we want to have answers to hyperbolic scenarios, while we hope for a God that is easy to explain.

Luke 20:41-44

The kids are running around the office getting peanut butter & jelly all over themselves and the walls. Interruptions erupt. My wife is out of town and I'm not much of a juggler. I'll be quick before the next bathroom break becomes another panic.

We write in-between.

Jesus is calm. He asks how people can say that the Christ is the son of David. David said in the Book of Psalms: The Lord said to my Lord, Sit at My right hand Till I make Your enemies Your footstool. If David calls Him Lord, how is He then his Son?

Was this an argument? Can he be both lord and son? I've heard it said that the Christ was both fully God and fully man. Is this what is being argued? Not being part of the conversation, I can't say for sure. I do know that David, a king, wouldn't call his descendant Lord unless he was more than just a descendant. David wouldn't even know about his descendant unless he preexisted him. Now there's one for the theologians. I have no more time.

I have been praying lately. Call it an experiment or a test or something. I don't know why. But I have been praying just to see what will happen. What happens is prayer changes you. You look differently. You don't yell as much. I thought of prayer as talking to an invisible God. Asking for stuff. Believe me, there has been a lot of that. But silence. In the quiet, my day changes. Five minutes a day. It works into your fabric. I pray and it all seems possible. Prayer has become shutting up and looking outside. No voices. Once I get past pondering all my screw ups, adding them up to estimate my measly worth, I feel loved. I can't say it another way. Feeling loved in those moments, I don't spend so much of my day trying to feel loved. I don't worry as much. I feel content every once in a while. I hope this isn't a phase like every exercise regimen. I pray. I'm a prayer. I feel small and I don't care. Prayer is the new writing. But I won't quit my day job just yet. Phases are great, but what will last?

Luke 20:45-47

I'm a fake, a fraud. That's not a gimmicky thought or the opening line to a sleight-of-hand. It's not even a hyperbole. It's the truth. It's an emotion. I've hardly ever been this low. My son is yelling. He calls me a liar. I know he hasn't gone to the bathroom, cleaned his room, washed his hands, brushed his teeth. He tells me he has. He calls me the liar. My younger kids are crying. I'm yelling now between my teeth. My jaw tightens. Do not talk to me that way! I am practically throwing my son into his room. The windows are open and I am sure I am stopping traffic, girls on bikes. One asks the other if they think there is a lion inside. I'm completely out of control. Don't roar him, Levi says. I snap in two. I sit and listen to the crying that comes right through the walls. My head in my hands. My fingers stuck in tangled hair. I'm dizzy. What kind of father am I? How large of a scar will I leave?

Which am I? The writer or the yeller? I'm more patient with words. I've been described as laidback. I make small resolutions year round. One step forward for theories, a giant leap back for follow-through.

Why write it down?

Why no secrets?

How am I to be believed otherwise?

Sometimes truth comes in all the wrong places.

Believe me, I still have my secrets no matter how much I write, I'm always worse. My thoughts are still my own no matter how much I pretend to lay it all out. He's not very good at his job, but I do have an editor upstairs.

It's with sour eyes that I read about Jesus telling his disciples to watch out for the scribes, who wear long robes, who love public greetings and honored seating at church and feasts, who eat up the homes of widows and make long prayers under pretense. These will receive greater condemnation, Jesus says.

At first, I visualize these scribes. I see them plainly. I berate them momentarily in my mind. Then I look closer to home. I recognize myself. I might attempt to conceal it, but there's a scribe inside. I can say (or write) all I like but words only live long enough to give way to a higher communicative medium: what I do. Come home with me and see how I treat my wife and kids. Swim my thoughts. Ride in my car at rush hour. See what happens when I know I'm right but no one else does. Mail a package with me. Forget words. Take me to the airport to see if I make it through the security check with my jaw unlocked and volume turned down to slow jazz.

twenty-one

Luke 21:1-4

I'm sitting in my office, nothing completed. It's an exciting story. I want to write the great American novel, but I sit here instead. I don't write much. Life is a freezer with promises. I'm not sure if even accomplishment is worth a dime.

Jesus looks up and sees the rich giving to the treasury. There is also a poor widow offering the only pennies (mites) she has. Jesus says the poor widow has put in more than anyone else. Most give out of their overflow to God. That is their offering. But she. She gives out of her poverty. It's her livelihood she gives.

It's her faith she gives.

It's her belief she gives.

It's her control she gives.

It's a better life she gives.

It's a better life she hopes in.

First a belief in God, then trust. A gift. Faith. Pennies, then everything else.

Luke 21:5-6

Some guy says live in the moment. It's a concert. He says have a pet giraffe if you want one. I'm not sure what he meant, but I don't care either. It sounded good to me. He was enthusiastic and some of that enthusiasm is rubbing off on me even as I sit at my computer wondering what I should be working on. I'm an editor of a literary magazine that is more of a lazy idea than the idea implies. I tell no one because there is nothing to tell. There's no evidence more than the words in my mind that this literary magazine is a reality. Maybe a pet giraffe then. It makes just as much sense.

Jesus was speaking of the temple—not a giraffe—but with equal enthusiasm. He notes beautiful stones and donations. He says, you see it now, but the days will come when not one stone shall be left upon another. They will all be thrown down.

Luke 21:7-19

It's been a faith swap. First I should say that I don't typically work this late. There's not much to do here, but I forgot my bag. My wife's already asleep. It's been a long day. It's Sunday, 10 PM. I let my brother's dogs out and put them in their kennels. I stopped by the office for my bag. It has my books in it. I turned on the computer to check email, see if the Dodgers were still winning without Manny, and update myself on fantasy baseball scores. I opened up my file to reread a couple of sections that were bothering me. Now I'm writing.

The woman next to me at church was in tears. She was happy. She sang loudly. She was the only one there. I love her. I took some of her faith.

My wife loves worship music. She wasn't up playing the guitar today. She was taking the week off. She sat beside me. She stood and she sang. She has no doubts.

What? I ask. She just smiles at me. Wraps herself around my arm. Tells me I don't need to steal her faith.

We were arguing this morning about politics, what else? I had said it seems like only Republicans are welcome at church. Is being a Christian or a Republican more important? What if I am only one of these?

I'm afraid to say I'm a Democrat if it comes down to choosing.

Oops. I just lost 65% of my readers. I've caught a Democratic flu from time to time. You may call it a disease. Some have told me it's an error in judgment or even a serious character flaw. I sometimes agree with Republicans. All Republicans don't even agree. I just lost the rest. No readers. Just me and my computer and my confusion and my borrowed faith. I just wish there was more disagreement because then there might be more honest conversation. Now I have a Utopian fever. I'm useless, but at least my views are unpopular amongst my peers. I have that going for me. So, it's faith I borrow.

You can't borrow faith... but if you could, I would.

I'm riffling through my bag looking for some notes I had scribbled down to keep me on track when they asked him, Teacher, when will this all happen? What sign is there that will let us know these things are about to happen?

Jesus maybe sighs, then answers, don't be deceived. Many will come saying I am The ONE and The Time is Near (I read that sign this morning). I say don't follow them. However, when you hear of wars and commotions, don't be terrified. These things must come first, but the end will not come immediately. (Well, that clears that up. It sounds like every age. Nothing changes but the direction of the wind.)

Jesus continues despite my weak thoughts. Nation will rise up against nation, and kingdom against kingdom. There will be great earthquakes and famines and pestilences. There will be fearful sights and great signs from heaven above. (Sounding somewhat familiar.) However, before all these things, they will lay hands on you and persecute you and deliver you to the synagogues and prisons. You will be brought before kings and rulers because of me, because of my name, my words. Words. This will become your testimony. (At least they know what they are getting into, I guess. They asked for the sign after all, but I bet this wasn't what they were expecting. When you go to jail, you'll know it has begun.)

Jesus concludes, therefore, save it in your heart and don't spend your time in meditation over your answers for I will give you both a mouth and wisdom to fill it. Your adversaries will be unable to contradict or resist you. (I've taken care of it all ahead of time. Don't worry, as if that ever stopped anyone from worrying.)

However, Jesus has more to say, know this. You will be betrayed even by parents and brothers, relatives and friends. Some of you will die. You will be hated because of me. Listen more: not a hair of your head will be lost. In patience, you will possess your souls. (All will not be laughter. All will not understand your commitment. It will get worse before it gets better. Though great turmoil is ahead, victory is assured. No secrets. No sugar. Only what is what and what will be. Asked and answered.)

Did he say your family will betray you?

Luke 21:20-24

You'll see Jerusalem surrounded by armies. What but desolation could be near? Jesus speaking of course, not me. Don't be confused. Never be confused. Confusion is not allowed. Confusion is sin, my silly words from my condemning heart. Back to Jesus. Back to authority. Back to wisdom. Back to sentences that don't begin with Back. Let those who are in Judea run to the mountains, let those in the midst of her depart, and let not those who are in the outskirts enter her once more. These are the days of vengeance (haven't you been desiring vengeance all along? Isn't justice your primary excuse for everything?) What is written will be fulfilled. The word created it all. Those days are not for the pregnant or those nursing babies—timing couldn't be worse. There will be great distress sprouting in the land, wrath. The sword will be showing off, making slaves not just to death but to other nations. Immigrants will trample Jerusalem until their time is fulfilled. Anti-immigration lobbyists are saying I told you so.

It's a grim picture. I can see the paint of it dripping down. It's not all daisies. It's amazing that so many can't wait. It's amazing that so many feel justified. My heart is a disgusting hairball. Seriously. I am selfish and spontaneously self-serving if you understand the difference. No difference. I'm irritable and not just before coffee. I let worry choke faith every time. I think when I should be listening. But let's talk no more about me. Let's leave that subject for a while. If someone told this to your face, would you be pining after the "End Times" with a sign and a blow horn? Would you be picketing a downtown establishment with anti-you views? Would you be on your knees?

Let me ask the real question: In the face of absolute truth, how are we to respond? I say humility, reality, and dancing. Others say we need to tell everyone in the world that we are right and more importantly... wait... and more importantly... wait... and more importantly... that they are WRONG. Spell it for them. It feels good doesn't it? WRONG. WRONG. W-R-O-N-G. WRONG. The truth will set them free. It's tough love. It's our duty. I'm glad to do it. I will suffer for God. WRONG.

I say take a step back. I say think through your delivery. I say be thoughtful. I say community, relationship first. I say if someone claims to be speaking for God, they better be. There is nothing scarier to me than misquoting God. That's one journalistic mistake I hope I never make.

I take a deep breath. My editor says I've gone too far this time. I say what is all this worth if I don't lay it out there? I wouldn't do it face to face, but sometimes here in this office I've got to have it out. I have to box my own reflection with the words I've swallowed down so often like a Men's multivitamin. People call them horse pills. I've never seen a horse pill but I believe the simile nonetheless. I'm so gullible. So afraid. So hoping readers have followed me away from that tirade that was even annoying me.

What next?

Have a pet giraffe if you want.

Luke 21:25-28

I have a new discipline. Don't think me wacky. It is going to sound wacky. Discipline is wacky in my ears. Here is my new discipline: to listen. Not just to people, although I want to be a better listener all around, but to the quiet so that like many have told me—especially those I tell I'm starting a Lit mag or writing about Luke (not many)—I might hear the "still quiet voice" of God. I don't know if I believe it's possible, but I will. I will listen. I will meditate on silence even though silence doesn't exist and scares me. I will listen. The quiet has a way of engulfing you even as your mind yells, you're wasting valuable time! I'll listen. I'll risk it. Jesus says have ears.

My mind says go help someone rather than wasting your time. I think my mind is right. Do something. Read a book or something. Accomplish something. Check something off that long list you keep in your backpack. You spend more time on adding to the list. I can't quiet my mind. My mind is a motor mouth. I stay the course because listening is now an item on that list. I want to check it off.

One thing: I'm not so angry anymore.

This quiet has feet.

My prayers become single words. Sometimes names. I let the others words be filled in by the quiet all around. All is added to them.

There is a dog—next door maybe—barking.

When I can't listen anymore, the laughter begins. It doesn't make a sound.

Jesus is saying there will be signs in the sun and in the moon and in the stars. (In the trees and ocean too? Under rocks? Hidden between words?) On the earth the nations distress, are perplexed. The seas and the waves roar (lions? An angry father?). Hearts falter from fear and the expectation of those things that are coming to the earth. The powers of the heavens will be shaken (thunder?). Then, Jesus continues, they will see the Son of Man coming in a cloud with great power and glory. When these things begin to happen, look up, lift your heads, because your redemption draws near.

Those who have ears.

Luke 21:29-33

No one can create or even gather the words of listening.

After so much straight talk, Jesus tells another parable to illuminate. Look at the fig tree, he says, and all the trees. When they have begun to bud, you see, and know that summer is near. No one has to tell you. (I know summer is near because my 80-year-old neighbor is shirtless in the garden mumbling. I pretend not to watch. He walks his old hunting dog around the block. He mumbles. He talks to his wife and is surprised she isn't there to answer. He's shirtless. Summer is near. The trees bud unashamed.) Know also, Jesus breaks through my worthless commentary, just as you interpret these signs that the kingdom of God is also near. Furthermore, I tell you that this generation will by no means pass away until all things have taken place. (Is that true?) Heaven and earth will pass away (despite your doubts or boasts) but My words (Jesus's words) will by no means pass away.

His words will outwrestle even heaven and earth.

Luke 21:34-38

I listen. I fade to the backdrop. I see behind the curtain. Watch and listen. Listen and watch. Both.

The narrator has a question for himself and you, reader, can listen in if you like, or skip, if it has no value for you: Does this writing mirror my life or does my life imitate this writing? I can hear my wife saying it's always a little of both. No answer is always one or the other. I love my wife! She is so much a part of everything I do, I hear her even in my thoughts. Our relationship goes on unceasing, no matter how far away we are. Pray without ceasing, Jesus says. I think I just came up with a model for that. Or someone did. I'm not sure who I am anymore. I know who she is. She's the best of us. You can't believe all I say about my wife, can you?

A phone call. A person at my door. Another dog barking. I try to stay in the moment. I've lost some momentum. I try to stay in the moment. Each moment can be a moment. Each moment can be a vacation or a word or a line drive to the gap. Each moment is coal, prediamond. So I stay here. I fight against moving to the next moment until the nectar is sucked dry. I listen. I pray. I forget everything. I'm a blank page, a moment in neutral. My face is red and reddening. But here I am. I'm in my office. I'm typing. It's all made up of moments, and the small decisions encased therein. My face reddens a little more.

In a moment, Jesus's voice breaks through again. A warning. (Where have all the complete sentences gone? There's no time.) Jesus says to take heed—to watch, to listen—lest your hearts be a rock solidified by carousing, drunkenness, and cares of this life. That day will come to your door, into your bedroom, your office, unexpectedly like death itself. It will come as a snare, Jesus says, for all those who are at home, on the face that is this earth. Watch, he adds, and pray always that you may be weighed worthy to escape all these things that will come to pass, for they will surely come to pass, and so you can stand before the Son of Man. (Who can stand in such times?)

It was daytime, Luke records. Jesus was teaching in the temple. That night he went out. He hiked the Olivet Mountain. Then early the next morning all the people came to him. They came to the temple to hear him, to listen.

I sit here. I remain here. The story might as well go on without me. The words gather, huddle together. My mind is off to other things, doing chores at home, tucking the kids in for bed. Saying those prayers.

twenty-two
twenty-three
twenty-four

Luke 22-24

I felt like I was there I guess. Or at least I tried to feel like I was there. I was still an outsider. They didn't really notice the typing. It was Passover, a holiday I knew harkened back to the mass exodus from Egypt, and how the angel of death killed all the first-born sons in Egypt because the pharaoh would not let God's people go. I wasn't there. I didn't see all the blood. But the angel of death passed by all those doors of the Israelites because they had spread blood on them, as they were told to do by God through Moses. But you probably know all of this. It's called setting the scene. I was there and wasn't. Or at least I was imagining I was there. I am attempting to inject a little humor now because there might not be much humor going forward. So maybe I was there and maybe I was laughing at a good joke.

Meanwhile, I heard whispers. I heard whispers because I was there but no one noticed me. They whispered, but I could hear. They didn't seem to notice. Nobody notices the narrator. I don't think Luke was there. At least I don't see him, but this is the story he gathered. He knew the Exodus story. He knew about Passover. If you have more questions you might want to ask him.

I was laughing. They were whispering. In this case the whisperers were the chief priest and scribes, who sought a way to kill Jesus. It had to be stealth because Jesus had followers. Satan entered one of the twelve, not yet famous but a byword now, named Judas Iscariot. Judas came to whisper and conspire. They were glad to see him. There was a whispered cheer. We'll pay you they said. Judas said, I can get him away from the multitude. Judas left, people smiled.

It was time for the Passover, a killing for remembrance. Jesus was telling Peter and John to prepare the Passover, so they could all eat together. Where can we meet, they ask.

Jesus says in the city a man will meet you carrying a pitcher of water, so enter his house and ask the owner if we can use his guest room. He will show you a large, furnished, upper room. Make that place ready. So they did. I followed along, typing away. It was a cool afternoon. Jesus and his twelve sat around a low table. There was a buzz around the table. It was a time of somber remembrance and conversation. Sandals were removed. Dust wandered around the room. The roof was open and the evening has sheen and air whirled. It quieted as Jesus began to speak. His voice wasn't booming, but it had timbre. It traveled. He speaks and somehow it reaches everyone's ears despite being not much more than whisper. I am glad to be here to share the Passover with you before my suffering begins, Jesus says. The disciples make subtle eye contact with one another. I will no longer eat of it until all is fulfilled in the kingdom of God. Another look around. A cool breeze. Jesus takes the cup, giving thanks to God, telling them to divide it among them. I will not drink of the fruit of the vine until the kingdom of God comes, he says. Jesus also took the bread and after giving thanks, he broke it and gave it to them, saying this is my body given for you, do this to remember. They ate not in hunger but as if they were swallowing his words, his teaching, his life. After they had eaten, he took the cup, saying this is the new covenant in my blood, shed for you. This also was a new teaching. I could see that it wasn't easy to swallow what had been called his body and blood. This was a difficult teaching to visualize. But Jesus went on, my betrayer is here with me at this table and truly the Son of Man submits to what has already been decided; however, the betrayer has a destiny too and woe to him. The laughter and conversation has ended. Only quiet. I inch toward the exit. I shouldn't be here.

A buzz. This body and blood. Who would betray Jesus? I hear people ask. Is it you? Is it you? It's on the tip of their tongues. A dispute begins to erupt. The disciples argue over who is the greatest among them. So quickly division seeps in. The exit is closer, within reach. Jesus interrupts, saying, the kings of the Gentiles have lordship, exercising authority, their benefactors. But this is not so among you. The greatest among you should be like the youth: He who governs should serve. Are you great because you have been invited to sit at this table or is it he who serves? Those serving the meal perk up. I serve, Jesus says.

Quiet. A long beat.

But you have continued with me through my trials so I give you what I have been given, a kingdom which My Father has bestowed upon me. So eat and drink at my table in my kingdom. Take your seat on the thrones judging the twelve tribes of Israel.

It was difficult to digest, I could tell, the food, the drink, the words, the man.

Jesus looks over at Peter. A pause. The wind. Peter, Jesus exclaims in a quiet boom, Satan has asked for you, that you may be sifted like wheat, but I've prayed for you, that your faith should not fail. After you have returned to me, strengthen your family.

Peter's eyes are two moons. He peeks around. Confusion rushes his face. Lord, he says, standing now, I'm ready to go with you now, both to prison and to death!

Calmly, eyes alight, Jesus says, the rooster won't crow today before you deny me three times. You'll say you don't even know me.

A beat.

Jesus addresses the twelve again as a group, as a huddled flock. When I sent you without money, knapsack, or sandals, did you lack?

No.

But now, he who has money, let him take it and his knapsack. He who has no sword, let him sell his clothes and buy one. What has been written is still to be accomplished, which is "And he was numbered with the transgressors." These things concerning me have an end.

We have two swords.

It's enough.

Enough.

Jesus leaves. The swords are heavy in their hands.

Leaving their table, Jesus walks to the Mount of Olives as he is accustomed. His disciples follow, as do I. Jesus says, Pray that you may not be tempted, and he withdraws a stone's throw. He kneels. He prays. I close my eyes, but hear, Father, if it is Your will, take this cup from me. But. Not my will, yours be done.

An angel. From heaven. White light. Strength. Agony engulfs Jesus, who is praying even more earnestly. My eyes are open. Jesus is sweating profusely. His sweat comes in great droplets like blood falling to the ground, like hail.

Jesus is up again. The day is long. All are asleep, sorrow a blanket.

Why do you sleep? Rise up and pray, temptation is all around, is a dream. Ghosts. Demons. Blood and body.

A number of men rush up. Judas is leading them. He kisses Jesus.

—Judas, do you betray the Son of Man with this kiss?

Shall we strike with the sword? Before the answer, one sword is swung, slicing the right ear of the high priest cleanly off. It happens in a vacuum.

Permit even this. Jesus reaches down and heals him. The ear is new.

To them, Jesus says, have you come out as against a thief with clubs and swords? I was in the temple daily and you did not seize me. This is your hour. This is the power of darkness.

They take him away. No one resists. An angel. A sword. Healing. Arrest.

They take Jesus to the high priest's house. Victory is about them. I follow, behind Peter, at a distance. A fire rises up in the courtyard. Many sit. Peter sits. A young girl sees him sitting there, his hands near the fire. She looks him over. This man was with him, she says, a finger out.

Woman, I don't know him.

Peter gets up, walks away. But others see him. You were also among them, they say.

Man, I am not!

Peter picks up momentum, hides. Others find him, a group. Surely, this fellow was also with him for he is a Galilean, we can see that. Why else would he be here?

Man, I do not know what you are saying!

The rooster crows like thunder.

Jesus turns, looking at Peter now. Peter remembers his words. He has denied him these three times.

Peter runs, but cannot escape his bitter tears.

I run with him.

I am afraid.

Men surround Jesus. They throw words. They throw fists. Blood appears as if painted there. They blindfold him, punch his face and ask, prophesy for us now. Whose fist is this? Who strikes you? They yell. They accuse. They beat. Many join, find pleasure in it.

No sleep. The night finally gives way, has mercy. With the sun still peaking, the chief priests and scribes drag Jesus to their council. If you are the Christ just tell us now, they command.

–You won't believe what I tell you. I also can ask you, but no matter the words you will not answer me or let me go. From here the Son of Man will sit on the right hand of the power of God.

Are you then the Son of God?

Yes, that's right.

What further testimony do we need? For we have heard it ourselves, straight from his mouth.

I am under a rock. I continue to pray. I continue to listen. Nothing happens really, but over time... I can say this, I have a thought. It's unproven, but I think God might be greater than my mind, or my prayers, or my heart. At least I hope this is true. I'm under a rock.

I follow Jesus as he is led to Pilate. We found this guy perverting the nation, telling people not to pay taxes to Caesar, and saying he is the Christ, A KING!, say Jesus's accusers.

Are you the King of the Jews, Pilate asks. This guy gets right to the point.

—It is as you say.

—I find no fault in this man.

Anger.

—He stirs up the people. He teaches throughout Judea. He has taught all the way from Galilee to here.

—Is he a Galilean? Then he's under Herod's jurisdiction. Let him go to Herod. He is also in Jerusalem right now.

Joy was on Herod's face, even I could see that. Herod had heard many things about Jesus. He wanted to see a miracle for himself. Herod had a thousand questions. They bounced around the walls sounding like basketball practice. But Jesus wasn't responding.

The chief priests and scribes were on their feet, accusing him, words spitting out.

Herod was in a fit. He brought his warriors forward, mocking Jesus for his contemplative silence. They gave him a royal robe, sending him back to Pilate. No one wants to deal with Jesus.

Pilate and Herod, antagonists to this point, become friends.

Pilate brought the chief priests, rulers, and other people together.

—You brought this man to me because you say he misleads the masses. I've examined him in your presence and see no fault. Neither did Herod for that matter. Certainly there is nothing here deserving death. I will reprimand him and release him as is customary during the feast. One will be freed.

—Away with this man. Don't let him be free. Release Barabbas.

–I wish to release Jesus.

–Crucify him! CRUCIFY HIM!

–Why? What evil has he done? I find no reason for him to die. I will chastise him and let him go.

–CRUCIFY!

Loud voices prevailed. I listened, dumbfounded and dumb, as Pilate was pressured into sentencing him. He released Barabbas (the rebellious one, the murderer). He delivered Jesus to his death, which was their will.

They lead Jesus away now. When he can carry it no longer, they have Simon, a Cyrenian who was coming from the country, bear his cross.

Many are gathering now. I am lost in a sea of people. Women are crying out and lamenting. Their words float above the sea. Like an ear-boxed fighter, Jesus turns to them. –Daughters of Jerusalem, don't cry for me. Cry for you and your children. The days are coming when the barren will be blessed. People will pray for the mountains to fall on them and for the hills to cover them. These things are done in the green wood, what then will be done in the dry?

A murmur.

–What does he mean?

Two criminals are being led away with him. They have come to Calvary, where they will be crucified, one criminal on the left, one on the right.

Jesus says, Father, forgive them, they don't know what they are doing. They divided his clothes by casting lots, while we all watched.

–He saved others, let him save himself if he is the Christ, the chosen one of God.

Justification grows.

The soldiers continue to mock. They offer sour wine.

–If you are the King of the Jews, save yourself!

In Greek, Latin, and Hebrew, this is written above him: THIS IS THE KING OF THE JEWS.

One of the criminals even ridicules. –If you are the Christ, save yourself... and us.

The other rebukes him. —Do you not even fear God given that you are condemned alongside him? We deserve this because of what we have done, but this man is blameless. To Jesus: Lord, remember me when you come into your kingdom.

Jesus: Today you will be with me in Paradise.

I closed my eyes. I wasn't really and was there. I'm exhausted by it all. It's no exercise. I'm useless but to repeat.

Darkness. The sun is swallowed, the veil of the temple is torn in two.

Jesus: Father, into your hands I commit my spirit.

His last breath. (It is finished.)

A centurion: Certainly this was a righteous Man!

Many beat their breasts and returned.

Jesus's friends and acquaintances, the women who followed Him from Galilee, huddled together in the distance, and watched these things come to pass.

Joseph, a council member who was known to be a just and good man, had not consented to this deed. He was from Arimathea, a city of the Jews. He was waiting for the kingdom of God. He went to Pilate and asked for Jesus's body. He took him, wrapped him in linen, and laid him in a tomb cut from rock. No one had laid there before. It was the day of preparation. The Sabbath drew near.

The women who had followed Jesus from Galilee watched, saw where he was laid. They returned, preparing spices and fragrant oils. They rested on the Sabbath according to the commandment.

I listened. I watched. I had nothing to add. I was useless but to repeat.

It was Monday. The morning was cool, reminiscent of camping on the Oregon coast. The sky looked like iced tea with the sun becoming a bit less of a rumor each moment. Monday. The women had to wait for the curtain to close on the Sabbath and now it was slowly reopening. They brought the spices they had prepared. The tomb was before them. I heard a discouraging *What?* coming closer, I saw that the massive stone had been rolled away from the entrance. The braver among them went inside. They couldn't find Jesus's body. Those faithful women were beside themselves. They began searching. Suddenly two men stood before them. Their clothes were bright, maybe shining. It was difficult to explain. The women prostrated themselves; I hid.

—Why do you look for the living among the dead? He's not here. He's risen!

Echo to silence.

—Remember what he told you when he was in Galilee? He said the Son of Man must be delivered into the hands of sinful men and crucified. The third day he will rise again. That's what he said and that's what he did.

They remembered. They returned quickly from the tomb. It was crazy. I was a whirlwind. It was like you stepped outside your life. You looked around and everything was different. A morning run was salvation. All was salvation.

Mary Magdalene, Joanna, Mary—the mother of James—and many other women told the eleven and everyone. The faithful women knew first. They were there first. They beat the sun and the iced-tea morning that smelled of ocean. The huge stone was rolled away. Nothing inside. Shiny men. Words rise. He has risen. Salvation. They believed.

The apostles, they thought it sounded like fairytales. Jack & the Beanstock. Fish stories, a few said. Peter, however, ran. The tomb was empty but for the linens lying by themselves. He left swept up in his marveling at what had transpired. Just three days.

Two were traveling to Emmaus, a seven-mile walk from Jerusalem. They were discussing and reasoning through all that had changed in the last several hours. What would life look like now? Another walked beside them. They ignored him. They whispered the more.

—What kind of conversation is this? Why are you sad?

Cleopas (who is Cleopas?): You must be a stranger to Jerusalem if you don't know what's going on.

—What things?

—What things? Those things concerning Jesus of Nazareth, who was a prophet mighty in deed and word before God and all the people. The chief priest and our ruler delivered Him to condemnation, crucifixion. The cross. Suffocation. But we were hoping that Jesus was the one who would redeem Israel. And that's not the crazy part. This is the third day since his crucifixion and now certain women of our company, who arrived at the tomb this morning ahead of us, have astonished us. They didn't find his body in the tomb. They came saying that they also saw angels. The angels announced that Jesus is alive. And there's even more: Several others in our party went to the tomb and found it just as the women had described. Jesus's body was gone.

—You fools. You are slow of heart to believe in all the prophets have spoken! Wasn't the Christ supposed to suffer these things and then enter into his glory?

The question hung in the air like a foul smell.

Who is this man?

Beginning with Moses and all the prophets, he expounded to them all the things that had been foretold concerning himself, but still they didn't know him.

They wished now that the trip was longer for they were drawing near the village where they were headed. The man indicated that he would have gone farther, but they said please no. Stay with us. It's evening. The day is far spent (I liked that, the day as currency). He went in to stay with them.

At the table, expectation flavored the food and drink. Jesus took the bread, blessed and broke it, and gave it to them. Their eyes finally opened. They recognized him.

And, he vanished.

—Was your heart burning within you while he talked with us on the road, opening the scriptures to us like a gatekeeper opens a door?

Even with the day nearly spent, they rose and rushed to Jerusalem. They found the eleven and those who gathered beside them.

—The Lord is risen indeed, and has appeared to Simon!

They told of the road and the broken bread.

As they were relaying their tale, Jesus appeared among them, saying, Peace to you.

A ghost!

—Why are you troubled? Why is your heart tumored with doubts? Look at my hands and my feet. You will see that I am myself. Touch and see. What ghost has flesh and bones and the scars of crucifixion?

Tall tales. Wives' tales. Lies. Misdirections. Conspiracies. Political subterfuge. War. Power. Lies. Lies. Lies. Ghost. Flesh. Words. Words. Words. Words. My mind is painting it all.

He showed them his hands and his feet. They marveled, but there was no joy. Still terror maybe.

—Do you have any food?

They gave him broiled fish and honeycomb.

He ate it.

—These are the words I spoke to you while I was still with you, that all things must be fulfilled which were written in the Law of Moses and the Prophets and the Psalms concerning me.

Like an old, rotten door, he opened their understanding so that they might comprehend the scriptures.

—This is how it was written. It is necessary for the Christ to suffer and to rise from the dead on the third day. It is also necessary that repentance and remission of sins should be preached in his name to all nations beginning in Jerusalem. You are the witnesses of these things.

—I sent the promise of my Father.

—Tarry in Jerusalem only a short time until you receive power from on high, your endowment.

Jesus led them out as far as Bethany. He lifted up his hands. He blessed them. Still with his hands reaching up further and further, he departed. He was swept up into heaven.

They worshiped him. They returned to Jerusalem with great joy like rain in July. They continually were praising God.

I was with them for a short while. I was caught up, swept up, rained on.

They were in the temple. They were on the roads. They were dusty. They were everywhere.

They continually praised God.

And Luke says, Amen.
—Amen.

I am not a witness. I have no authority. Despite my transparent narrative strategy and quick slips into preachiness on his (or my own) behalf, the truth is I never met Jesus before or after the grave, but I see his effects on the earth. I know this: He restarted time like an old Buick. He's a cosmic mechanic, physician, carpenter. I know this also: Those who seek become better people, citizens (almost always) (because sometimes politics...). I must decide. There's no doubt.

My heart is tumored with doubts and selfishness.

There's sickness. Words don't heal. Something must be done. After all, I'm a father, a husband. I'm responsible for a number of hearts.

In the end, I'm more Christian than not Christian, but how worthless is that?

On the fence. Straddling the mean, the median, the average.

Some will ridicule me for not believing when it is so obvious to them. Some will ridicule because I've crossed a line and become one of "them." I am too Christian. I am not Christian enough.

You're a bad writer.

Count the costs.

It's not obvious to me.

What next then?

You stubborn chump.

A fire from the heart of hearts will burn it all. But will it incinerate or purify?

Words. Words. Words.

The evidence is there, if the evidence can be believed.

Science. Religion. Politics. Jesus. I choose all, not one.

I've been to the mountaintop, why must I stumble down?

I've seen the angels. He has risen! Doubt tackles all.

My mind is a map of which I am all over.

I swing on a pendulum.

I love the man Jesus. I love his stories. I love a lot of his words (some mix me up—trip me—I must admit). Is that enough? I know it's not.

Words are their own snafu.

It's stuck in my midriff—one arm reaching out for my dreams or desires while the other arm runs and hides, plays it safe, close to the sleeve. The midriff is not easily broken... or wildly successful. It's balance. It's safety. It's diversified. It's safe. It's an addiction. I'm addicted to self-security. I like eating my cake and having it too. Sometimes both is better.

Sometimes I'm a wuss. I know this about me.

I'm addicted to the midriff.

The heart. The head. The arms.

Here's the truth:

I'm not very religious.

I'm as religious as any other old junky.

> *At least I think I am.*

Love. Joy. Peace. Patience. Kindness. Goodness. Faithfulness. Gentleness. Self-Control.

epilogue

Afterward, he said his prayers. He walked. He worked. He continued his start-up. He maybe yelled less, but just as passionate. He changed diapers and drove to t-ball, soccer, school plays, dance. Afterward, he said his prayers. He still argued about science and politics. He was too liberal for some, too conservative for others. He grappled with the shadow of his entire life, even that still to come.

"It needs more dialogue," his wife was saying.

"Answer me," she says.

"More dialogue."

Dinner is getting bone cold.
Chicken. Fried.
Vegetables. Steamed.
Potatoes. Mashed with Johnny's Garlic.
A table.
Three kids.
A beautiful wife.
He said their prayers.
They ate.

Complaints were heard.
They filled the room.

Ink.
He slumps.
    Then he sees it.
    There is something shiny in their faces.
    Light.
    He saw that they were surrounded,
    but not outnumbered.
    It's something that might last.

"You guys want a pet giraffe?"

ABOUT THE AUTHOR

Chris DeVore, author of *A Palatable Past* (2009), *Catching the Flathead Monster* (2006), and *The Literary Detective* (2004), is a freelance writer, journalist, and bookshop owner. His writing has also recently appeared in IDAHO magazine, *The Whistle Pig* literary journal, and The Cabin's *DETOUR: Writers in the Attic*. DeVore serves on the Mountain Home Arts Council's board of directors, and is the editor of Elmore County's literary journal. He grew up in Polson, Montana, and earned his literature degree from the University of Puget Sound. After stints in Tacoma, Seattle, and Ellensburg, Washington, and Albany, Oregon, DeVore currently resides in Mountain Home, Idaho, with his wife, Hannah, and their three young children.